Wicked Beast

Gail Faulkner

Ellora's Cave
Romantica®
ELLORASCAVE.COM

An Ellora's Cave Publication

www.ellorascave.com

Wicked Beast

ISBN 9781419968280

Edited by Mary Moran.
Cover Design and Photography by Syneca.
Model: Giorgio.

Electronic book publication October 2011
Trade paperback publication 2013

Chapter One

Pain burned past his nose with a sulfur sting, followed by the barely there scent of rose petals. Seeking more of the last sweet smell in his hazy, half-dream state, Cord inhaled deeply.

Abruptly fire bit low in his back and jerked him awake. He jackknifed to a sitting position and dazedly swung his head around. Nobody in the dark room with him. More than human senses made him certain.

The burn snaked up his spine. He shook his head and glanced at the clock.

Four a.m. What the hell?

Suddenly pain washed over him as every cell in his body screamed with primal demand. The invisible wave of torture was a force of nature, totally uncontrollable, inescapable. Cord fell forward, head sinking between knees to breathe through wrenching agony. Perhaps he was dying. Was this what happened when there was finally nothing more?

The consuming pain evaporated into a rose-scented mist. Cord frowned. What did flowers have to do with dying? He'd smelled all the scents of death, and the flower crap never marked it until a funeral event occurred.

The fire eating his spine spread to his shoulder blades. He gingerly stood and found he was steady. Kicking an empty bottle of scotch out of his way, he stumbled to the kitchen, jerked on the faucet and thrust his head beneath the spigot.

Icy well water penetrated masses of tangled hair and scotch-induced fog. Cord gritted his teeth and endured a little longer just to make sure. Flipping ropes of coal-black hair out of his eyes, he straightened.

The excruciating burn was not death, but it was damn close. His eyes narrowed as focus returned, dark pupils elongated to slits, the beast beneath man-skin came fully awake.

The call hit him again, *"Come now!"*

It came on the wings of white power with the kick of a bolt arrow to the gut. The jolt slammed him across the galley kitchen and up against the wall. Unprepared for the hit, he nearly blacked out as it thundered through him. Power sizzled out his extremities. He looked down at his hands to be sure they were still there.

White power! Where the hell had that come from? It'd been thrown at him with dangerously clumsy strength. Cautiously he breathed deeply, testing the scents left in the wake of the hit. Yes, there it was, the trail whispered low in the air. Not rose mist but something he didn't recognize, a scent that could only originate with the sender.

His lip curled silently as he took the scent into his body, marking it. He'd waited a damn long time for the end of the world, who knew it'd call his ass? Time to go kill it.

Cord strode from the cabin, not bothering to change clothes. Grimly, he swung into the truck. He had no other thought besides finding the source, no other option.

This time he scented the white power coming and braced for the hit. The only reason he'd missed it before was he'd been unconscious. Five minutes ago the world was safe and white power didn't exist anymore, hadn't since before time as humans marked it. Five minutes ago the beast required to kill it hadn't walked this world either. It did now.

The hit was more potent than last time, it pounded through him, but he was able to absorb the energy, using it instead of letting it escape his starved body. Ignoring the burn as long-unused faculties fed on the extreme injections of fuel, he drove on. Being sober helped. The first shot had evaporated the scotch.

The excessive concentration of life-force power meant he couldn't control involuntary responses and tears streaked down his cheeks. It was unimaginable that the wielder had no idea what they were doing, but in this reality, that seemed the case. Ignorance was no shield for the responsibility of white power—it just made his job simple. Preserving the sender's ignorance about his intentions was not even a question. Cord sent a response.

"Calm. You must calm down. I'm coming." He hoped the sender could read him. He'd put as much push as he could afford on the thought, infusing peace and security into it.

He immediately felt the answer, puzzlingly faint in a trembling whisper, *"Now, now!"*

That was confusing, considering the strength of the wielder. He hadn't felt this type of ability since... Okay, perhaps he'd never felt something exactly like this. Even back in the time before, he'd never encountered this concentration of power in one individual.

And he knew it was one person. There were no melodious strains of music to the power. No harmonious voices melding together to throw it. This was a single voice that didn't sing. The person had simply hurled command at him as if it were a ball to be tossed about.

Barreling down the mountain, he skidded around curves. Speed didn't bother him. The wielder bothered him. He had no option but to respond, and that'd never happened before. Questions about this event bloomed but they were pointless. He was aimed at the wielder with one mission, to end the voice and the threat it posed. There would be no question-and-answer session.

Cord automatically slowed as he neared town. The mystery scent intensified. Power pulled him at the same time it forced its way into his body. His eyes burned as did every vertebra down his back. His hands and feet tingled with the endless sting of needles stabbing in nonstop staccato.

"Be calm. I'm coming!" he sent again, trying to get the wielder to tone it down. The power being force-fed into his starved frame was merciless to assimilate this way. It lanced through every joint and system.

"Much hurry!" was the insistent response. The wielder didn't tone down the compulsion.

A child? Could this be a child? It didn't seem possible. Deep within him, the beast rumbled. His nostrils flared on the smell of that response. Baby powder? No damn way! He didn't even know what baby powder smelled like.

Pulling into the drive of the house that compelled him, he sat panting and looked at the tidy little Cape Cod cottage. The house glowed in ultraviolet white power, outside the human sight spectrum but plain as day to a creature like him.

Cord half fell out of the truck, only closing the door because he needed to lean on the truck a moment to ensure he could stand. The path to the front door was short but it was the few steps into eternity for him. He was almost there when the door opened. He stumbled as a punch of power flooded his system. He came to a stunned halt. The power called him with the painful vengeance of an attack—he should have been prepared.

Framed by the lights behind her, stood three feet of trembling, sobbing, pink footy pajamas, clutching a purple bear. Tears slid silently down plump cheeks already glassy with misery. Cord pulled himself through the power she was forcing into him and dropped to a knee on the bottom step of the porch. He should have been ending her life, not lounging on her steps. That thought slipped away as his senses read the child. The innocent, completely vulnerable and utterly trusting little sender, powerful beyond imagining, drew him in. So perhaps he could just see what she was, in the interest of doing a thorough job. Yeah, that was it.

Rigidly controlling his eyes, forcing them to appear human, Cord gritted as gently as he could, "Please, sweetheart. Try to calm down."

"Mommy! Bassent!"

He mounted the stairs slowly, waiting for the terror to hit her. Currently his frame was six feet and lean. He hadn't shaved in at least a month and didn't recall the last time he'd had his hair cut. Bathing might have occurred last week. He was a mess. Burning eyes sent tears dripping into his beard and haggard would have been a kind word for what was visible of his face.

Reaching out with his senses, he flashed through the house, looking for occupants. Only one other life force in the house, and it was quiet. Hesitation was not part of his nature, but at this moment, he couldn't make sense of any damn thing. The child was human and she was…not. But not un-human in the way he was or any other way he'd ever known. She was his target, and yet she was nothing at all like the projected target. And she was feeding him!

Power like hers might be able to kill him with a thought. She didn't try. That earned her at least a few minutes to make him understand what the hell was going on. The fuel ripping through him was accumulating fast, so there really was no risk in investigating.

"Honey, I'm here to help. You've got to believe me," he crooned gently, hoping to reach her with friendly intentions.

"Yes, yes. Hurry." The clear tones of her voice held no fear. No fear of him at least. Her little hand reached out and grabbed his. Pale as paper white lilies, her fingers curled around one of his to drag him inside. "Dagon hurry. Mommy bassent!"

As soon as she touched him, pain dissipated and he was able to concentrate as footy pajamas led him to the kitchen. His eyes caught every detail. Boxes stacked against the wall. Some open on the floor. Things stacked on chairs. The occupants were moving in or out.

Across the big country kitchen a door was standing open. Feeble light punctured the damp darkness below, and the scent of rose petals misted up from the depths.

"Mommy, bassent!"

Cord looked down into her tearful face. The little miracle in footy pajamas compelled his future. Her fingers couldn't even close around one if his grubby digits. She clutched him, extending perfect faith that he'd rescue her mommy.

He couldn't read her, not like regular humans, but he could feel her. She knew exactly *what* he was. She knew everything and she knew nothing. Impossible as her abilities were, it was her knowledge that carved new space in his brain. Something no one had ever imagined, even the majestic minds that had made this reality possible hadn't been able to dream big enough to envision her.

At the door to the basement, she let go of his finger and stepped back, hugging the purple bear. Thankfully she was calmer and the thundering power emanating from her churning emotions was a less-painful roar. It was a roar of confidence that everything would be fixed now. He couldn't resist the need to go down those steps. Not really for her, but he suspected that was part of it, mostly he went to see where this new reality was going. He'd not seen something new in a very long time.

"Stay right here, sweetheart." He tried to sound parental so she'd understand the importance of remaining in close proximity to the basement door.

Little Miss Miracle nodded and jammed a thumb in her mouth.

Cord turned to the darkness and hurried down the stairs. His eyes didn't need the pitiful light from the bare bulb to see the problem. It was his nose that told him he was in real trouble. The woman passed out on the floor was the rose petals. The shattering power emanating from the little miracle upstairs had shielded his senses from the real danger.

Her scent. Oh dear God in heaven, no!

Staring at the woman for less than a second was all it took. The world had indeed ended today. Expecting to die was a lot easier than knowing he was going to live and that was exactly what he faced. There was really no choice, he literally had no choice. She was fast losing her choices too.

A feral growl built in his chest as the animal responded to seeing her trapped and injured. There was no repressing it. She lay with a very old, hulking water heater tank crushing her left leg. He could tell she'd been there awhile, trapped and alone. He was thankful she'd passed out.

Remnant scents of her emotions were strong enough to tell him what she'd been through. If she'd had an implement, it's possible she would have damaged herself to get out and back to her daughter. She'd considered removing the leg. Wisps of that determination offended his system so badly he nearly lost the bitter remains of the scotch he'd drugged himself with.

Sliding to his knees beside her head, his hand shook as he brushed wisps of hair off her face. Words breathed out his mouth. Words no one had spoken since the time when his kind disappeared from this world. The words gave her peace, ensuring her sleep was deep and dreamless, protecting her from pain.

Her skin was alabaster with shock. Looking at her face, he knew it had all the regular features a woman should have, to him it was stunning. The beast within was silent as he drank in the sight of her. Drawing a deep breath, he closed his eyes and felt her scent sink into the center of his being, where it belonged. Everything he'd known was wrong. Apparently.

The tank on her leg must have been brought down in pieces and built in place, perhaps a hundred years ago. At full strength he could have easily lifted it, but he was nowhere near that. Currently he was a starved, gaunt shadow of a being and had almost no hope of moving it. Almost didn't mean none.

Hurrying up the stairs, he dropped to one knee in front of Miss Miracle. "What's your name, sweetheart?" he asked as calmly as he could.

The thumb came out. She glanced at the open door and back at him, her forehead wrinkled in distress. "Bing Mommy."

"Yes, I will bring Mommy, but I need your help. Please tell me your name, and then we'll get Mommy."

"Minuet."

"Minuet, have you seen Mommy?"

Light shimmered off flaming curls as her head shook. "Minuet skeered bassent," she confessed solemnly.

Damn, not good.

"You know what I am, honey?" he asked cautiously to see how much she was actually conscious of.

"Dagon. You airs dagon."

Again he was stunned with her innocent, clear understanding that was uncluttered with normal human perceptions. "Yes. Air dragon. Do you know why I look like this?"

Minuet frowned. "Dagon sick?"

"Exactly. Dragon sick, but I need to lift a very heavy thing to help Mommy. Will you help me?"

"Minuet small," she informed him, holding out a hand to show him, her look telling him she was concerned that he'd missed this critical point.

He took her extended hand and folded it in his. The connection with pure power snapped with the force of an electric current. He was as depleted as a polio victim, not just weak, but one whose muscles had actually wasted away.

"Do you feel what happens when you hold my hand, Minuet?" He searched her eyes, desperately hoping shock and revulsion would not suddenly bloom there, unable to quite figure out why it didn't.

"Dagon better?"

"Much better. Minuet is medicine. Will you come with me to help Mommy?"

Big eyes glanced at the door to the basement and back at his. Her forehead wrinkled in concentration and she stepped closer to him. "Me skeered bassent," she repeated directly into his face with a slow cadence as if he didn't hear her the first time.

"I know, sweetheart, but Mommy needs both of us. You don't have to walk down. Just climb on my back, close your eyes and hold on. I'll bring you both up the stairs and then you can open your eyes. Can you do that for Mommy?"

Nodding, she placed the bear carefully on the floor and held up her arms. Cord helped her climb onto his back, her little arms clamped around his neck. The two pink-covered feet couldn't reach very far around his chest, but she had the clinging ability of the very young in any species.

"Close your eyes. You must be calm to help," he cautioned. "Ready?"

"Yes."

The little body on his back, acting like a power pack, Cord loped down the stairs. He lifted the huge cylinder and set it aside, being careful to place it so it appeared he'd been able to tip it off. Scooping up the woman, he tried to ignore the burst of need exploding up his body. Carefully he carried his burdens up the stairs.

Carrying both of them created an enthralling mix of power and pleasure pouring into his starved frame. What they were to him was magnified by the years he'd endured without even a taste of what he craved much less this new, indefinable mix of whatever it was they supplied.

Placing the woman carefully on the floor, his hand went to her leg without hesitation. She was in shorts, the damage painfully evident. Passing over it, he felt crushed bones, mangled arteries and dying muscle. Even with the little one on his back he didn't have the strength to fix it all, so he swiftly did what he could with the arteries and veins she needed to ensure a healthy leg. The rest modern medicine could set, but the tiny blood vessels would have been beyond them.

He grabbed a kitchen towel off the back of a chair and draped it over her leg to hide the ugly reality from the little miracle on his back. No child should see that. He shifted so Minuet would be facing away from the pale form of her mother when she opened her eyes.

"Okay. You can open your eyes and get off, honey."

Her little body slid off and she dashed around him, grabbing the purple bear as she went to her mother's side.

"Mommy, wakes up!" Grasping a limp hand, she franticly shook it. Power was building in the room as Minuet struggled to wake her mother.

Cord gathered deceptively frail pink shoulders under his arm. "Mommy is sleeping and that's good. Her leg would hurt her very much if she were awake," he tried to explain and calm the tearful child. Her vibrations at this level of distress could echo too far. She was so young. There was no way to explain the cost of that much white power flowing across the countryside. His own actions were compounding those dangers, but he couldn't do otherwise.

From the first rose petal scent to penetrate his booze-induced fog he'd be helpless to overcome the instincts that brought them to this moment. Rose petals and pink pajamas. Who knew these were the tools that compelled him to forsake sacred vows and his last hope of redemption from a God who didn't know him.

The directive he'd rejected was a perfect theory, long and involved yet elegantly simple. His commitment to the mission had dragged him through endless decades of remaining sentient for one last service required by his beloved creator. To save the humans, all he had to do was kill the woman and her child.

Chapter Two

This isn't right, pounded through his brain. Nothing was as it should be. The plan had been perfect, freaking brilliant, but no one had said anything about a tiny white power miracle, pink pajamas or rose petals. And how was his animal nature actually offended at the thought of killing them? Animals don't get offended.

Minuet wasn't exactly a white witch. She was something else. The little girl clutching her mother's hand was so much more than anyone had been before. He'd like to use that as an excuse for his inability to follow the plan. She was a new development, a twist of fate and genetics who might save them all. It could happen. Apparently anything could happen in this new reality.

His eyes went to the alabaster face of her unconscious mother and he knew the truth. Minuet might indeed save them, but every drop of innocent blood shed from this moment forward would be on his head. He wasn't strong enough to kill this woman.

Merciless animal instincts came with a price it seemed. Logic was not an unstoppable response, logic was always a choice. What his creators seemed to have miscalculated on was the amount of instinct remaining in his system.

Cord's hand tightened on Minuet's shoulder. "Where is the phone, honey?"

Minuet never took her eyes off her mother's pale face. "Phone man sick. Him come tomorrow."

So they were moving in, not out. That explained his not being aware of them. "Does Mommy have a cell phone?"

Minuet nodded. "In a floor."

"Where? I need it to call help for Mommy. Try to remember exactly where the cell phone is."

A fresh tear raced down her cheek. "I dop it inna floor. Mommy put me bed and go find phone. No more Mommy." Her silvery voice shook as she finished her story.

"Mommy is going to be fine. She's just sleeping real deep." Cord glanced at the ornate grate cover on the floor heating vents. The swirling brass was decorative but certainly left enough room for a cell phone to fall through. "It went down one of those?" he asked while pointing at the kitchen vent.

"I sorry," Minuet whispered. "I didn't mean to."

"Shhhh," he comforted as her guilt added to the mix of emotions she was projecting. "No one is mad, honey. We need to call the doctor to help Mommy. Have you met the people in the house next door?"

Cord had several problems now. He didn't have a cell phone. He didn't have anything to tie him to this century except the necessity of a vehicle. He looked like a scary homeless person and he had to get these two into the hands of medical professionals. Normal people would take one look at him and assume he'd broken in and attacked them.

"Aunt Molly. She coming," Minuet responded as if he should have heard the footsteps hurrying across the lawn.

She was right, he should have. Damn! An aunt person would really dislike finding him bending over these two. He had to be acceptable to this family unit. It was imperative. Fuck!

"Minuet, would you help me one more time?" he asked softly. There was no time to do things the right way. No time to explain what he was about to ask her.

The little tear-streaked face turned up to his with a tiny smile. "I does it. Aunt Molly afeared of messy dagon. Now you pretty." The last was said as someone hurried up the porch steps.

Cord glanced down at himself in mild panic. Minuet's idea of making pretty gave him an instant image of a pink puppy. Thankfully he only had two legs and jeans were still on them, but the cloth was clean instead of dirt streaked. Above them his T-shirt had lost both stains and wrinkles. His hand went to his chin and found a close-cut beard.

"Be good dagon. No magic. It a rule," Minuet informed him in a whisper.

"Good rule," Cord agreed, and turned his head as a woman opened the front door calling for Minuet and Kelly.

So that was her name, Kelly. It fit. "Minuet, my name is Cord. Let me do the explaining when she comes in. Okay?" he whispered quickly.

Little Miss Miracle nodded just as the woman entered the kitchen and gasped.

Cord straightened slowly so he wouldn't startle the short, dark-haired woman. She didn't look a bit like Minuet or Kelly. In her housecoat, it wasn't hard to see that her body size held none of the long, lean lines Kelly possessed, though she wasn't fat.

"Oh my God! What happened?" she exclaimed, pausing in shock at the scene.

Cord nodded seriously. "There was an accident in the basement. Minuet flagged me down. Do you have a cell phone, ma'am? I'm afraid I left mine at home this morning and I can't locate a phone to call paramedics."

Cord attempted to appear sincere and concerned as the woman at the kitchen door added a punch of earthy power to the emotions swirling around the room. He was forced to breathe shallowly to avoid an overload, but it didn't matter. There were three in the room with him, three powerful elements of nature.

Deep beneath, the muscles of his back moved to the inevitable response to the power surrounding him. Two of them were upset, seeking assistance. The third was in jeopardy. He'd known this would happen. He hadn't known they were three. Apparently they didn't know they were three either.

If Minuet was forbidden from letting Molly see her magic, Kelly had no idea Molly was gifted. They certainly weren't blood sisters.

Molly rushed toward Kelly, her eyes on the kitchen towel covering Kelly's leg from the knee down. "How bad is it? Oh Minuet, Aunt Molly's here. Everything will be all right. I promise, baby. Who are you? I saw the lights. I knew something was wrong…"

Her words rushed together as the woman sank down beside Minuet. Cord stepped back as he felt her gathering her gift. Molly was very busy trying to distract everyone with the deluge of words. Her hand fluttered to Kelly's ankle and Cord grabbed the back of a kitchen chair to keep from falling on his ass.

Molly drew on the earth as she demanded it heal the serious wounds in Kelly. Ruthlessly she took from the surroundings. Power rushed through Molly into Kelly's leg, and Molly's eyes flashed up to Cord in wide-eyed surprise.

Apparently she had no idea what he was. None of them seemed to know anything about what they were. He almost laughed at the absurdity of it. Cord was a creature of the earth. His kind were created, not born, they were the earth as much as they were flesh. Animal was as close as human words could come to identify them, but they certainly weren't any type of beast this world knew. They had blood DNA but it was the mix of elements that made them the soulless creatures that they were.

To heal Kelly, Molly had gathered life force indiscriminately, thinking she was calling on the organic world to lend its assistance. And she was. Earth Witch simply had no idea organic could walk on two legs. Her call had required a response from his body and she'd pretty much drained him with it.

Pulling out the kitchen chair, he sat down heavily. The fact that he could bleed, that his body usually resembled a mammal didn't make him a true one. Trees bled. Even rocks could in their own fashion. The stark reminder of what he was didn't change what he wanted. What he was no longer willing to live without.

"What…what are you?" Molly stuttered as she stared at him from the floor beside Kelly.

Kelly coughed as her body jerked slightly. Minuet clutched her mother's hand to her wet cheek.

"Mommy? Mommy, wake up?" she asked hesitantly.

"Soon, baby," Cord responded to Minuet first. Kelly wasn't waking up if he couldn't help her, and Molly had done a damn good job of stripping him of most abilities. He lurched to his feet and concentrated on moving normally as he stepped around Kelly's head and went down to one knee beside Minuet.

He regarded Molly. "You done?"

"I don't know. Depends," Molly answered cautiously. "What are you?"

"Not a threat to you. You know that now. I helped her sleep so she wouldn't feel the pain. I have to help her wake up. Do you understand?"

He was asking her to understand what she'd just felt. She knew enough to use her gift and feel the power she'd bled out of him. Mostly he wanted her to come to the conclusion she could control him if she wanted to. It would make her feel safe and accept him more readily. There was truth in that conclusion. It just wasn't the whole truth.

As Molly stared at him, Cord's hand drifted over Minuet's hair in a light caress and came to rest on her shoulder. It appeared he was gently giving the child physical comfort. Again that was true, mostly. Molly's slight dip of chin was grudging consent but enough to work with.

He slowly laid his other hand on Kelly's brow, his eyes on Molly to strengthen the impression that she could stop him at any time. Kelly moaned softly.

That was all the attention he could give Molly. Looking down at the beautiful woman slowly opening violet-blue eyes was an action he had no hope of resisting. In that moment, her consciousness came to life and he was truly lost. She awoke and he would never be forgiven. So be it. Cord smiled into the eyes of the future.

"Hey. How are you feeling?" he asked softly.

"Mommy!"

Minuet launched herself on top of her mother, trying to wrap arms around her neck. Kelly struggled to sit up and hold her baby. Cord slid an arm under Kelly's back to lift both so Kelly was sitting with Minuet in her lap. The move was natural. His hand remained lightly supporting them.

For a moment, Kelly's head dipped to rest on Minuet's head, both of them sheltered under his body. Cord dragged in a deep breath, soaking up the perfection of that moment.

All too soon Kelly's head lifted, bringing their faces intimately close. "Who are you?" she whispered. The hesitancy in her voice brought him back to reality.

"I'm the guy Minuet called when you were in trouble," he answered calmly.

"Right. I thought you said she flagged you down," Molly declared with a frown.

Kelly's head jerked to look at Molly in surprise. Cord immediately shifted to help Kelly stand. Minuet clung to her mother, making getting up difficult. Cord helped Kelly. Lifting easily, he maneuvered her into the chair he'd been sitting in.

"Minuet does not make mistakes about people," he told Kelly conversationally, ignoring Molly for the moment as she also stood.

Sitting in the kitchen chair, clutching Minuet, Kelly's expression was priceless as she glanced at Molly, as if afraid Cord would say something she couldn't explain.

Cord straightened. "You're right, Molly, I did lie. That was before you *helped* Kelly feel better. The need for subterfuge has passed."

"Ah." Molly's hand nervously fluttered to her neck. "Um. Well. I don't think... I mean, I saw the lights..." Her glance touched Minuet's head.

"Minuet called you telepathically after I carried Kelly up from the basement," Cord stated flatly. "She's too young and upset to be coherent, but you brought your cell phone in the housecoat pocket, didn't you?"

Molly's hand grasped the right pocket of her housecoat reflexively, giving away the truth. Cord continued looking down at Kelly.

"You have always tried to conceal Minuet's abilities, just like your mother taught you to blend in and appear normal. Just like your friend Molly is so good at appearing normal. Why do you think the two of you are such good friends? You are sisters. Not by blood, you are drawn to each other by something much more binding. The three of you keep secrets. You don't need too. Not from each other."

"Molly?" Kelly asked hesitantly.

Her first question going to Molly told Cord how deeply Kelly trusted Minuet's judgment. It would have been far more natural for her to question the strange man in her house, but she didn't need to. Minuet had called him.

Cord pulled out a kitchen chair for Molly and invited her to sit with a sweep of his hand. She did so with a deep sigh, her eyes moving from Cord to Kelly.

"I have a...um...a gift. I don't talk about it because it's so strange to normal people. I can sort of use the energy of living things. Not animals or people, I use, ah, draw from plants, the earth." She paused as her eyes went to Cord again.

He could feel her looking at his back as he opened a cupboard for glasses. She reached for him with her senses, trying to probe him. This time he blocked her. Molly tried again and he gently pushed back as he filled two glasses with water and set them on the table in front of the women.

"You're being nosy, Molly," he said softly.

"What are you?" Molly asked again.

Kelly's eyes bounced between them. "What's going on?"

Minuet was sitting quietly in her mother's lap, her head on her shoulder, nearly asleep. Cord reached down and picked up the child.

"Come to Cord, honey. Mommy needs to drink and rest."

Minuet went to him willingly, wrapping little legs around his chest as arms circled his neck, her head dropping to his shoulder. Kelly's jaw went slack for a second as her daughter relaxed in the tall man's arms.

Cord pulled another chair away from the table and sat facing them. "We'll get to me. How about you?" he nodded to Kelly.

Both women stared at him as Kelly started speaking. "I have a thing too. A lot like yours only my strength comes from air. I can influence the wind. I know where it's been. It tells me things and it strengthens me."

Molly nodded but didn't take her eyes off Cord. "That leaves you," she said with a frown.

"My name is Cord Windweaver. I have a place up on Correl Mountain. Minuet called me when she realized you were trapped in the basement," he stated to Kelly. "You'd passed out by the time I arrived. The old heater tank had crushed your leg. When I got you into the kitchen, I couldn't find a phone to call the paramedics so Minuet called your friend Molly. Miss Molly used her gift to repair your leg. Then you woke up."

Both women drank the entire glasses of water he'd set in front of them, replenishing power. He wondered if they knew why they needed it. There was silence for a few moments.

"Cord, that wasn't the question. Why is my daughter, who is very uncomfortable with strangers and men in particular, sleeping on your shoulder?" Kelly asked. "I know she reads people. That's why she has a hard time interacting with them. I'll give you the latitude her trust earns. Now tell me why she contacted you?"

Looking into Kelly's eyes, Cord struggled with his answer. He couldn't lie. Damn it to hell. If it were Molly pressing him for an answer, he could give her just enough to stem her questions. But it was Kelly, and his response to her was writing the future. She deserved to know that, but he would do almost anything to keep that burden from her. Seemed there were a few more things he didn't know about what was happening now. Apparently his drive to protect her was a rock-solid mandate he couldn't escape. Along with it came the impulse to shield her from...well, anything that she might not like.

Minuet lifted her head. "Cord dagon. Him save mommy and Minuet."

"Dragon?" Kelley asked her daughter softly. "You mean he's the friend you sometimes talk to? The one Mommy thought was an imaginary friend?"

"No, dat my dagon. Cord Mommy's dagon."

Cord controlled his features to remain calm. Such simple words, the logic of a child and it was entirely complete. It was frighteningly revealing.

The two women were struggling with the concept of dragon. Cord took advantage of their silence.

"Honey, what's your dragon's name?" he asked, smiling down at Minuet encouragingly. They had no idea how important that was. The little power pack in his arms had abilities he could barely fathom. She was certainly capable of calling the creatures Cord's entire world had sacrificed itself to contain. Now it seemed the worst might have already happened.

Minuet laid her head back on Cord's shoulder, her eyes already closed. "My dagon sleep. Him name is, My Dagon."

"Dragon? Is she saying dragon?" Molly asked in consternation. "There is no such thing as dragons."

Cord looked at her and smiled. "Nor are there really women with unique powers that might make other people call them witches. Right?"

Molly's mouth thinned as she clamped it shut.

"Why does she think you are my dragon?" Kelly interjected.

Cord turned to her, such a perfect goddess. Her kind was called witch, but their title should have been goddess.

Kelly's scent perfumed his every breath, and he wanted to lick it out of the air. The pale warmth of her now-glowing skin was a fine shade of temptation, and he intended to taste every inch of it. He had no right to what he wanted, but he had sacrificed eternity for the opportunity.

"I am a protector. In this age, you would call me a bodyguard. You're the one I am here to protect. Minuet reads that in me."

"I don't need protection." Kelly shook her head. "Why does she need a protection dragon?"

"I'm afraid you do. So does Molly," he added. "The two of you are mistresses of natural elements. You've both hidden that power, but it's out now. Minuet's distress could easily have disclosed your secret to forces whose most merciful choice would be to kill you. They have never been known for their mercy.

"She calls me dragon because I am." He nodded at Molly. "You're right. Dragons should not exist. We are not natural to this planet. That doesn't mean we don't exist. Being unnatural, our lives are not bound by what humans call the laws of nature."

Cord laid his arm on the table, palm up, close to Kelly. "Put your hand in mine and feel with your gifts, Kelly," he invited softly.

"Protection from whom?" Molly pressed, her eyes narrowed on Cord as Kelly hesitated.

Cord didn't look away from Kelly as he answered. "From the dragons created specifically to capture you."

"By dragons do you mean big lizards, flying, fire breathing? Or some bike gang with scary jackets?" Molly wanted to know.

"Take my hand and know what I am," Cord invited Kelly. He really didn't want to be in charge of the explaining. Letting them draw their own conclusions would absolve him from deception. What they came up with would be correct, just limited without the history involved. They weren't ready for the history.

Kelly's hand slowly descended to rest on his. Skin to skin involved fierce control of the starved beast. That selfish, depraved animal who was stealing her future. She was air. His air. Surrounding him, invading him. Delicate as a breeze, powerful as any hurricane gale, Kelly touched him and he drank her.

He didn't close his fingers around her hand, just let her rest there. He wanted her in control of the touching, adding the illusion of safety. Placing herself in Cord's hands was a personal choice. One he was determined she would make on her own.

Her eyes were on their joined hands, but as she reached inside him, her eyes rose to his. Understanding, amazement, acceptance. She gave him all of these things because she didn't know he was still hiding a part of himself from her, using her ignorance to conceal what would hurt her to know. He couldn't have her frightened of him. Not now. So he ensured her trust with truth, truth that concealed.

What else could one expect from a soulless abomination?

Chapter Three

"Oh," Kelly breathed, looking into his eyes. She absorbed him. Glided into his world and took her place at the center, right where she belonged. He let her see all that, and she innocently thought she knew him. Knew his motives, his desires, what he intended and needed.

"Well?" Molly prompted impatiently. "You're holding his hand. Does it magically tell you what he is?"

"Yes." Kelly smiled at Cord, her eyes glanced away from his shyly only to return. The shyness was still there but there was trust too.

He controlled his response and gave her a gentle smile. "Explain it. I'm not sure what words she'll understand," he encouraged in an intimate tone.

Kelly nodded and focused on Molly. "You know that scene in *Terminator II* where the mother realizes the machine is really there to protect? He'll never get tired. He'll never leave. Never stop. That's what Cord is. Not a machine, I mean the protector part," Kelly clarified.

"He's Arnold Schwarzenegger?" Molly asked skeptically.

"He's Cord," Kelly corrected.

"That still doesn't tell me what he is. When I healed your leg, I gathered power from the organic world. Too late I realize I was getting life force from him. Is he a talking rock? A big fungus? What is he?" she demanded in frustration.

"Perhaps your dragon will know how to explain it to you," Cord responded. "Kelly needs to rest. Minuet is already sleeping. For right now everyone is safe. It'd be a good idea if you ladies took advantage of the peace and slept."

"My dragon?" Molly exclaimed. "I don't have a dragon."

"Sure you do, and he's on his way," Cord assured her. "I'd rather you didn't go back to an empty house. I'm not at full strength and can't protect you that far away. Legion would be upset. He's unpredictable when he's mad."

"Legion?" both Molly and Kelly said in unison.

Cord frowned at Kelly. "He's a big, ugly earth dragon, sorta like a giant mole. You probably will not like him. I'm the wind dragon, much better looking."

"You're vain about being so handsome?" Kelly asked in surprise.

She thought he was handsome. Cord smiled as her statement bloomed in him. No, not just handsome, *so* handsome. That went a long way toward soothing his initial reaction to her interest in Legion.

"You know what I am," he evaded her direct question. "Mostly I'm trying to get the three of you in bed and failing. That should tell you something."

Light teasing would only get him so far. These two women were gifted in every way. Not being stupid went without saying. He'd brought up Legion because he needed them prepared for the large, dark dragon when he appeared. Implying he was benevolent was a reach, a guess or a hope. Cord's responses were forcing conclusions that went against everything he thought he believed. If those conclusions were true in him, they would likely be true in his two counterparts.

Legion had endured the same amount of time without power and would be as diminished as Cord had been. That was Cord's only advantage. Contact with Kelly and Minuet gave him an edge. He'd need it to buy the time to explain how the plan had changed, but as soon as Legion saw Molly, Cord had a feeling all bets would be off.

If he were a gambler, he'd let Legion run into Molly first, but he couldn't take that chance. What if Legion didn't react as he had to Kelly, he'd kill Molly. If Cord didn't let him see

Molly, he'd have no reason to change the plan, so he'd try to kill them all.

Cord had spent time with Legion before. The dragon was all things earth. Calling him dark, passionate, volatile and strong in the physical sense was a serious mistake. Those words did not begin to cover the minimum facts, but they were the best Cord could do in English. Legion was also huge. There was nothing streamlined or aerodynamic about the earth dragon. He had a wicked sense of humor and an appetite for physical gratification.

This meeting was going to be fun in the really deadly sense of the word. Cord needed to soak up as much power as he could before Legion arrived. He would not allow things to go wrong. Legion would have one chance, if he didn't get with the new program, Cord would take care of it in the only way possible.

"Do you mean we each have a dragon? How do you expect us to sleep if we don't know what's going on?" Kelly insisted.

Cord closed his hand over hers as she spoke. She didn't object. Mostly he did it to draw what he needed from her as he was doing with Minuet. But that wasn't the irresistible reason. No. Touching her was. He had traded a soul for the right to touch her. He was betting Legion would do the same for Molly.

That's how strong the driving hunger was. It was more important than his will to live. That huge malfunction was something no one had mentioned. He had to conclude the need of this woman was built into his nature as surely as the drive to protect her was. His creators didn't make mistakes and they were very good at secrets. The fact that their secrets where part of who he was, what he was, made it crystal clear that he was a tool as opposed to possessing the free will he'd always believed was his.

"Let me make this simple," Cord explained as he controlled his response to his own revelations. "You and Molly are gifted. You are air, she is earth. Some would call you witches. Back when the world was young, everyone knew such people existed. What you call magic was as prevalent in that age as your age uses electronics. The problem was the gifts were exclusive to a few.

"Originally dragons were created to defend or attack, the product of too much knowledge and very little forethought. Created by wizards who believed they would rule the world through the strength of an undefeatable army.

"The three ladies who held the keys to this planet had to answer the threat of dragons and did so by coming up with a separate version. New and improved, second-generation-type beings with a few surprises built in.

"Brings us to our other problem, there are only two of you. If you are here, there is a third witch. We have to find her. Do you have a redheaded friend you're abnormally close too?"

"What about Minuet?" Kelly asked softly.

Cord couldn't be less than honest. It was too important. "She is not water. She is a different type of power. One I've never encountered before."

"So I have a dragon, just as Kelly does," Molly clarified. "And there is another woman gifted with water and she has a dragon protector? And there are other dragons who want to kill us? How can this be? Neither of us has ever seen a dragon."

Cord carefully filtered information before he answered. "There are only three walking dragons currently on the Earth. The others are still here, but you could say they are sleeping, inanimate is a better explanation."

Kelly sucked in a deep breath. "Sleeping? Minuet said she speaks with a dragon but he's sleeping. Is he a protector?"

Cord couldn't reassure her as he wanted to. If the worst were true, Kelly would have to be prepared. "I don't know. She didn't give a name. I suspect she can call us all."

Kelly's hand tightened in his. "That's bad? How many are there?"

Cord sighed. This wasn't what he wanted Kelly focused on. She had so much to learn before she faced this. She should have been able to get out of the basement herself. Was it possible she didn't know the strength of her gift? Or was it she didn't trust it? If she was totally untrained, it could be a problem. Every minute of Minuet's life presented the danger her mother had just voiced. His inability to end that life while the child was too young and weak to stop him had created the danger.

"I will not let it happen," he promised rashly. He had no idea if he could stop it. "I'm here, I'll teach her how to shield from them. You're safe."

"How many?" Kelly pressed.

Cord lifted her hand to his lips, kissing the back as he answered. "They can blacken the sky with their wings. The last time I saw them gathered was in a battle. I didn't have time to count."

"A battle? You won?" Kelly asked softly.

"In a manner of speaking."

"That doesn't sound like winning," Molly stated firmly.

"I'm here. They are not. That's winning in the end," Cord responded.

Molly pursed her lips as she frowned at him across the table, her eyes disapproving at the way he cradled Kelly's hand. "That's double talk for something sneaky. You just said they are sleeping, so they are not dead. How did you make them sleep? Why didn't you kill them if it was a battle?"

"I also said what seems normal to humans does not apply to dragons. It is very difficult to kill a dragon, hence our value in combat.

"Let me put Minuet in her bed. I don't want to have this conversation over her head. There is no telling what her subconscious picks up," he evaded. "Then you can tell me where her father is."

Kelly stood. "I'll show you to her room."

Molly pushed back from the table too. "If I can't go home, I have to cook," she stated.

"Fine." Kelly waved a hand at the kitchen distractedly. "Do whatever you want. We'll be right back."

Cord smiled inwardly. Molly hadn't asked. She'd announced what she was going to do. She was earth, creative and energetic. It would be amusing to watch Legion handle that. If it went that way, he cautioned himself.

Kelly went up the steps ahead of him. Not even a hitch in her gait from her recently crushed leg. Those long columns of perfection were unblemished. Her shorts framed her bottom and he had to look away.

Carrying the child helped him remember what he was here for. And there was the unresolved issue of Minuet's father. He couldn't sense a male's mark in the house. Not even a hint. He'd been trying to find one since he walked in the door.

The hall at the top of the stairs was short. One way led to a single door, the other had two. Kelly led him into a beautiful pink dream of a little girl's room. He raked it with a ruthless search, using both senses and eyes. Laying Minuet on the bed, he remained leaning over her as she settled under the covers. Kelly was close beside him, but Minuet didn't wake.

Cord guided Kelly out of the room with a hand at the small of her back, pulling the door almost closed. He stopped at the top of the stairs.

"Her father?" he asked softly.

Kelly leaned on the wall to look up. "He was murdered six years ago."

Cord frowned. "Minuet is about three. How is that possible?"

Kelly smiled, it was a bit sad but there was humor as well. "Dragons don't know everything?" she teased gently.

Cord moved closer. He had to. Her teasing, the humor drew him. "Explain it to me. Use small words. What happened?"

Her hands rested lightly on his chest, not pushing him away. "The murder is unsolved. Minuet is the result of artificial insemination. We were ready to start the next week. But then I couldn't for a long time. Do I need to explain?"

"No." He placed his hands on the wall, one on either side of her head. "You waited 'til you were done mourning? Are you still in love with him?" He was leaning down, his mouth a few inches from hers.

"I will always love him," she confessed softly. "He is part of my daughter."

Cord let the hushed purr of her words sink in. He waited for it, any minute now that confession should back him up off her. It didn't. He didn't care. Perhaps he couldn't care, not even a little bit. Well, he did care, he was glad he didn't have to take her from the man.

Shadows and reality swirled, merged. Suspicion raked his predatory senses. This story had the smell of an old evil, but the rose petals overwhelmed even that stench. Everything was wrong with the way he was reacting. She was taking up too much of the present. He couldn't back down. Getting what he needed was more than a compulsion.

Dawn was not here yet. A single night-light lit the floor and little more, the top of the stairwell enclosed them in intimate darkness. He could feel Minuet sleeping undisturbed at the other end of the hall. Molly was doing something down in the kitchen that involved a lot of muttering.

Cord's hands left the wall to cover the back of her hands on his chest and pressed her palms into his flesh. He dragged her hands up, wrapping them around his neck as his body slowly crowded her, trapping her. His fingers trailed down the undersides of her arms, coming to rest on the sides of her breasts, thumbs caressing the swells in lazy sweeps.

Kelly didn't stop him. Her large violet eyes watched him but there was no fear, no rejection as he wrapped her arms around his neck and pressed his body to her from knees to chest. Nor was there any doubt of his response. His hips rocked into her abdomen as he watched her eyes. It was her mouth he should have been watching. Lush lips opened in a tiny gasp as she felt his heavy length.

That was his, the air she breathed, and he had to have it. His mouth took hers and he couldn't be slow anymore. He'd given her every opportunity to object, to stop him. She'd accepted.

His lips on hers weren't near enough. Firmly pushing into her mouth, he was rewarded as she opened for him. Her taste, her delicious, addictive taste exploded through his senses as he delved into her. She tentatively sucked his tongue and all hell broke loose, triggering a chain of responses he'd never experienced before. Lust backdrafted through him with white-hot demand.

Cord ripped his hands off her, flattening them on the wall beside her body. The rush of sexual aggression left little besides the drive to complete his possession of her. He was dimly aware his reaction could manifest in talons to ensure she did not evade him.

A low growl rumbled around them as his weight shifted into her, the need to pin her beneath him lashed at what little restraint he could manage. Muscles tensed in his neck as the kiss intensified. He needed more—more taste, more sensation, more of everything she was. Hunger like nothing he'd ever known roared through him even as she fed him with her kiss and he knew there was nothing, nothing he wouldn't do to have this woman.

It was her soft, wheezing moan as she struggled for air that controlled his response. With a stifled snarl, he wrenched himself off her, flinging his body to the opposite wall as he stared at her blankly.

Kelly gasped in air, her eyes wide as she watched him. Cord had no idea what his expression was but it couldn't be good. There was a flicker of fear on her face. Damn it, she should be afraid. He was freaking terrified of what had almost happened. Almost? No, it had happened and there was no going back. Why? Why hadn't Marelda told him?

"I'm sorry," he ground out softly.

"For kissing me?" Kelly whispered.

"No, baby, for much more than that." He ran a hand down his face and tried to make sense of the changes he'd just forced on both of them. The secrets kept from him within his own body.

Marelda and her cohorts were indeed brilliant. He'd known they were masters of nuance, their end plan lush with detail. This detail changed everything and he hadn't known about it. Ignorance was his only excuse and that was a damn useless set of words. He had to explain it to her.

"You didn't offend me," she continued softly.

Cord managed a half smile. "I will, give me a minute."

"What's wrong? A kiss isn't the end of the world. I wanted it. You couldn't have missed that."

"You should have slapped my face and told me to keep my animal paws off you."

Her brows went up. "How could I do that? Reading you in the kitchen was informative. You think my daughter is a miracle. You would give your life to protect her. But that's not the reason I wanted that kiss, Cord. When you think of me, you are loyalty, protection, defense and you think I'm hot. You want me and that's a huge turn-on. You're also sexy as hell. Knowing as much as I do about your need to protect me makes it easy to ignore common sense and enjoy what we both want a little bit."

Cord crossed the space between them and cupped her face with both hands. "No, baby, you don't read me like you think. You read what you want to see. Those intentions are true, but not the only truth, Kelly girl." His nose almost touched hers as he held her gently. "Look again. Tell me what you see."

Her eyes on his, her spirit spread through his consciousness. She became an inquisitive spring breeze that touched him from the inside out. His response was powerful, surging to meet her, surrounding her, blending with her. He didn't shield its depth from the beautiful Wind Witch who stroked him with her attention.

"Possession," she gasped.

"Yes," he gritted. "Complete, irrevocable possession. I mentioned I was the product of brilliant minds. Notice I didn't say 'the child of'. I used the words *product of*. I was made by using DNA gathered from many sources. The flesh DNA mostly came from predators, some you know, some no longer exist, but the significance of those species was not just their skill as deadly aggressors. Before this morning, I never realize the importance of their mating habits. Now I can't ignore them. Every one of the predators used in my makeup mates for life."

He took his hands off her, flattening them on the wall. He wasn't harmless or gentle. He wasn't some casual thrill because it had been so long for her. She needed to understand that he was her last thrill.

Her brows drew together as she regarded him. "It's not like…"

"It's not your fault. I'm not a man." Even though she was the Wind Witch, she was still thinking in terms of him being something with human reactions.

"I'm not even an animal. I'm the product of desperate times. A creature made to endure the end of the world when dragons ruled. I exist to support the fragile hope that humans could survive if they were given a second chance." Cord stopped. This wasn't making sense to her. He could see it on her face. Of course it wasn't.

"Maybe this will make more sense. When we're animated, dragons eat and drink, but that's not what fuels us. The brilliance of dragon design was making a perfect weapon that could not be killed by normal human methods. An endless energy source was the key. We drink human emotions. Sexual desire is delicious. It drives us to seek more. Do you know what really packs a satisfying punch? They are emotions humans have in endless supply. Adoration or terror."

Chapter Four

"You were feeding? Is that what you're telling me?" Kelly asked, offended comprehension raising her voice.

"No," he denied but had to amend. "Yes. I was feeding but it's different with you." His voice deepened as he saw the bitter disbelief on her face. He should give her some space to work through the information but he didn't have time. Nor did he have the will to move away from her. He had to make her understand.

"That line wasn't believable when I was sixteen," she stated flatly, withdrawing all emotion from her face as she now regarded him coldly.

"It's not a line. I was created by a Wind Witch for the next Wind Witch. You. She didn't tell me that important fact. I didn't know until Minuet brought me here.

"Kelly, listen to me. Dragons are thinking, learning beasts. The originals soon did not need their weak, human creators, wizards. About the only thing they shared with the ones who designed them was greed.

"The shortsighted, greedy wizards intentionally created dragons with a constant, limitless hunger, thinking it would be a means to control the army and a weapon when unleashed on an enemy. Very shortly the highly intelligent, impossible-to-kill and veraciously hungry beasts disposed of their masters. They have no built-in control such as a conscious, a sense of right and wrong. There is only the drive for more of what a dragon needs. The more hideous the abuse, the stronger emotions humans gave, and the dragon could become powerful beyond imagining. A well-fed dragon can continue to develop both size and strength if he wants too.

"The three witches realized that love was the only edge humans had. That emotion can dominate all others. If a dragon's need could be refined to only feed on human pleasure, he could become powerful without being out of control. If he found the most pure source of power was the sexual satisfaction of a woman, then giving him the genetic handicap of having a single mate would ensure he never strayed to the darker gratification of fear and abuse."

Cord carefully took his hands from the wall beside her head. He backed to the other side of the stairwell as he watched her work through what he'd just said. He continued softly.

"Not telling the dragon he could be trapped by a single female ensured he didn't know enough to resist her and stay away. The failsafe was telling him his mission was to kill the next Wind Witch who appeared on Earth. If he killed her, he'd never become powerful enough to be dangerous to humans. If he didn't kill her, he'd still be leashed to her."

Cord paused as he realized the promise of a soul, redemption from a God who named the creatures he did not create abominations, had been incentive. A lie.

The three witches' plan had worked perfectly. He'd done exactly what they'd programmed him to do. Bile rose in his throat. Being used, forced into servitude was a long way from what he had thought he was. It had never actually been his choice to take the so-called mission, just as he never really had a choice where Kelly was concerned. However, there was something they hadn't foreseen. Something they couldn't control.

"What they didn't know was that it is possible for there to be a dragon caller. One who can reanimate them without loving or hating. One who's power is so pure it draws dragons from the sleep of ages. Minuet."

Her eyes widened as fear bloomed across her face. Her glance darted down the hall and then swung back to him.

"Call them? Which ones?" she wanted to know.

"All of them, any of them," he confirmed. "And they are not like me. There are only two others like me. I promised I could protect you both. I was wrong. I can't unless we..." He paused, looking into her eyes he let the realization dawn on her without the words. Said this way, it was so damn crude. When he saw her grasp the facts, he continued. "I'll reach full strength and you will be tied to me forever."

She took a few minutes but her gaze never left his as she processed their situation. Cord had to give her credit for fearlessness as she looked at the face of the stranger who'd just told her he'd be having her body if she wanted to protect her daughter.

He knew exactly when she got over that. Her eyes narrowed as she leaned toward him from her wall. "Alone? You could protect us from some unknown number of vicious dragons by yourself?"

"It would help if Legion mated Molly and we found the third witch. Then there would be three witches, a perfect circle, and three extreme dragons," he admitted to her question, which led him directly a bitter truth. "The thing that can't work about this is you cannot love me on command. Humans don't work that way, especially freeborn, non-genetically engineered ones. And there is no guarantee Molly will like Legion, much less love him."

He had to turn away from the woman trapped with him in this nightmare. "For God's sake, what were they thinking?" he demanded in frustration, his base instincts reacting to his anger. Betrayal by the women he had considered a mother on such a grand scale might have made him sick to begin with, now he just wanted to kill something.

Kelly grabbed his arm. "Come downstairs if you're going to start roaring," she hissed.

Her hand on his body was the shackle he'd been designed to make it. His anger didn't dissipate, if anything it increased as they moved down the stairs. He let her think she was leading him, perhaps she was. His inability to separate from her was the bottom line.

Kelly stopped just outside the kitchen to look up into his face. "You're too angry," she said softly. "I understand most of your story. You feel trapped and betrayed. Stop thinking this is all about you."

"What? This is all about you, Kelly. I can't change what I am. Now you have no choices."

"I happen to disagree. There is always a choice and I choose my daughter, whatever it takes." Kelly frowned up at him and poked her finger into his chest to make her point. "You had choices and you made them. You chose not to kill us. So you betrayed your witch and her plan before you learned how she'd programmed you. That tells me you're not as programmed as you seem to think you are."

Cord scowled and conceded she might be right to some degree. He'd made his own choice. Who was to say if Marelda had programmed it into him or simply guessed it was the one he would make.

He reached out, his hands spanning her waist, and drew her lower body flush against his. She grasped his forearms but didn't protest as he surrounded her.

"I don't have a choice about this," he gritted out as his cock rested hot and hard against her soft belly. Even through both sets of clothes there was no hiding his response to her. "And now you don't either. I'm not a man. I'm more predator than anything and I am possessive."

Kelly's bottom lip sucked in under her teeth as she regarded him. "Does that mean we don't have to use condoms?"

A smile crept through his anger and onto his face. Somehow the twinkle in her eyes as her hands glided up his arms to circle his neck had the power to displace all that indignation, righteous anger and bitter resentment. Just like that.

"You know what one of the most powerful things in the world is?" he asked her in a low growl.

"Tell me," Kelly invited with her lips as the rest of her invited everything else.

"Laughter, sweet Kelly Wind Witch," he informed her as his mouth ate all those invitations she was making.

"Kelly, enough crawling over the big fungus. We don't know where it's been," Molly interrupted. "I was willing to pretend I couldn't hear every word of the argument from the kitchen door, but I draw the line at copulation."

Kelly reluctantly turned her head to face her friend. He had one arm snaking up her back, she wasn't pulling away. Cord didn't feel there was any reason to stop tasting so continued down her cheek and around her ear.

"Not to worry. Copulation will not…um, oh…" Kelly seemed to lose her train of thought as his tongue dragged slowly down the side of her neck. "Relax, Molly, you're turn is coming," she managed to croak.

"Oh really?" Molly faced them from the stove, one hand on a hip the other brandishing a wooden spoon. "Fungus thinks he's getting some witch sandwich action? Kelly, you might think he's all portabella in garlic butter, but he just became poop-fur to me."

The rumble of laughter in his chest was a welcome interruption. Cord's head lifted from Kelly's body as he chuckled and slowly let Kelly go. "That's a good one, Mol. Sure you don't want to save poop-fur for Legion? It's particularly disgusting."

Kelly grabbed Cord's hand, edging him to the table. "This one is mine, Molly," she stated firmly, but laughter laced each word. "You'll have to settle for your own dragon. I don't share."

Molly was still frowning at them. The housecoat was swallowed under a long apron that was obviously Kelly's. Molly would be giving in to wishful thinking to call herself five foot four inches tall. Kelly was easily six foot.

"He's grown!" Molly exclaimed as they stepped into the kitchen. "Kelly, look at him. He's gotten all big." The spoon wavered at she pointed it at Cord.

"Is something burning?" Cord asked, leaving Kelly's side to stride toward Molly and the stove.

"Oh my God. The biscuits. Potholders. I need potholders." Molly's voice betrayed her stress as she turned to pull out draws and snapped them shut in frustration.

Cord opened the oven and pulled out a tray of golden biscuits, placing them carefully on cooling rack by the stove. Both Kelly and Molly froze.

"Your hand?" Kelly breathed in concern.

"Dragons have a thing about fire," Cord commented. "It doesn't exactly burn us." He held up his hand so both women could see his unscathed palm.

"Oh." Molly gulped, and backed up a step.

"But we don't know shit about cooking. Should I stir this gravy while you get over it?" Cord asked Molly conversationally. "Smells too good to let it burn over a little shock."

Molly nodded and Cord plucked the wooden spoon out of her hand. "Thanks," she responded automatically. "I cook when I'm nervous, or..." Her words dropped off as she stared at Cord stirring her gravy and backed closer to Kelly.

"I think we're in trouble," Molly said after a brief silence.

"Yeah," Kelly agreed with her.

"This is really happening," Molly continued.

Cord took the gravy off the stove, placing it beside the biscuits. "Mind if I eat while we discus what's happening?" He hadn't ingested food in quite awhile. Though he didn't need it to live, it was a pleasure he'd not bothered with. Molly's breakfast smelled good.

"No, um, yes, of course," Molly agreed. "Where are the plates? I can't find anything in this kitchen," she accused Kelly as if that were the root of all her problems.

"I don't know. We've been using paper plates. I don't think I've unpacked the dishes yet," Kelly stated as she glanced around her own kitchen.

Cord opened the second cabinet from the stove and pulled out three plates. "Saw these while looking for glasses," he explained casually.

Kelly was quiet through the meal. Eating thoughtfully and glancing at him under lowered lashes. He was more interested in what was going on in her head than explaining the stalking skills of evil creatures.

The plates were clean and sitting in the drain by the time Molly had mulled things over enough to ask questions. "Bottom line, will the dragons you said were designed to kill us start showing up soon? And if they do, don't you think the government will notice and do something about it?"

Cord raised a brow. "Would you have known I was anything but a normal guy if Kelly hadn't needed healing? We are very good at stealth. I don't know if any of them have animated, but I'm pretty sure the presence of natural-born white witches in the world again means there are Silver-phin Wizards as well. Those are the guys who thought it would be cool to invent creatures that feed on terror with an insatiable hunger."

"Well, why haven't we noticed your wizards or dragons before? What do they want from us?" Molly wanted to know.

"Minuet," he stated.

"Explain," Molly demanded.

Kelly looked up from under her lashes, her eyes on his face. Cord was captivated with the look. It was innocently seductive but speculative too.

"She is a dragon caller. I've never heard of such a person before, but then, apparently there are a lot of things I was not told." Cord glanced at Molly. "She is power, pure power. Isn't that the root of all conflict? Doesn't matter if they know she can call dragons. The wizards get a whiff of her and they will do anything to acquire her. If one of the original dragons realizes what she is, he'll do anything to get her under his control."

Kelly's hands were clutched together on the table. Feeling her stress, Cord reached over and covered them with one of his. "There are only supposed to be three animated dragons. We know what happened last time and we're not giving them tips. It might be different this time. The only thing we know for sure is the white witches are women of the earth and elements. As a unit, they can work together to save the planet. Or they can destroy it and everything on it."

Both Kelly and Molly frowned. "Destroy it? We'd never do that."

"You would if there was no other choice. You'd come up with a plan if the forces working to enslave humans were so strong that they would soon destroy you, the last power fighting for freedom. You'd do it to give your people another chance at freedom." Cord's hand tightened on Kelly's as she shuddered at the picture he painted.

Molly sat back and crossed her arms. "You're talking destruction in Biblical proportions."

Kelly stood up without letting go of Cord's hand. Calmly she stepped around and backed into his lap.

"What? What are you doing?" Molly demanded as she watched Cord open his arms and settle her.

"We need him uber strong," Kelly said. "Explain it to her."

"I'd rather the new tree in your front yard grew a pair and got his ass in here. He can explain it to her."

"He's here?" Kelly asked as she leaned forward to peer out the kitchen window. "He's been watching? Oh, that's good, isn't it?"

Dawn was streaking the sky with the promise of a clear day.

Molly shot out of her chair, went to the window, scowling. "You're right, that tree wasn't there yesterday."

"It could be good," Cord answered Kelly, taking the moment to lick her neck.

Molly was firmly focused on the oak in Kelly's front yard. Cord had noticed it when they came downstairs. Unsure if it was who he thought, he'd waited to see if it became a threat.

It'd become clear Legion was figuring things out the same way he had. Only he was out there letting Cord do all the work handling his woman. Cord wanted to handle his own woman.

Kelly's acceptance of his physical needs wasn't a puzzle. Her reasons for being on the lap of the creature she'd met a few hours ago were exactly what he deserved. She was doing whatever she had to. Protecting her child required he have access to power, her power. Here she was on his lap.

"Are you telling me that the big stump out there is a dragon?" Molly demanded. There was an edge to her voice. She'd already proved she was aware of her natural talents, and Cord suspected she used them much more than she let on.

Kelly was the one who didn't seem to have any idea how powerful she was. Why had she been in the basement physically looking for her cell phone? A Wind Witch should have called it back up the pipe. Nor should she have been stuck under the tank. What was the problem? Was she simply not using her powers? Or was she as dangerously unaware of them as her daughter?

There were a lot of questions Cord would have liked to ask, but Molly abruptly turned on her heel and exited the kitchen, headed for the front door.

"Wait a sec, Molly," Cord called after her as he set Kelly in the chair next to him, Cord got to the front door but not fast enough. He grabbed Molly's arm to stop her marching into the front yard. "Will you hold on, woman? He might be dangerous."

Molly's head whipped around, her body half turning to say something to Cord but she never had the chance.

"Hands off her, Windweaver," gravelly tones demanded.

There was no longer an oak in the yard. Behind Molly stood over seven feet of hard, male. His skin the color of rich soil, he appeared more rock than man. Simple T-shirt and jeans covered massive muscles that moved in fluid grace as his large palm slid around Molly's waist to pull her against his abdomen. Tall, dark and gravelly turned her with the move so they both faced Cord, who held her arm. Standing in front of Legion, with her jaw hanging open, Molly's head reached the bottom of his pecs.

Kelly's gasp of shock warmed Cord's neck as she saw the exceeding large male. Cord's other arm flashed behind him to hold her there, making sure she stayed back.

"The lady's choice," Cord replied in calm tones.

The bastard was huge, not a gaunt molecule in his form. Cord's eyes didn't flicker as he surveyed Legion. "Though considering how well fed you appear, I'm guessing you've been hanging around for a while? Perhaps you can clear something up for me since the old ones were obviously full of shit. Do dragons really go a little blind from beating it that much?"

Cord's eyes flick down to Molly's round ones. "Been having hot dreams lately? We feed on sexual energy and the boy looks well fed."

A little gasping, "Oh," escaped Molly as she stared at Cord. Then the shock on her face did an amazing transformation into indignant anger. "*Oh!*"

Her head twisted around to look up at the male holding her. "Let. Me. Go!"

Kelly's hands fluttered on Cord's back. "Um…is he safe."

Cord remained in ready stance but his voice was relaxed. "Oh yeah. Big boy has been here awhile. He figured it out long before I did."

Legion immediately released Molly and stepped back as the ground rolled beneath their feet. "Shut up and get your hands off her, Cord."

His hold on Molly was loose. She easily pulled her arm away. "Seriously? Sexual energy?" she asked Cord.

"Listen, it's not like that," Legion started behind her.

Molly simply held up a hand at his face without bothering to turn her head and look at him. "I'm not speaking to you, Rot Wood. Fungus can explain it."

A slow smile spread across Cord's face as he relaxed to lean against the doorjamb. His arm drew Kelly around beside him. "Well, it's like this," he began.

"Enough!" Legion growled. "You've helped me enough, Windweaver. Molly, calm yourself," he commanded.

"Oh, so not a good idea," Molly replied in a quietly controlled tone, still not looking at the tall male. "I think I'll go home. If anyone here is so stupid as to follow me, I am from the Islands and very aware of my craft. You will end up a twig with a bad case of termites." She nodded at Kelly. "Thank you for breakfast."

"You cooked it," Kelly murmured.

Molly had already turned and was heading to her house. Legion scowled after her and glanced at Cord. "You talk too much."

"You could have talked a little more. How long have you been here?" Cord shot back. "A warning would have been welcome."

"When? You've been in a bottle since the last moon phase. You were in no shape to protect the child. It was my duty."

Cord raised a brow and motioned with his chin at Molly's retreating form. "And you have such a handle on your duty?"

Legion grunted and turned to follow Molly.

"Bottle? What does he mean by you were in a bottle?" Kelly asked as Cord shut the door.

"He means I preferred the oblivion of scotch to being aware of how hungry I was," Cord confessed as he looked down at her. He wasn't quite sure which way he wanted to go. Back to the kitchen or the other way to the box-jammed sitting room? He glanced up the stairs and rejected that temptation.

"Are you an alcoholic?" Kelly wanted to know.

She was planted in front of him, frowning, and he realized how serious a subject this was for her. Of course it would be if he were human.

"Kelly, I'm an addict. Consider me a crack junkie. My drug is you." He resisted the drive to touch her as she looked at him.

He had no choices and neither did she. To protect her daughter she'd do precisely what he needed. The one possession he had, the thing they could not program out of him was what he was determined to give her now. The truth.

Chapter Five

"Cord, that is an amazingly sweet thing to say in a really weird way, but I'm being serious. Do you have a drinking problem?"

Her hands were on her hips, and if she'd had a tail, it would be fluffed in irritation. Did he find her irritation cute because he was programmed to? Or was she really adorable when she was annoyed? What did it matter, his reaction to her would only grow.

"Sweet? I'm being direct. Using the illustration of an addict is not a ploy. It's as close as humans can come to what's been programmed into me. The only thing I can choose to give you is a little time to grasp what I am. I don't even have much of that. The rest—protection, defense, these things are yours whether you want them or not." He continued after a brief pause, it was all he could manage to make sure she heard this part. "The way you get rid of me is to refuse contact. I'll become diminished and one of your attackers will eventually figure out how to kill me."

Kelly's head cocked to the side as she listened to him, and then she reached for his hand. "Come here."

She led him into the living room, around a haphazard stack of boxes and to the couch. "Sit."

Cord sank down on the couch. Kelly girl wasn't processing the information he was trying to give her in the manner he'd expected. Sure, he expected her to be ticked, who wouldn't be when they became a possession as opposed to a free woman? Mad at him was a natural response. He was the monster and she had no alternative but to accept him into her life in the most intimate way imaginable. But she didn't seem mad at him for reasons he couldn't fathom.

She stood between his wide-spread legs and frowned down at him as if he were messing things up.

"Do you know what I see when I look at you?" she asked.

Cord resisted the urge to run a hand through his hair. "No."

"Give me your hands," she requested softly.

He held them up and Kelly grasped them, letting him take her weight as she slid both knees onto the couch, straddling his hips. She then sat back on his thighs and laced their fingers together. Holding his hands, her eyes studied his face.

Cord didn't move. She was touching him. His body tightened as he savored the feel of her weight on him. She'd placed herself on his lap as if it were natural for her to sit there. Why she would do that didn't have much time to bother him. The globes of her perfect ass resting on his thighs took too much of his attention.

"I see midnight in your hair, so dark the black becomes purple when I glance away and I have to look again. My fingers want to touch it to feel the night. Your eyes are the steel gray of winter morning. Lush lashes can't soften the coldness there, but when you look at me, they become the color of steam rising from the fire within."

Her voice moved through him, a melody of sounds that almost drowned her words. It was intimate, softly open.

Letting go of his hand, the back of her knuckles feathered down his cheek. "High cheekbones, a straight, arrogant nose and those amazing lips. The close-cut beard brings night's shadow to your face without disguising its strength. A male face that is so perfect it's a mask, except when you look at me." Her eyes lingered on his lips a moment then met his gaze as she continued.

"I refuse to believe the honor holding you still under my hands is some programmed thing. I feel your body shudder and I'm not so ignorant as to think it's sweet emotion moving you. If you are even a little bit of what you say, the choice to give me this freedom is one you are making every second, isn't it? Comparing yourself with a drug addict is unacceptable. Please do not."

"What would you like me to do then?" Cord asked tightly.

Kelly let go of his other hand. As her hands settled on his shoulders in light exploration, she smiled into his eyes. "Like yourself a little," she murmured.

Cord leaned his head back on the couch and closed his eyes. His hands started at her knees and slowly glided up silky flesh, curving around the back of her thighs to pull her up and into his body. She flowed into him just as he'd asked her to with the gentle pull. Keeping his eyes closed to give her a little more gentleness, he grimaced sadly.

"Kelly, we both know what you're doing. If even half of what I've said is true, you need me to protect Minuet. Knowing your response is what feeds me, strengthens the beast, you're willing to try. If you want to ascribe some sort of honor to me because it helps you deal with this, I'm all for it."

Her hands framed his face as she demanded, "Open your eyes. Look at me."

His lids lifted in lazy sensuality. Her face hovered over his and there had never been a sexier sight than Kelly panting slightly and little bit mad.

His caress grew bolder as knowing fingers played over soft inner thighs then trailed down her legs to casually caress the backs of her knees and upper calves. He felt her pulse quicken. The sweet fire of desire was well kindled low in her belly. He would keep building it. Carefully, slowly, knowingly drawing her deeper and deeper into sexual abandon.

His body drank her pleasure and he'd take that substance from her until she was helpless in a sexual frenzy. There was nothing he wouldn't do to get more of her and when he was done, there would be nothing she wouldn't do for him.

He knew exactly how to get what he needed from a woman. But she had no idea what he'd take from her. She was already feeding the beast, giving him her soul. What she asked of him was impossible. She'd understand that eventually. He was a user and she was the drug.

"Kiss me," she breathed into his mouth as she lowered her lips to his.

Her touch was not tentative as she opened and kissed him with fierce female claim. His response was a flash fire of demand. He ignored it, letting her take what she needed from him. Perhaps he could give her this, this little bit of control. It wouldn't last, but she needed it right now.

Sucking her tongue deep in his mouth he stroked it as she withdrew, his head lifting off the sofa to follow the nectar, demanding she enter again. Her hips took up the rhythm, pressing into him and retreating as he continued the light touches along the length of her legs. The gliding caress was no longer enough.

Her body asked for more and he denied her, only giving her his mouth in full abandon. Her hands became claws, raking from his hair to his shoulders. Kelly moaned into his mouth and that was the trigger he couldn't refuse. Abruptly it was his tongue invading her with a hard push as his body shifted in a liquid ripple of muscle, turning them to lay her back on the couch, his body blanketing her.

Steel thighs pushed between her legs, giving her no other option but to wrap those long columns of perfection around his hips. His fly thrust into the crotch of her shorts, driving material between soft wet folds. There was no mimicking going on anymore. He stroked her with a hard length of distended jeans. The layers of clothing between them added to her frustration.

Soft hands grabbed fistfuls of shirt and wrenched it out of his jeans. Finding the moving flesh of his back at last, she was desperate to touch all of it.

His hands remained fisted in the couch cushions beside her body. Bulging biceps trembled with the effort of restraint as he kept most of his weight off her. His hips and mouth engaged her with pounding response, but he would let her see where they were going. This one time.

Friction on her sensitive folds drove her up the sensual ladder. Her response sank into his starved body and it felt better than anything he'd experience before. It had been so long since he'd indulged sexual hunger. Then it had been good, this was nothing like that. Bursting spears of pleasure pierced every cell in his body.

Her legs locked around him, heels digging into his ass, and he felt the electric flash fire wash over her. She was close and exactly where he needed her to be. His hips slowed. Pressing his cock down on her clit, he let the material tease, keeping her on the edge of release. His mouth ate her as her hands grew more demanding. She raked down his back with nails, and Cord growled in satisfaction.

He gave her several hard thrusts in reward and she arched into him, trying to get more, needing the push over the edge. He withheld it.

Her hands thrust down the back of his jeans, greedily clenching into his ass, pressing him into her. He lifted his crotch off her as her hands raked up to the small of his back. Yes, that's what he needed from her.

The power of her desire poured into him with each twist and pull of her body. She was more, so much more gratifying than he'd thought a woman could be. Pleasure snaked around his brain, infused his body, jumping with the snap of electric current from unused muscles to sleeping bone. She ignited him and they were fully clothed.

She wrenched her mouth from him, but he couldn't give up contact. Open mouthed, he dragged his tongue down her neck, seeking the sensitive nerves he knew were there. He was rewarded as soon as he licked over them. Her response speared him and his mouth smiled into her neck, licking lightly. The feathering strumming resulted in her head arching back and her hands clutching the back of his nearly shredded shirt in frustration.

The sound of material ripping and woman hissing through clenched teeth was an interesting mix. He liked it. His lips fastened down and he sucked that bit of flesh into his mouth as his hips thrust hard up the valley of her legs. One hand shot up over her mouth, the other reached down and clamped around her hip to hold her as he push his hips over her clothes-covered crotch.

He could feel the lightning racing through her body. Drinking it, he tasted how close she was. His lips lifted and the hand at her hip skillfully worked snap and zipper. The soft flesh of her belly met his palm and he slid thick fingers under damp silk to reach the center of her. Two fingers spread plump folds, uncovering her clit for a third finger's attention. Strumming that sensitized group of nerves, with each touch he enjoyed the burst of pleasure she couldn't contain.

He held her on the edge with light contact. Her hips rocked up into his grasp, but he wouldn't let her take control. Pleasure was white hot and ripping through her. Still he refused.

Kelly's teeth closed on his palm and Cord jerked in response. As she bit down, his long forefinger left her clit to slide into the tight opening clenching below. The heel of his palm slammed down on her clit, grinding in a circular motion as he invaded her.

Kelly exploded. Her body clenched in ridged shock then convulsed under him. His hand on her mouth muffled her vocal response but he was pretty sure there were a few curse words in the screaming moan.

She came into him with such a punch of power he nearly lost control. Fire raced through every joint and muscle. It burned deep in his back and lanced down his legs. For a moment he was drunk with it. Intoxicating, excruciating in this volume.

His mouth let go of her neck as he clamped it shut to hold back the roar of fulfillment and cut off his own answer to her release. Not this time. This one was hers alone. Eyes squeezed shut, the pleasure became pain as he refused his response to her gift of power.

Their bodies gradually stilled, his hips resting heavily between her legs. His hand released her mouth and he opened his eyes to look down at the woman beneath him. She was looking back. He might be mistaken but the round eyes and slightly slack mouth as she panted looked a lot like shock.

He held her with his weight and let her work through it. There was no way he'd crawl off her now and pretend they'd just been necking and indulging a little heavy petting. They'd been doing a lot more than that, and she needed to face it head-on. He'd be taking more than that from her very soon.

"Kiss me," she whispered into the silence.

He gave it to her, slow and deep. She wanted to feel cherished and he had no problem with that. He cherished the hell out of her. There was no adequate way to express how deeply he valued her, but nor was he capable of what she was looking for now, and that burned deep in his mind. He could pretend though. If it made her happy, he could be any freaking thing she needed. Ruthlessly, relentlessly.

She melted into the kiss, meeting him with gentle hands and closed eyes, soaking in his act. She wanted to him to pretend they were falling in love. She needed that emotional human validation for what had just happened.

He would create an illusion of anything she wanted, anything at all, but he couldn't give the real thing. He wasn't capable of it. The bitter reality smoldered in useless anger. He was not capable of the one thing she wanted desperately. Soulless creations could be a shitload of things, but all of them were hard and demanding. Love was not something that could be mixed in a lab and added to the beast.

Illusions were easy though. Reading her desires and using them to create what she needed was one of the things his kind was very good at. Sly, deceptive, manipulative, all natural abilities that were part of being a predator who took what he wanted by any means. A dragon always got what he wanted from a human and most animals.

For a dragon there are no rules, no morals, no regrets a soul would hamper them with. But his creators had found a way to leash him. They'd wrapped it up in pretty words and high ideals, convincing him that he was different, cruelly giving him the illusion of choice.

Holding this woman, drinking her, he knew with complete clarity that there was no choice and there never would be. He would do anything to keep her in his arms, giving him this. Any deception, any lie, any act of violence. For her, he'd be as fully dragon as any killer from that bygone age. And that was exactly what they'd built him for. It was working perfectly. He hated them with the same intensity he needed her.

She deserved more, and in making him, they had stolen her future as surely as they'd written his into the biological cement of DNA. She would never be free. Her choices would be manipulated, bent to his will. Even if she eventually suspected it, there would be no freedom for her. By that time she would crave what he gave her.

A soft light broke over the dark path his thoughts had taken him down. Above them in a blindingly pink bedroom, hope stirred in her bed. There was the one thing the old ones could not control. The reality they hadn't thought big enough to conceive. Proof they could not be in command of every life. Dangerous, incomprehensibly precious, a miracle who would make the future one that belonged solely to this age.

Her mother and he might not have a choice, but Minuet had every choice imaginable.

Cord lifted his head, feathering kisses over Kelley's face. Her eyes opened in lazy pleasure as he licked down her neck.

"That was not nice," Kelly murmured.

"No? I was pretty sure you enjoyed it," Cord growled back, unwilling to lift his head off her skin very long.

"I was lonely."

That did jerk his head up to look into her eyes. "Lonely? Honey, there is only one way I could have been closer to you."

"Uh-huh, and you ran away from me," she accused.

Cord regarded her as he tried to understand what it was she thought he'd done. "I was being careful not to rush you."

"You were being a coward."

"Because I didn't bang you within hours of meeting you?"

"Because you were afraid to trust me emotionally," Kelly told him.

Cord sat up slowly, pulling her up as he did. "What makes you think that?"

Those lovely eyes were a little sad as she opened her mouth to respond. She abruptly shut it as little feet pounded down the stairs. Cord stealthily adjusted Kelly's clothes telepathically, closing shorts in the nick of time.

Without hesitation Minuet ran in beaming, launching herself from a few feet away. Cord shifted slightly to make sure his body took most of her weight as she landed on them. Laughing, she was totally confident she'd be caught.

"Cord gow'ed big," Minuet exclaimed as she lay across them. "Now you pretty."

"I am not pretty, little woman," he corrected in mock seriousness while making sure Minuet and Kelly could feel his humor in the air around them. "Guys are never pretty."

Kelly was laughing and holding Minuet's shoulders as Cord wrapped an arm around her kicking legs and threatened to tickle. "Say I'm not pretty or the tickle dragon gets you."

Shrieks of wiggling laughing met his threat. Cord let her struggle out of his hold and wrap little arms and legs around her mother. Regarding him triumphantly, she laid out the rules as she saw them.

"No tickle when Mommy holding me."

"That's not fair," he challenged.

"I no tickle when Mommy holding you."

Cord nodded. "I guess you're right."

"Time for breakfast," Kelly interrupted them.

"Is Cord eat too?" Minuet wanted to know.

"If he wants to," Kelly agreed as she stood, letting Minuet slide to the floor.

Cord stood with them and smiled down at Minute. "I'd like to see you and Mommy a lot now. How do you feel about that?"

Minuet looked up at her mother a moment. Kelly smiled and raised a brow, giving Minuet permission to say whatever she liked.

At her request of raised arms, he quickly scooped her up and set her on his hip as he smiled into her serious face. Minuet placed two small hands on his cheeks to hold his head in place.

"I happy. Bad birds all gone."

"What?" Kelly questioned in concern.

"You have bad birds?" Cord asked casually as he took Kelly's hand and sauntered toward the kitchen with his little armful.

"They gone," Minuet assured him as he sat her in the kitchen chair with a booster seat.

Kelly sat down beside her daughter, worriedly taking her hand. "Honey, tell Mommy about the bad birds. What did they do?"

Cord gave them a little space. Getting a bowl from the cabinet, he carefully cut a biscuit in it then poured gravy over it, heating it for twenty seconds in the microwave. At the table, Minuet tried to explain.

"They fly an talk. I not talk birds. They bitey." She made snapping motions with her hands as if they were clicking beaks.

Grabbing a spoon, Cord brought the bowl to the table and handed them to Kelly. He sat on the other side of Minuet as her mother tested it for heat.

"Bighty?" Kelly asked "What is bighty?"

"Bitey. They big moufs. Scary."

"Good girl," Cord approved. "Never talk to strangers, even strange birds. Mommy taught you that, right?"

"Yes. I hide pillow. But I hear dem."

Kelly inserted a spoonful of food in Minuet's mouth. "I'm very proud of you. But you should have told Mommy about the birds."

"You not hear?" Minuet asked in surprise as her mother raised the spoon again.

"No. When were they here?"

"Comes wif boxes truck. Talking all a time. Go wif truck. They come back. Flying, flying."

"Well, they are gone now. I'll make sure they don't come back," Cord assured Minuet. "But in case I don't hear them first, be sure and tell me when they come back. Don't tell me in my mind, they might hear that."

Minuet chewed and swallowed before she could reply. "I know dat. They wanna hear in my head."

Her tone told him she thought that was evident to anyone.

"Exactly right," he agreed. "We don't let anyone hear us in our heads. Right?"

Minuet glanced at her mother and shook her head while chewing the next spoonful. Cord looked up over her head and raised a brow at Kelly, asking what the look was about.

"We've been very careful not to use the other ways," Kelly explained conversationally. "It's a big no-no."

Well, that explained a lot. These two actually worked at not testing and controlling their skills. Cord got up and moved to the sink, turning on the water to do the dishes. Mostly he needed to keep out of the conversation until he had a chance to talk to Kelly. Not contradicting her rules in front of Minuet was important. He knew that much about parenting.

Kelly didn't give him a lot of room to work with though. She wanted Minuet reassured that she was safe, so she pressed him.

"Cord is going to take care of the nosy birds. Aren't you?" Kelly stated confidently.

Cord turned from the sink to face her. "I'll protect you from them, but it would be best if we left them alone. Minuet had the right idea when she was quiet. They can't know you ladies are here if you don't give them a sign."

"Why they talk us?" Minuet wanted to know.

Kelly's hand trembled slightly as she shoved another spoonful in Minuet's mouth.

Cord considered his answer. "I think they are looking for anyone who can hear them. You said they are birds because they look like birds? Or do they just feel like birds?"

"Black wif wings. Birds," Minuet clarified.

"In that case, someone is using the birds, honey. You know how you can talk in someone's mind? Sometimes a person who can do that will take control of a little animal and use it. That person can see and hear everything the little animal does and so they don't have to go everywhere the animal can," Cord explained. "I need you to be very careful of animals. If you feel one watching you, you have to tell me or Mommy."

"Okay," Minuet agreed, obviously bored with the animal conversation and ready to be done with it.

"If it's okay with Mommy, I'll teach you how to make sure they can't reach into your mind and hear you," Cord offered, watching Kelly's reaction to the offer.

Kelly's eyes rose to his. There was no fear in them, just sadness. "I think that would be a good idea. It's important to be able to protect ourselves."

"But you said no-no magics." Minuet frowned at her mother.

"Yes, baby, I did. It wasn't safe for us. Weren't you afraid of the loud birds?" Kelly paused as Minuet nodded. "Cord is here to help us now. It's okay to do exactly what he shows us how to do. Do you understand, Minuet? No trying anything unless you tell Mommy or Cord. No matter what."

Minuet's eyes glanced between them and a huge smile appeared on her face. "Cord make daddy?"

Chapter Six

He couldn't say Little Miss Miracle was slow on the uptake. She nailed them with the one question he was more than willing to answer but suspected he shouldn't.

Kelly hesitated a moment, glancing at Cord. "He is our very good friend. It takes time to be a daddy."

"How much?" Minuet wanted to know.

"Honey, being a daddy is about loving us, loving us with all his heart. You can't expect it from someone who just met us and it's not polite to ask," Kelly explained as she fed another spoon of food into Minuet.

Minuet frowned and chewed. Taking a big swallow, she leaned toward Kelly and whispered loudly, "How we see him love us?"

"Let's just be happy we have a new friend. Okay?" Kelly stated, trying to cut off the endless questions.

Cord decided it was time to give Kelly a break and distract Minuet from the subject. "Minuet, I have a very important question for you. Don't be afraid of answering honestly. Taking responsibility for what we do makes everything much better. You know you can tell me anything. Right?"

Serious little face chewed and nodded as she looked into his eyes.

"Why do you think the loud birds followed the truck that brought your boxes? Was there magic they could feel in it?" Cord asked.

Minuet looked down at her bowl but answered clearly. "I not magic anyting we pack. Mommy said no-no. So I magiced truck, no breaking. Maybe birds feels it."

"Minuet." Kelly frowned at her daughter. "You know that was wrong."

Minuet defended. "No magics our stuffs. Smelly man's truck is all."

Cord interrupted. "When does the magic end, honey?"

"End?" Minuet asked puzzled.

"You didn't put an end on the magic?" he asked.

"No. How do dat?" she wanted to know.

"Mommy didn't teach you to end the magic?"

"Mommy not like magics," Minuet explained seriously.

"I didn't teach her to spell either," Kelly said calmly, "she knows how though."

Cord looked at Kelly. "A natural gift. She'll be fine with a few lessons," he stated as if it were a simple thing. "The smelly man's truck just became his best machine. It will never break. However, someone felt Minuet's power. They will follow the truck for a while, but eventually they'll give up and backtrack. I'm guessing we have maybe two months."

"Two months before what?" Kelly asked then glanced at the little face swiveling between them. "Never mind. So we might move again?"

"This is a good place for a while. You two can learn how to handle the craft. That's the most important thing," Cord emphasized seriously. "Especially Minuet. She has to be taught, Kelly. Next time she could unwittingly cause damage. You can't act like she doesn't have the gift."

"I know. It's just, well, things have changed," Kelly finished softly while she pasted on a smile for Minuet, who was watching the adults with sharp eyes. "What about my job, our life?" she couldn't resist asking in the next breath.

"You've recently came into a huge inheritance," Cord informed her with a half smile. "From a great-aunt. She left you everything. Quitting your job will be understandable. Besides, you just moved here, right? No big deal."

Kelly frowned. "Do not think I'm about to become dependent on you. I can support my daughter, thank you very much. Molly got me the job at the place she works. I do not want to make her look bad. Besides, it's a very good position."

"Molly inherited more than you did. How difficult do you suppose it is for an earth dragon to find a vein of gold? Or diamonds? Or any other thing he might need? Molly will not be working there either," Cord informed her.

Kelly raised a brow. "Can you even afford us? Wind doesn't exactly make money."

Cord chuckled. "When an investor has been around long enough, he owns a share in every bank, every company, everything worth investing in. Inventing shell companies made me invisible and has been very profitable. But the point you're not getting is all of it really is yours. I was created for you. Everything I might own is yours."

Minuet took the spoon out of her mother's hand and continued eating.

Kelly cocked her head and narrowed her eyes. "No, it's not and you're not. I don't own living beings. No one is owned."

Cord reached around behind Minuet and lightly traced a finger down Kelly's cheek as he said softly, "Yes they are and you do, but it's going to work a bit different than you're thinking."

She got his message. He could see it in her unblinking stare and soft gasp. She did own him and everything he was. It would be his pleasure to show her how that was going to benefit her.

"You have to think of Minuet," Cord continued in a normal voice, pulling the trump card. "Sending her to daycare while you work might not be a good idea. We've been given a small window of time for both of you to learn a great deal of skill. I can teach you, but not in the evenings when you're both tired from a long day. Your new job has to be helping your daughter master her talents while honing your own. Your lives depend on it."

"You really think… I mean, we don't even know who the birds are from." Kelly stumbled around, voicing her real concerns in front of Minuet. "Surely it's not as serious as all that."

"There is a truck rolling around the country with a powerful, endless spell on it. Obviously the wielder does not have to be near it for the spell to continue at full strength. The best we can hope for is only one interested party has noticed it and wishes to find the source of such never-ending power," Cord said conversationally to shield the importance of the statements from Minuet. "I'm not that optimistic by nature."

"Oh. Can't we find the truck and un-spell it?" Kelly asked.

"Sure, but you or I can't. The little lady responsible would have to, and I don't think she has the skill at the moment. Removing is always harder than putting on. If she made up the spell on her own, the words could be tricky. We can't risk the explosion of power a mistake would cause."

"I sorry," Minuet said quietly, proving she was following the conversation much more closely than the adults wanted her to.

"Sweetie, it's okay. Mommy and Cord will take care of it. All you need to worry about is not doing something in secret again," Kelly cautioned.

Big eyes blinked as she looked at her mother. "I pomise."

"Good girl." Cord smiled into the worried little face. "We will not be making that mistake again." He picked up her empty bowl and took it to the sink.

"Am I gowned?" Minuet asked Kelly.

"Gowned? You can put on your dress-up gown if you want," Kelly assured her. "We unpacked dress up a few days ago."

"No. Gowneded for being bad," Minuet insisted. "No dress up."

"Grounded? Is that what you mean?"

Minuet nodded.

"Where did you learn that word? You can't be grounded, honey. You don't drive or use the phone," Kelly explained to her worried daughter.

"I see TV. Gownding is da worst." Minuet nodded confidently as she said it. "Can I play Coco? She waiting."

Cord had felt the little dog sitting at the back door too. The animal hadn't made a sound and he'd waited to see if, as he suspected, it communicated with Minuet. Quickly he questioned the relationship. "Who owns Coco?"

"She is Molly's," Kelly explained. "A sweet little border collie who has as much energy as Minuet. They spend hours running each other into the ground with fetch and chase."

"Minuet, does Coco ever use words when she talks to you?" he asked seriously.

"No. She happy," Minuet responded.

"This is important." Cord looked into Minuet's eyes. "If any animal, even one you know, uses words to talk to you, call me right away. Do you understand? Small animals are easy for bad people to control. Always use words out loud when you talk to them. Do not use mind pictures."

Minuet nodded. "I no talk Coco. Play now?"

"Honey, go put on play clothes. Do you need my help?" Kelly asked.

"By myself." Minuet's statement was left behind as she dashed out of the kitchen at her normal speed.

"Is it safe?" Kelly asked in concern. "Should I call Molly and tell her about this?"

"It's fine," Cord assured her. "I can shield an area. Nothing will happen in the backyard I don't know about. I wouldn't worry about Molly, she should know all about small animals. She's much more in tune with her craft than you are."

The child shedding pajamas and pulling on clothes was easily heard and monitored by both Cord and Kelly. Movement only slowed for the few seconds it took to pull on socks and jam feet into shoes. The soft scrunch of Velcro fastenings pulled tight and she was barreling down the stairs again.

Kelly looked worriedly at the back door as Minuet dashed through it with a laugh for the little dog jumping about in welcome. "Molly and I never talked about it. Are you sure?"

"I'm sure, but we'll ask if you want. Interrupting her and Root Rot should be fun right about now. Or did she call him Wood Rot?"

Kelly smiled and stood up. "Let's sit on the back patio and you can explain shielding to me. I think the lawn chairs are in the living room."

"Of course they are. Wouldn't you rather we unpack while we talk?" Cord asked as he dried his hands.

"Unpacking just dropped to the bottom of my to-do list," Kelly commented as she turned to the living room to find the folding lawn chairs.

"I didn't mean actually handling the boxes. I meant commanding the items to go where they belong. We can sit and watch Minuet and unpack."

Kelly stopped in the door and frowned at him. "How do things know where to go? How will I know where they are? Wouldn't that cause the explosion of power you're talking about that would draw attention?"

"Shielding is multifunctional. You've got to learn how to do this stuff," Cord explained, walking up to her. His arms went around his Wind Witch to pull her to the side as lawn chairs floated past her and across the kitchen, out the back door and set themselves up on the small concrete patio.

"That's the long way of doing things," he explained while nuzzling her hairline. "Here is the short way." Boxes in the kitchen disappeared.

Kelly melted into the tall, broad man who gently pulled her into his body. She was aware of the lawn chairs moving behind her and abstractly watched the back door open on its own and the suspended chairs moved through it and settle on the patio. The vanishing boxes were disturbing enough for her to interrupt his nuzzling.

"Hey. I know where the chairs went, but I can barely remember where I put things by hand in this kitchen. Now how am I supposed to know where those things are?"

Cord turned her to the back door. "You think of the item you want and draw it to you. Why are you so resistant to using the abilities you were born with?"

They moved outside. The morning was warm as sunlight splashed over the lawn. Minuet's laughter lilted on the air as she and Coco raced around, chasing a ball.

"Family roots in New England," Kelly stated as she sat. "And a religious, fundamentalist family makes for a closed view of what you call talent."

Cord took a deep breath. There was a world of information she wasn't sharing in that short explanation. "None of your family are talented?" he pushed.

Kelly shrugged. "If they are, no one is talking about it. I've never asked. Until I had Minuet, it wasn't a concern." Her smile was a little sad as she watched her daughter plop down and laugh as the border collie bounded up with the ball. The two bodies became a squealing mass of giggles and yaps.

"You moved out here to get away from them?" Cord asked shrewdly. What could make a single mother choose to move away from her family to a place where she had one friend and no one else to help with the burden of rearing a very talented child?

Kelly nodded. "It was safer for everyone. I know whatever is in me is untrained and uncontrollable when I get mad. A mother defending her child is a dangerous type of mad. A child blindly trying to defend her mother could be worse though. It was time to leave."

Cord nodded and figured he'd have time later to delve into that subject.

The yard was fenced with a short chain link. The fence was shared by two other yards, Molly's on the right and the other neighbor on the left. Out the back beyond the chain link was a brush-covered strip of land sloping down to a stream. On the other side of the steam was a wooded area.

"Time to start training your gift," Cord stated. "What does the breeze tell you? Who do you see in it?"

Kelly closed her eyes and tipped her head back. "There are three deer in the woods. Two raccoon dens sorta close," she stated. "There is a sleeping owl, quite a few types of birds, lots of mice and rabbits behaving normally."

"Very good. Being aware of how the wild animals are acting is important. They are extremely sensitive to the old ways. Domesticated animals are harder to read. They behave in ways they think their humans want them to. Now pick an animal and try to feel the world through it. Start with a very small one and just touch its mind."

Kelly frowned, her eyes still closed as she tried to do as instructed. The breeze picked up, turning tree leaves over to show silver backs.

"Easy," Cord murmured softly. "Go small and gentle. Deep breathes."

The pull of air quieted and Kelly's chest rose in a deep but controlled breath as she narrowed her focus. A rabbit was grazing on the other side of the stream. Slowly she flowed around it, feeling her way to see with its eyes. The bunny jerked alert as its long ears picked up a loud banging.

Kelly started and jumped to her feet. The banging was muted when hearing it with her own ears, but it was still there, coming from Molly's house.

Cord slid down farther in his chair and stretched long legs in front of him, crossing them at the ankle. Hands stacked behind his head, he watched Kelly spring out of her chair with the same alarm the rabbit had felt at the new noise.

"Cord. Do you hear that?" she gasped in alarm.

"Yep." He grinned.

"It's coming from Molly's place. Should we go see what all the banging is? It sounds like a fight." Kelly hadn't looked at him as she gazed at her neighbor's back door.

"Oh, it could be a fight, but I doubt it. Feel the air around the house. Listen to the rhythm of the noise," he instructed softly. "Do you really want to go over there?"

"Oh!" Kelly backed up a step in surprise and kicked her lawn chair over. "Oh. Ah, perhaps not. Wow. That's just not right."

Cord chuckled. "I'm sure it's very right or Molly's back door would not be rattling on its hinges. My only fear is they will knock it off the wall and fall out the door."

Kelly straightened her chair and sat down jerkily. "No. It's not right that we can tell what they're doing. We should go inside and um, shield or something."

Cord did laugh then. "Shield? Can't be done. The pure emotional power of sex doesn't allow complete shielding. A sensitive will always know if they are in the area. Those two are not concerned at the moment. Besides, it's natural."

"That does not sound natural to me. Good heavens, are you listening to this?"

"Yeah," Cord purred softly.

Kelly's head whipped around to look at him.

He raised a wicked brow and half smiled as her eyes swept down his long body. The bulge behind his zipper snagged her gaze. Her eyes jerked up to his face and there was a frown between her brows.

"You've changed size physically since earlier. I know you explained that we feed you somehow but…um…does everything change? I mean is there some point you stop expanding? Ah, growing. Getting stronger, taller and all?"

"Not 'we'. You feed me," he corrected softly. "In human form, I'll gain a few more inches. Taller," he tacked on wickedly. "What you're concerned about is something you'll have to investigate firsthand. As a shapeshifter, there is no limit to what I can do for you, but nor would I harm you, little Wind Witch."

"Oh. Um, yes, I mean…I see. I think. Dang it, I'm not little, you know. I'm a very tall person," she huffed in frustration at her nervous responses.

"If you say so," he agreed while his smile told her she was his little anything he wanted.

Kelly turned away from the sensuality in his look. Gray eyes were warm pools of steam that beckoned. The close-cut beard promised sensation in the most intimate ways and then there were his lips. If she watched them while he spoke for another second, she'd have to taste them.

Looking away meant gazing at Molly's house and realizing the noise had gotten louder, the rhythm, womb-clenching fast. Just what she needed, a reminder of how damn lusty these dragons were. Dragons…now there was a thought to ponder.

Glancing at him, she asked casually, "So you shapeshift into a big lizard with wings?"

Cord dragged in a deep breath to savor the spice of her arousal. She was intoxicating. His eyes scanned the yard though he already knew the exact location of child and dog. He needed a moment before he answered.

"I suppose," he agreed lazily, unwilling to describe the reality of what a dragon looked like or why that form was so different from the current human assumption. "Dragon form is armor. Only engaged when someone or something is about to die. I've mentioned we're hard to kill. In true dragon form it's been impossible, as far as I know."

"What about St. George who killed the dragon? I mean, he is a saint and all. What exactly did he kill? Or do you know?" Kelly asked.

"Kelly, George probably wanted to impress a girl," Cord scoffed. "If there was a dragon involved who let him live, it had to be Harrison, the water dragon. He'd think it was funny. They put way too much dolphin in his DNA."

"So you don't think St. George killed anything? He was really a big liar and they made him a saint?"

Cord shrugged. "He might have believed he killed something, but it wasn't a real dragon."

The sound that interrupted them was the low rumble of an earthquake. The muted boom of tectonic plates shifting, but it came from the house next door and the earth in Kelly's yard remained still.

"Seriously?" Kelly murmured as she looked over at the innocent-looking Cape Cod that matched her own. "Everyone in the neighborhood has to know? Every time? That really cuts down on the romance."

"They are earth creatures. Both powerful in their gifts," Cord commented. "Wind folk are not the same."

"Are you saying we'll not be alerting the township every time?" Kelly demanded. "Because I'm not interested in the public being able to keep score."

Cord gazed at the disgruntled Wind Witch as her slightly aroused, a little annoyed, mostly curious mood washed over him. She was everything sweet yet spicy with that strong streak of delectable dark-candy danger. The woman was driving him crazy and doing it while sitting three feet away. She had no idea how powerful she was.

"I'll keep that in mind," he promised with a wicked smile. Teasing her yielded a sexy mix of humor spiced with lusty fear. She fed him without even meaning to. Greedily absorbing her essence was his pleasure, his addiction, his sentence, his prison. Cord closed his eyes and let the smirk shadow on his face for her benefit.

"Humph," she sniffed. "Do that."

Minuet raced up to them, leaping into her mother's lap. "You hear Aunt Molly laughing?" she wanted to know.

"Laughing?" Kelly was surprised but smiled at the innocent interpretation. "Yes, honey. It's okay."

"I know. She happy," Minuet stated with a kiss to her mother's cheek. "Mommy happy too."

"Oh?" Kelly questioned. "Why do you say that, honey?"

Minuet cocked her head as she looked at her mother. "Bown all gone. Mommy sparkly."

"Mommy was brown?" Kelly asked cautiously.

"No Mommy, da airs round Mommy. Now pretty," Minuet explained. "You know, the pretties laughing are."

Coco was wriggling at Kelly's feet, holding her stick and trying to get her playmate's attention. Minuet hopped down and the dog took off, triggering the game of chase again.

"I didn't know she sees peoples' auras," Kelly said thoughtfully.

"She's unique," Cord agreed. "She'll consider her view of the world normal for several more years. Children do. It'll not be a burden until she realizes she's the only one with that view."

"What can we do for her? How do we make that easier?" Kelly asked worriedly.

"Love her," Cord answered softly. "Ultimate power is love. Beyond that, she'll have to make her world."

Kelly's worry was a good one. Minuet was amazing, but the magnitude of her gift would set her apart. If they all lived long enough for her to become an adult, would she be alone forever? She had the power to call up the armies of hell and perhaps the power to destroy them, something he'd never seen in one being.

The desperate battle for survival of the human species had been won on the strength of the three elemental witches. They hadn't been able to kill the dragons. Only disengage them from the power that animated them in a savage sacrifice.

And yet dragon lore whispered around the globe. On every continent, in every culture there were old stories, exaggerated depictions. Humans didn't believe, but they suspected.

Now there was Minuet. Whatever the outcome, evil would not be denied and dragons might get their second chance as well.

Finding the Water Witch was imperative. Cord was using precious time to allow Kelly and Minuet to grow in their craft, but the ladies had to know their power to use it. Finding the third witch would be useless if no one knew what to do. It was also possible the Water Witch didn't know her power either. Looked as if locating Harrison was the first priority.

The water dragon shouldn't be that difficult to track down. Cord already knew where Harrison spent most of his time. Loch Ness, Scotland.

Chapter Seven

Evening shadows stalked the lawn as Cord sat in the kitchen and watched his two ladies discuss supper. Since being released from the long-held fear of experimenting with powers that came so naturally to them, they had spent the day trying everything.

Cord was tired and it was his own fault. Using too much energy to shield their exuberant experiments had drained him. But he couldn't bring himself to take what he needed. Gorgeous, graceful Kelly was what he needed, and yet watching over her and Minuet was a pleasure he wanted to savor a little longer.

He didn't even have the freedom to offer them his protection simply because it was the right thing to do. He wasn't sure when he'd developed hero envy, but there it was. He wasn't the hero, he was the user. Hiding fatigue, he smiled as Minuet insisted on cooking.

"Mommy taste," she proclaimed triumphantly as a steaming bowl of macaroni and cheese appeared on the kitchen counter.

"I don't know. What did you put in this one?" Kelly asked cautiously as she eyed the normal-looking dish.

"I tells it read box and make. Jus like you said," Minuet insisted.

"No more additions? You're sure?" Kelly checked as she took a spoon and dipped into the bowl of pasta.

"No chocolate, Mommy said not in mac."

Kelly put the spoon in her mouth. "Very good!"

"I make, I make." Minuet beamed at Cord.

"Good job. Let's have supper," he encouraged.

Kelly turned her smile on him then sobered as her eyes studied his face. "What is it?" she asked softly.

Cord raised a brow. "What?"

"Something's not right." She glided away from the counter toward him.

"How do you know?" he asked, unwilling to let any opportunity slip by that made her more aware of her gifts.

"I feel... You feel..." Her hand reached for his.

As soon as she touched him there was a soft jolt as her power flowed through the flesh on flesh connection. There was no hiding how drained he was. He wanted her to know that. Know what she was to him. He could give her knowledge, skill and protection but only if she let him use her.

So this was need. Her touch was life-giving but apparently that wasn't enough to ensure his compliance. Of course it wasn't, he was a dragon. Somehow his creators had programmed his need of this woman in such detail that he wanted more. Perhaps it was just his natural arrogance. Who the fuck knew anymore, but he wanted Kelly to touch him for reasons that had nothing to do with their current situation.

He'd never felt the constraint of intangible needs before and it showed him another side of the woman who'd made him. In the time before, he'd known he derived power from females he seduced. He had excelled at finding willing power sources. Now he understood the intangible emotion he wanted from Kelly was the real strength and the fatal weakness that would shackle him forever.

What the hell had those witches been thinking? They'd come up with an incredibly complex plan that depended on what? Luck? There was no way the three dragons could force this generation's witches to love them. Love was the ultimate intangible. It could not be demanded, controlled or commanded. If it wasn't a selfless gift, it was nothing.

Kelly unexpectedly sank onto Cord's lap. He adjusted for her naturally but raised a brow.

"You're tired," she accused.

"Yes." There was no denying it.

"You should have told me."

"I'm fine for now," he stated. His eyes went to Minuet who was setting the table by floating plates and spoons out of the cabinets. "Both of you are doing well."

"I can feel the hunger. You could have asked," she continued softly.

"And lose the pleasure of you touching me just because you want too? It was bound to be a one-time event. Soon as you felt the exchange, you'd be doing it for other reasons," he explained quietly. "You weren't in danger. I'd never let myself get that weak for selfish reasons."

"Kiss him," Minuet directed as she brought the bowl of macaroni and cheese to the table. "Cord good, we eat."

"Kissing is private," Kelly said.

Minuet cocked her head as she regarded them. "You like it. He like it. I not umbarr…em…I like too. Happy Mommy. I seen Aunt Penny kiss Uncle Hank for long time."

"Aunt Penny and Uncle Hank are married. It's okay for married people to kiss. Did you see them doing anything else?" Kelly wanted to know.

"No. I hug dem. Dey happy and pretty colors. Den we go play park swing." Minuet sat at her plate. "You marry Cord. He need kisses."

"Penny is my younger sister. Hank is her husband. They're newlyweds and babysat Minuet several times before we moved," Kelly explained to Cord. Her eyes remained glued to his chest as she studiously ignored Minuet's last comment.

"Let's eat," Cord suggested as he lifted Kelly to her chair.

"She didn't kiss you," Minuet stated as she looked at them.

"Mommy's kisses are special, right?" Cord asked. "Mommy has to be careful with them." Cord winked at Minuet. "I think I'll let her decide when I've been good enough to get one."

Kelly distracted Minuet by filling her plate with not only macaroni and cheese but sliced tomatoes and baby carrots. Both favorites but not yet part of the three-year-old's meal planning.

The atmosphere relaxed considerably as the conversation moved to the possibility of Barney being a good dragon in hiding. Explaining that he was a person walking around in a Barney suit proved complicated. The concept perplexed Minuet. She couldn't get over the fact that a man was standing in the Barney suit and lying to all the children.

Minuet turned to Cord and frowned. "Can you make Barney?"

"Ah, you mean shapeshift to look like this Barney?" Cord asked cautiously.

"Yes. Make Barney but not a clothes. Be Barney?" she questioned seriously.

"Honey, shapeshifting does not mean a person can be someone else. It just means they look different. I could look like Barney but it would always be Cord inside."

"Please make Barney," she asked with such a hopeful expression on her face.

"I can't right now. I've never seen Barney," he confessed with the appropriate humility. Minuet was satisfied but not done with him. "Barney tomorrow. He on TV in a morning."

"Oh honey." Kelly reached over and laid a hand on Cord's arm as she laughed and continued. "Cord might not want to be Barney when he sees him."

Power flowed from her touch in a flood of unexpected heat. She was laughing and yet her emotions were colored with such a mix of intriguing delight that Cord sat back and smiled at her. Taking her hand in his to enjoy the connection, he turned it over and kissed the back. "Why not?"

"Have you ever watched children's TV?" she asked.

"No," he confessed. "But it can't be that difficult to mimic a figure."

"Ah, probably not," she agreed. "But remember, you can change your mind."

There was silence for a few minutes as food disappeared.

"Cord no have TV?" Minuet wanted to know.

Cord nodded at her puzzled face. "Nope, I don't. If I want to hear the news, I use the radio."

"We let you look ours," she consoled him as if he were sad.

Done with her meal, Minuet left her chair to come to his other side and climb onto his lap. Sitting on his thigh, leaning into his body as one of his arms circled her securely, she proceeded to discuss the Barney issue. Kelly hadn't let go of his other hand, and Cord discovered the most amazing sensations he'd ever experienced.

Minuet's trust flowed through him with jewel-bright sincerity. She didn't just believe in him, as she had this morning, there was more. Her emotions were personal, filled with her affection and trust. Kelly's connection mingled with it as she laughed softly, leaning across him to kiss her daughter's cheek. The round table allowed the three of them an intimate closeness. In that moment, Cord found something huge.

It was bigger than his mission, bigger than all of the history piling up on them. This was more important than any past betrayal or alliance. He had no word for what they brought him, who he was with them, but it was entirely different from the creature he'd been this morning.

Minuet yawned but pressed on with her case. "Cord be good Barney. No lying."

"The man in the Barney suit is not lying. He's playing a part. Acting," Kelly assured her.

"Honey, if you want to see Barney, I'll do my best, but you have to remember, its Cord inside," he promised. "Tomorrow I'll watch him and see if we can manage it. I might need your help."

"I help," Minuet promised solemnly with big, unblinking eyes.

Looking down at her snuggled into his chest, Cord knew he'd probably promise her the impossible and do it because she believed in him. Not because she was the amazing twist in fate that she'd prove to be. No, simply because she was Minuet.

Kelly leaned into his shoulder and smiled at her daughter as she pushed riotous curls behind Minuet's ear. "It's bath time. We'll talk about Barney tomorrow."

Minuet slid off Cord's leg. "I make water," she declared, and ran toward the stairs, excited to test her new abilities in a way she hadn't thought of yet.

Kelly hurried after her. "Only enough water for a bath. Be careful," she directed as she rushed up the stairs after the little witch who couldn't wait to play in the water.

Cord gazed after them. What had just happened?

Both of them had worked hard today. He'd tried to make the lessons part of their normal activities to get them used to the unusual. Easing it into their world without shock or the harsh reality of how ugly unusual could be. He suspected that would come soon enough. Even though they'd done relatively normal things, it hadn't been easy.

Believing in themselves wasn't enough. To work magic, one had to infuse confidence into each command. Knowing a thing could be done and believing oneself capable of making it happen were two different things. It had been easier for Minuet. She was too young to be loaded down with self-doubt. Kelly had struggled.

Focusing on the empty kitchen, Cord waved a hand and dispatched the dishes back to the cabinets, now clean and ready for the next meal. He sat there trying to work through the change in himself.

Was it possible for there to be too much of a good thing? No, that wasn't it. His hunger was not less. It was more. More in a way that included Minuet as a part of Kelly. One of them in his world would not be enough, both of them had to be safe, cared for, treasured. His need of them was more than physical hunger for the substance they provided him. The peace of this kitchen was what he needed. Knowing they were happy. Peace.

Like love, peace was an intangible. Something worth fighting for, dying for, but at the end of the day, peace could not be given to another.

A dragon's life was supposed to be simple. Jesus! One day with them and he was craving things that didn't exist, couldn't be "gathered", had nothing to do with his nature.

Dragons were creatures created by finite beings. Monsters designed for one purpose or another, be it war or defense. Even he had been made by the hand of a programmer. A programmer who worked in DNA, but it did not make him a God-created creature. He had no inborn right to evolve. He was made to do one thing, ensure the other dragons did not rise again.

This mission had been his only reason for living. It had consumed eons of time. Hard, empty time when he'd hungered without end, and now this? This impossible need to have what could never be captured, taken or contained? Hungering for such things with a dragon's appetite was a danger. His instincts would not allow him to back away from the drive to attain everything that had been out of humankind's reach since the creation of man.

Small feet rushed down the stairs, this time muffled a bit. Cord stood and turned to the door. Minuet launched herself into the air and he caught the bundle of pink footy pajamas.

She laughed in glee as he lifted her high above his head and pretended to drop her, catching her again.

The power of her happiness shot through him with the zing of an adrenaline rush. Laughing Minuet commanded more force than most wizards could hope to leash. She was amazing. Cord was about to swing her around when Kelly stopped him from the doorway.

"Time to calm down. We came down to read a book before going to bed."

"Cord read," Minuet stated from her seat on his hip. "Cord read Barney. He need ta know it."

After two Barney books on the couch, Kelly took Minuet up to bed. Cord stretched out and let the hazy warmth of the last half-hour melt off him.

In some part of her brain, Minuet was aware she strengthened him by touching. She probably had no idea why, but the little miracle child had insisted on sitting on his leg as he read to her, making sure Mommy sat on the other side. She'd arranged them then relaxed into his hold.

The time reading had calmed her down so at the end she drooped with sleepy eyes, struggling to stay awake. Before going with her mother upstairs, she'd kissed his cheek in her muzzy way.

"You better, Cord?" she'd asked, blinking. "My bear makes me safe. You needs him?"

"I'm much better. Bear needs you, hon. Good night," he'd responded with a smile.

The two of them had trudged slowly upstairs.

The couch he was stretched out on had begun the day an average size. Now it's long, comfortable shape fit him perfectly. Magic had given Kelly the freedom to decorate exactly as she wanted. When she'd gotten over the unexpected delight, her house had taken shape rapidly with warm colors and contrasting jewel tones.

Cord closed his eyes and listened as the voices above him murmur soft, sleepy things. Those engaging murmurs bound him to them with ever tightening strings.

This day had been a time-traveling experience. Where they had been last evening bore almost no relation to where they were tonight. The problem was, they were riding a one-way express car and they were dragging the hounds of hell with them.

It was clear the horrific solution employed by the great ladies of the past had been no solution at all. In fact, it had been a very temporary fix. They had given humans a second chance to solve the same problem. The one they, in all their brilliant planning, had failed to correct.

He heard Kelly move out of Minuet's room, tiptoeing down the hall. She paused at the top of the stairs. It was only for a second, but he felt it. That moment of hesitation told him she was feeling that day's effects too. It spoke of her fear, her courage and made him want to rip something to shreds. She was afraid, but she had no choice.

She would walk in here and seduce him if she had to. Kelly was that strong and just that vulnerable. He couldn't afford to refuse her courage. She had no time for a courtship, no time to pretend that was something a creature like him could give her.

She appeared in the doorway, outlined by the dark entry behind her. Coming out of the shadows to him, the Wind Witch smiled with her lips, but her eyes could not.

Cord slowly stood as she stopped three feet away from him. Her gaze didn't waver as she raised her chin to look him in the eye.

"You're afraid," he observed softly.

"Yes."

"I'm sorry."

"Will you hurt me?" Kelly asked.

"Probably, but never by choice," he answered as honestly as he could.

"Are you afraid?" she wanted to know.

"Not of this, a little of you," he admitted.

"I scare you?" She did smile this time.

"More than you can know. But the problem isn't yours."

"No, it's not my problem. It makes me feel better though."

Cord took a small step and reached for her, he had to. Standing so close and discussing the distance fear was putting between them was a fine new form of torture. His palm ran down her arm from shoulder to elbow in a soft caress. He didn't close his fingers around silky flesh, didn't draw her to him. There was nothing he wanted more than to help her cross the cold space between them, but he refused to take that choice from her too.

All she had to do was ask and he'd gladly cross it for her. He suspected she knew that. She was looking at him from the safety of her old life. Coming to him now would shed that illusion forever.

Kelly stepped into his body, sliding her hands up his biceps in slow motion as she studied his eyes. His hands slipped around her waist to hold her in a loose embrace as she chose him over her fear.

"I can make you feel better about a lot of things," he murmured. "But what we have to fear in each other is not one of them." His head dipped to her mouth, going that final step for her. She had come to him and it was enough. Brushing her mouth with his lips in a damp caress, he concentrated on controlling the drive to possess.

She relaxed into his body. His beautiful Wind Witch stretched up to him with a little moan to press her mouth more firmly into his. Cord's hands briefly fisted at her back, resisting the response she triggered in him. Acceptance from this woman, no matter how small, inflamed a primal urge, the one that demanded her immediate surrender in the most basic terms.

He pulled his mouth off hers. "Close your eyes," he instructed. He remained perfectly still as she stared into his eyes. She needed to feel the fact that he expected her to comply with a direction. Her hesitation was acknowledged with his patience but that patience would not allow her any other option either.

Kelly's eyes closed, reluctantly. There it was, fear. A basic instinct of her own, but one he would do almost anything to ensure she never had to act on while in his arms. Those lessons started now.

Candles appeared on the surface of end tables, windowsills, across the top of the armoire and flickered in the empty fireplace. The couch beside them now had a soft cotton sheet draped down its long cushions.

He easily swung her up across his arms as he said, "You can look."

"Oh," Kelly breathed. The sensation of being held high in his arms as her eyes opened on the romantic scene he'd made of the living room was overwhelming. "It's lovely but you didn't have to."

"I wanted to," he said into her neck as he sat down with her in his lap. His mouth paused over her sensitive nerves there, she shivered. Her warm body squirmed and he didn't care if it was the glowing candles or his tongue, the aroma of desire was deepening in the room around them.

Kelly's head tilted in response to his tantalizing licking. "You were going to get lucky without them."

His head lifted from her skin. "If you don't like it, I'll get rid of them."

"I like, I like," Kelly assured him hastily. "What would make you think I didn't?" Her hands pulled his shirt up to delve under it. There was something irresistible about the feel of his warm flesh under her hands. She had to have it. "Can you get rid of the shirt?"

The T-shirt disappeared as he explained. "Getting rid of excess clothing will never be your problem," Cord growled as his Wind Witch surprised him. Removing his shirt at her request was a thoughtless response. Her reaction had driven all reason from his mind for a second.

Kelly's body twisted swiftly in his lap as her mouth sought his skin. She seemed fascinated with the taste of his neck, shoulders and was very busy working her way down his pectoral muscle. Her hands alternately raked and caressed. The sharp gratification of her nails followed by the tease of gentle hands exploring was sweet torture. Sensation piled on top of spiking sensation and bombarded his resistance in a concentrated attack.

Her hands skimmed down his sides and she slipped fingers in the waistband of his jeans and slid them around to his abdomen just as her lips reached the sensitive disk of his nipple. His involuntary gasp at her mouth closing and sucking on his chest gave her a moment and she took it. Her finger dove into his jeans and the tip of her forefinger lightly caressed the head of his cock.

Cord's hand immediately closed around her wrist, the other hand gently wrapped around her neck as he turned her face up to his. His hold controlled her so it was impossible to remove her fingers from down the front of his pants, and he held her looking up at him from just above his chest.

"What are you doing?" he snarled aggressively into her face.

Kelly blinked. "Seems obvious to me," she countered. "Now if you would kindly disappear the jeans for me, I'll be a happy girl." His big body shuddered under her, but his hands would not release their hold on her.

"No," he said slowly as if talking slowly made his point clear. "You will not seduce me. I will be the one doing the seducing."

Looking up at him from her frozen position, Kelly's eyes warmed in laughter. "We have to take turns? It's not a dragon buffet? I was feeling like a first come, first serve policy might be in order."

"Buffet? What does an eating establishment have to do… Oh." Cord's brain finally unscrambled enough to catch up. "No, little Wind Witch. The dragon buffet is closed until such time as the Kelly dinner has been consumed to my satisfaction."

In one swift move, he rolled them to the side. Kelly gasped, she was beneath his body and all clothes had been removed. There was no time for discomfort as her smug laugh turned to a moan.

His mouth was on her breast and he was not being gentle with his enjoyment. Sucking her hard, his body forced her legs around his hips. White-hot sensation ripped through her as hard cock came down on damp pussy with an intoxicating thrust. He wasn't entering her, he was overwhelming her. In the next instant, his teeth clamped down on her well-sucked nipple as his hips sawed that hard shaft over her sensitive folds. He thrust her into a vortex of sensation, and Kelly gave up to it.

There was nothing but the mind-bending pleasure as he handled her. Sensations came with the thunder of an approaching tornado in her head. As if from a distance, Kelly realized the low rumble was him. He purred as his mouth moved down her belly. His body smoothly slithered down her and suddenly his hands were behind her knees. There was no possibility of thought as he lifted and spread her, holding her open for his mouth.

Kelly arched in shuddering reaction, the pleasure coming at her too hard, one punching through the last with merciless intensity. Gasping for air, she couldn't even scream as he took her intimate flesh. His mouth consumed her with raw power. Right on the edge of ruthless, he drank from her body. His tongue commanding she surrender what he wanted.

She'd never known it could be like this. He was in what would usually be considered a submissive position, his head between her legs, and she was totally out of control. He demanded and she complied, and then there was more. Shatteringly more.

His tongue flicked over her clit in maddening staccato as two fingers pushed into her, creating an impact explosion. The ripples of power shot through her and Kelly's head whipped back. She grabbed a decorative pillow to jam over her mouth as he threw her into a hard, fast orgasm, driving her deeper into the vortex. His fingers sliding in and out of her, stretching her, commanding her, drawing out her response.

His head lifted to watch as he entered her for the first time. So beautiful. His Wind Witch poured her power into him and he had to clamp his mouth shut and pant through his teeth to control his response. Every breath was her scent, the taste on his tongue was her pleasure, and the beautiful channel straining around his fingers was the hottest portal to pleasure he'd ever known. She was so tight, so compellingly innocent and yet not. As he watched the last weak contractions around his invading fingers, Cord smiled.

Kelly had no idea how long it took for her brain to quit shooting thoughts around in drunken abandon. The return of reality found her stunned at the power of what they'd just shared. How easily he drew what he needed from her, and now she'd just noticed he was studying her response as his fingers pulled out and he dragged them over plump folds. The aftermath of orgasm was quickly overcome with the sizzle of embarrassment, swiftly followed by her acknowledging the erotic punch of her pleasure in that sensation. She was surprised.

Beneath him, she had one leg draped over the back of the couch, the other held wide, and he was looking at her as he fingered her. Her body was wantonly displayed and she moved under his fingers, shamelessly following them as much as she could. Her fully exposed channel clenched and dripped, and she liked it. The mix of shy embarrassment and naughty display made her aware of his control in a way she'd never experienced before. Who was this woman? Kelly had no idea.

He didn't give her time to process the unexpected impact of her pleasure in his control. A wicked smile touched his lips as he lifted fingers so he could drag a long lick up her sensitized folds. Then his body surged up her and his mouth was on her lips. She opened naturally under him and he thrust into her mouth.

Her own taste in her mouth was a shock, and yet Kelly couldn't deny the zing of erotic pleasure as he introduced her to it. Cord took her mouth in a demanding kiss that filled her, and it was amazing. His body heavily pressing down on her, the feel of steel between her legs as his cock dragged up her wet folds, all of it was overwhelming. Again he was rocking his cock over her clit. Hard, demanding, his body rubbed every inch, and she liked it.

Kelly's fingers curled into claws as she lost all hope of controlling her own responses and sank into his power. Her hips rolled with his every movement. Sensations were blowing through her, firing down her legs. Her nails dragged down his back.

The thick steel of his cock nudged her opening. Its head slick with his own lubricant mixed with her damp welcome and he pushed into her. His mouth pulled off her lips.

"Look at me," he commanded.

Kelly's eyes opened to gaze into his and Cord pushed. Thick cock stretched her channel. He stopped and slowly grasped her legs again, placing them over his shoulders. Then his elbows rested on the cushions as his hands grasped either side of her head, his eyes never leaving hers. She couldn't move unless he let her. Her body tilted to accept him, open and completely defenseless.

The spiral of sensation whirled off the charts as Kelly trembled beneath the huge male above her.

"That's it," he encouraged softly. "Feel it all, baby."

Kelly wasn't capable of a response as he pushed into her body. His thrust was not harsh, but it was forceful. He entered her. She felt her body strain around him and it seemed impossible there could be more. He kept pushing.

"Yes, more," he growled as her breath came in short pants. "That's it, feel how tight you are, baby. How perfect."

It seemed a long time before she felt him fully seated in her body. Thick, long and so hard. Her back had struggled to straighten as if to make room for him. But there was very little movement she could manage as his wide chest pressed down on her, forcing her knees close to her breasts. Her eyes widened as he held her gaze in ruthless openness. He gave her no place to hide, no option to shield her response to his demands.

Hardly had he fully impaled her and his hips were pulling out. Her mouth opened in a soundless gasp as he pulled over every nerve that was clamped around him. This time his thrust into her depths was a little faster, sharper. As he plunged into her, the hot head of the post he was jamming in her hit a bundle of nerves she'd never known was there. It must be attached to her backbone because the response was electric and shot through her on the impact.

Her body responded with such force Kelly would have wrenched away from him if she'd been able. She couldn't and he was already pulling back to pound down into her again, and damn it, she loved it.

One of his hands moved over her mouth as he muffled her scream. He slammed into her, and Kelly's eyes glazed over. She broke out in a sweat as heat bloomed from the inside out. And still his eyes commanded her, took her as surely as the cock ramming in and out of her body. He demanded more than she was. He was getting everything he wanted.

With each deep thrust he hit her internal pleasure-shock center. Gradually increasing the speed, he wound up the intensity, granting her no recovery time as new sensations crashed into each other, pounded through each other in an ever deeper decent into chaos. Helpless beneath him, Kelly surrendered to the mindless sensation. Her body responded to his demands, complying each time he decided she would feel more, take more.

Cord had known entering this woman would seal his future. What Kelly brought to this was more than any imaginings had prepared him for. Feeling her pleasure as he took control of their lovemaking had driven him as surely as any drug addict would do anything it took to get a fix. Pushing her into pleasure rewarded him in ways almost sinister in their grasp on his needs.

So he gave her more, taking control, letting her feel the hard need as he touched her, drank her, consumed her. With each demand, her pleasure spiraled higher. His little Wind Witch liked power in her lover. As he looked down into the eyes of the woman who owned him, he very nearly lost his mind trying to comprehend the absolute perfection she embodied. Her need, her acceptance, everything about her was perfect.

Driving into her hard and fast, the fierce beast within demanded he scream his claiming. Holding back his elemental statement took a toll, but it was nothing compared to the control required to keep from hurting her. What he wanted and what she could take were not even close at this point. But damn, what she gave him.

The tight clasp of her body as she clenched around him was never going to be enough. He plunged into her with carefully restrained power. Each forceful entry smacking her clit with his groin, twisting so slightly she was not aware of his method to increase her pleasure.

His hands framed her face, forcing her to look him in the eye. Looking into her soul, he read each shock wave of pleasure and drank it. He held nothing back, driving her to come for him. The power in her release washed through him and he had to break eye contact to control his response. Sinking down, he took her mouth in a deep, hard kiss. His body slowed, driving in and out of her with gradually declining intensity.

Lifting off her mouth, he smiled as he gazed into her wide eyes. He saw shock, a little fear perhaps, but mostly wonder. Pulling out of her slowly as she panted through the sensations, he repressed a chuckle at the ghost of a frown on her forehead. No, he was not done and neither was she. Her taste for his control meant he got to enjoy showing her without wasting time explaining it.

Cord burrowed his arms under her body to lift her with him as he sat up on the couch, turning her to face away from him. Her legs draped on the outside of his thighs, opening her completely as he pulled her back to his chest. She was still breathing harshly, and that was okay with him. There was no need for her to talk at this moment.

He relaxed back with her flattened against him. In this position, she was available to his hands in every way. He started with her breasts. Those sweet mounds he'd barely enjoyed so far. His began on her ribs and slid up to cup both breasts, gently kneading them. Her arms fluttered as if to grasp the back of his hands.

"Reach behind your neck and clasp your hands." His command rumbled in her ear.

Kelly felt the deep tones of his voice resonated in each bone of her body. He intended her to feel the acceptance of his right to handle her. She did it, exactly what he told her to. It was difficult and it was so easy. She straddled his lap with the hard length of his cock pressing against her open pussy, her back extended, leaning against his chest. Raising her arms to clasp her hands behind her neck presented her breasts.

Exposed and open, she shuddered in response to the emotional impact his commands drew from her soul. Yet there was no question in her mind that pleasure bloomed from this new Kelly. Where had this wanton, shameless woman been all her life? He had just screwed reality out of the room and now he asked for more. And it was amazing. The sensations zipping across her body as his hands closed around her breasts were a mix of shivering in the light and the dark pleasures he introduced her to.

"So beautiful," his deep voice rumbled in her ear as he looked down, watching the candlelight glow off her pale skin as he manipulated soft flesh. "So fucking beautiful."

Fingers and thumbs captured distended nipples, rolling them gently. At the new sensation, her hips shifted, pressing down on his stiff cock. He increased the pressure and twisted a little further, causing her pelvis to arch as she rubbed herself on him. Her body's damp response bathed his rigid cock as she moved. Low moans whispered from her mouth and he sucked in a deep breath, drinking the scent of her renewed excitement.

His hands remained on her sensitive flesh, increasing the pressure as her excitement rose in relation to his firm handling of her body. Her hips squirmed on him, giving back vibrations that fired along his nerve endings with the gentle sting of being naked and too close to a sparkler. She was magnificent.

"Fold your legs under your thighs," he directed.

Doing so, she was kneeling over him. "Now lift up, baby," he said softly. His hands on her breasts gently squeezed as he rolled her nipples. "That's a good girl. Lower that pretty thing on what it needs. Right there. Stay right there. I want you to feel cock rubbing that pretty cunt. That's it," he approved as she lowered her pussy to rest lightly on the thick head of his cock. At his command, her hips swayed, rubbing herself on him.

"So good, baby. Just like that. Feel it, feel how hard you make me."

His hands moved down her ribs, around to cup her belly in gentle massage as her body moved over him. He loved the feel of her moving under his hands, shifting over his cock in female demand as her pussy wept with acceptance. His hands glided across her hips and down to her straining thighs, around to the backs as muscles flexed, to cup the sweet globes of her ass. Petting over them gently at first, he enjoyed her excitement escalating with the intoxicating spice of sexual uncertainty.

He teased her with a light touch, trailing fingers down the top of her clenched crease. Coming up under those swaying globes to travel back to her waist on the outside. Again his hands drifted down over the mounds, but this time fingers pressed marginally into her cleft. Kelly trembled, but the sway of her hips never stopped.

Little witch didn't know whether to be afraid or excited. He would give her what she was unsure of but not yet. He would give her everything, anything, but only when she was ready. Only when he was sure she couldn't live without it. That didn't mean she couldn't enjoy this taste of surrender.

Chapter Eight

Cord slid his butt to the edge of the couch cushion, spreading his legs wider as he moved them. Relaxing back, he was half lying with her perched above him, his head lined up with her pretty bottom.

"Lean forward, put your head between my knees," he commanded, his hands resting lightly on her ass.

Electricity shot through Kelly as his words exploded in her head. She knew the view he was directing her to give him. The complete exposure was shocking and intoxicating. She had gone this far, and he wanted more.

Smoothly she complied with his direction. Her legs were now widely spread on either side of his hips, her upper body bent over as her hands clasped his knees. He was holding her bottom, but she was the one opening every secret of her body to his view.

"Now lower that sweet pussy and take the cock it wants."

His hands only lightly rested on her as his direction made her push herself down on him. He would watch her take his thick rod. Though the candles around them were a soft light, she knew he had no trouble viewing every detail as she wiggled down his cock. Bent as she was, it was not easy to get him in her. Her body stretched to its limits around living steel.

"That's it. You can take some more. Push."

The last was a firm command sending a shiver of fresh excitement to mix with the already chaotic sensations his direction and body were igniting in her.

Kelly gasped, sucking in air as she tried to comply. It was desperately important that she do exactly what he said. And yet there was a far-distant part of her that couldn't believe the shameless woman displaying herself this way was enjoying his attention. And she was enjoying it. The evidence of her excitement dripped down his cock and off his balls onto the floor.

"Move on it, baby."

Midnight stirred in his voice as he commanded her to fuck him as he watched. Wicked and wild was the rumble behind the words. Her bottom moved up and down, his hands still resting on it.

Gently his fingers clenched as he ordered more.

"That's a girl. You can do it faster."

And she did. God help her, but she was spinning out of control as he directed her. One of his hands moved around her hip to reach in front, and his fingers flicked over her clit in wicked encouragement. The sounds coming out of her mouth were guttural, animal sounds as the entire situation took her to a new place.

His talented fingers knew exactly what she needed. She was almost there. The stars swirled behind her tightly closed eyes then he stopped. His fingers left her and his hand again rested on her ass as she bounced up and down on his rigid cock.

"Not yet, sweet witch," he crooned as she shuddered over him. "This time is for me. My beautiful Wind Witch, fucking my cock is the most erotic thing I have ever seen. I want it to last. That's a good girl. Go ahead, fuck hard. I love watching this beautiful ass rising above me like this."

His hands caressed her moving bottom as he spoke. Sliding down the back of her thighs, he drew his hands back up to her ass with nails digging lightly across her flesh, skittering new sensations into the overwhelming mix.

Kelly gasped for air, straining, but she just couldn't find the power to push herself over the edge, and he knew it. She knew he knew, and yet she couldn't stop trying as his hands toyed with her and his eyes watched every move.

"Ready to come?" he asked with maddening calm.

"Yes," she hissed urgently.

"How much do you want it?"

"Now. I need it now."

"That wasn't the question," he responded as one hand lifted from her bottom and allowed her motion to deliver a light smack as she worked herself on and off his rigid cock. "I asked how much."

"Very much," she answered.

"Then tell me what you want. Want you need to feel."

"Please just touch me."

"How?" he asked softly.

"I don't care. Something, anything. I need," she demanded breathlessly.

"My sweet Wind Witch, you will learn not to use such sweeping statements," he told her. "This time though, you get what you desire. Next time..." He let the sentence trail off and it didn't matter. Kelly wasn't listening to the words.

His hands snaked around her hips, bringing his fingers into contact with her engorged clit. This time he clamped thumb and forefinger on it and squeeze gently as her body moved. It was more than enough. The slightly harsh sensation pitched her into orgasm.

Her head down between his knees, facing the couch, muffled her scream, but not enough. Cord captured the sound, drinking it in with her release. All of it exploded through him, in him, around him. The pleasure skittered down his spine with the soundless scream of a razor across polished steel.

He was almost at the end of his control. Watching her ride him to pleasure was almost too much, but not quite. Even as she relaxed onto his thighs, her body sinking over him in exhaustion, he knew he would take more. His hands petted her ass as she panted. Ah, this woman, this amazing creature, there would never be enough.

He reached around her rib cage to lift her off him and back into his arms, settling her across his lap so her body was half propped up on the arm of the couch. Leaning over her, his hand trailed down the side of her face and her eyes fluttered open. They gazed at each other a long time as he cupped her neck.

"I don't think..." she started softly. His finger dropped over her lips to quiet them.

"It's not time to think yet, just relax and enjoy," he instructed as his lips dropped to replace his finger.

The kiss was soft, feathering over her features. He worshiped her face as his hand drifted down her collarbone to cup a warm breast. His thumb lazily stroked back and forth over her erect nipple. There was no pressure, just a gentle caress as his mouth moved down her neck and around to go up to the other ear.

Kelly closed her eyes and let her head fall back on the couch arm. His mouth moved over her, his hands caressing, and she wasn't sure she could take any more. She was aware that though she was rapidly losing count of her own orgasms, he had yet to come. If he waited much longer, she would be asleep and it would be all his fault.

His mouth moved down to her neglected breast, sucking it in gently to lap at her nipple as he continued caressing the other one with his thumb. His attention kept her body burning on a low heat level. She was aware but didn't have the strength to even mention it. And why start now? Apparently she'd surrendered to his control a very long time ago. If he was dumb enough to exhaust the woman before he let himself join her in pleasure, he deserved the dead body in his lap now.

Cord shifted, pulling her down to the seat of the couch with him as he continued the gentle kisses and quiet murmurs. He stretched out beside her, enjoying the play of candlelight across her skin as he followed the shadows with his tongue. Kelly's eyes barely opened and he could feel the tremble of exhaustion in her thighs.

"Sleep," he murmured as he straightened to wrap his arms around her. Her only response was an intelligible mumble as she adjusted in his embrace. Her breathing indicated she'd dropped off into slumber.

Closing his eyes, he held his Wind Witch. She could nap, he was a long way from done and the night was young. A beast like him would never be satisfied, part of the problem humans had not understood the first time. Hunger for food was not the reason dragons always needed more fuel. Hunger was a human interpretation of the sensation.

He'd pushed her. She'd answered new sensations with growing excitement, meeting his demands. She'd been surprised. He'd smelled her initial response. Still he'd pushed, knowing he was taking her to the edge of her experience. Sweet, beautiful Kelly had glimpsed the beast.

It was his nature, a drive as elemental as survival. He knew he would keep pushing her, taking more. As he looked down at her face relaxed in sleep, a new sensation invaded his body. Doubt.

The dark question swirled in his mind, was he hurting her? Not physically, no, he had complete control of that. Was pushing her to explore the hidden submissive in her soul a mistake? Was he taking innocence?

His hand swept down her body in a light caress. He just needed to touch her, feel her skin under his hand. The compulsion to touch, connect with her physically would grow in him. In pushing her, he'd only been feeding the natural need in him. She wouldn't understand it.

Dragons were not human. His reactions were ruled in ways she still didn't grasp. He was fiercely territorial. A predator in the wild marked his territory and was willing to kill or be killed in its defense. There were no morals, no questions, no choices.

His kind had been created masters of the world, instantly the most deadly predator alive. They had never struggled to survive, been forced to evolve with the environment to create a balance in nature. Everything about them was a direct violation of natural law.

Crafted by brilliantly shortsighted humans, it had taken less than a mortal lifetime for dragons to free themselves from their masters. The species had continued to take, unfettered by fear of consequences to any action. The driving greed or hunger had been intended as a control, the humans being too arrogant to ever envision a world where a creature of their own creation became the master.

The three ladies of the Earth had solved that developmental flaw in dragon engineering. He was indeed leashed to the woman in his arms. Bound to her with all the ravenous greed dragons embodied. Whatever the original Earth Witches had done, it was working. There was nothing but grave consequences to any action he took.

Pushing her sexually for his gratification was not acceptable. He was worried about her response to his appetites and it was a new experience. Not worried that she would reject him, he knew too much about human females to fear that outcome. His concern was that he would change her. Would his needs create in her something that was never meant to be? Something unnatural to the woman that was Kelly.

Unnatural was bad. If anyone knew how bad unnatural could be, it was the three elemental dragons. There was no point in wishing he could be anything else but what he was, cursing the commands programmed into the core of his being. He couldn't change his nature, but there was a new pain below his breastbone. For her, for her future.

She stirred his arms, shifting slightly brought a soft moan to her lips. The scent of pain tinted the air, telling him she was sore. His hands moved over her, healing bruised muscles.

When she woke, there would be no pain. The last part of her to receive his attention was the lovely channel he could not get enough of. His hand slid between her legs, fingers lightly combing through damp curls.

This time the moan had nothing to do with pain as she shifted to open her legs, welcoming his touch even in her sleep. Cord clamped down on his response to her blind trust. That sweet, welcoming movement punched him in the gut with punishing power.

She should be running from him. He was the worst possible future and she would never get rid of him. Perhaps she would never know. He was a master of deception. A shapeshifter was a natural liar, deception built into every form by virtue of the fact that he can shift to another to suit himself.

His fingers between her legs stroked, petting her because she had asked him to with her movement. Even in this, he was an excellent liar. Touching her intimately was a desire that would never be sated. He would always want to, but the dragon knew so well how to make her want him to. Get her to ask for what he would always take.

Sleepy eyes opened to look up at him. Leaning over, propped up on one elbow as his other hand strummed plump folds between her legs, he wished he could smile for her. He was afraid attempting that would simply be a show of teeth. Apparently his ability to deceive her to her face was diminishing. A purring smile and sleepy eyes as her hips shifted eagerly translated to complete trust, and he had no defenses against that innocent gift.

His head sank to take her lips so her eyes would close. The kiss was deep and sweet, a soft plunder of her soul's secrets. He sucked her tongue into his mouth, keeping his ravenous cravings hidden behind a blind of gentle touches and sensuous requests.

One of her arms was trapped between them but the other hand rose to trail through the thick hair on his chest. She seemed fascinated with it as her mouth opened under his.

Between her legs, he carefully, ruthlessly stroked her with seemingly casual touches. His fingers gliding around her slick opening, drawing liquid up over her clit in quick passes and down again. He leaned farther, deepening the kiss, thrusting his tongue into her, but still gentleness was all she felt.

Kelly moaned as her body arched, inviting his attention with growing hunger. The hunger he was creating, encouraging, building. She was asking for exactly what he wanted. His lips trailed across her cheek, dropping light kisses as he found the sensitive nerves below her ear. Kelly turned her head so he could better reach what he wanted.

Knowing he was manipulating her did not make him any less of a dragon. He took what she offered, rewarding her with subtle stimulation to little-known nerve bundles directly beneath her skin. Sucking where he knew it would have an erotic response, kissing and nipping down to her collarbone. His body moved over hers and his head rose to gaze into her eyes as his hips settled between her legs.

She was ready for him. He'd made sure of it. His cock found the entrance to paradise and he pushed into her slowly. Kelly's knees came up in response, opening her center to his invasion. Her fingers threaded through his hair, pulling his head down to her mouth so as his body pushed into her fully they were kissing like lovers should.

Cord bent his will into channeling all his animal greed into being the gentle, sensual lover she deserved. This time he would be with her all the way, in every way it was possible for a dragon to pretend he was a man.

He didn't move in her until her little fingers curled into claws and scrape down his back. His hips pulled back slowly, savoring every inch of the journey, out then back to her body. She arched into his gentle thrust, trying to take him faster. His large hand clamped around her hip, not tight enough to bruise, but firmly.

This was for her, and she would endure being treasured. Establishing a slow rhythm of entry and retreat, he lifted his mouth from her lips. Her beautiful eyes were closed and her head naturally arched back, inviting his mouth to her skin. The bruise he had left on her alabaster neck this morning had long since disappeared. Something else he'd made sure of. But the spot that drove her crazy was right there beneath his nose.

He kissed around that temptation, refusing to take any shortcuts to her fulfillment.

"Cord," she whispered, her head still tilted back, eyes closed.

"Right here, baby," he rumbled into her neck.

"Kiss me like you did this morning," she requested in a trembling voice.

"It would be cheating," he admitted reluctantly.

"That doesn't make sense. Kiss me."

"I am kissing you."

"Please."

Little Wind Witch had found the whip. It didn't matter what he said, what his intentions were, she had just hit the master control button. He wasn't sure she was aware of it so it seemed prudent for him to simply shut up and do as she wanted.

Cord's mouth settled over that sensitive spot on her neck. Sucking gently, he felt the ripples of excitement wrap around the ever-rising flame deep in her abdomen. His hips picked up the rhythm of his mouth on her neck. The woman in his arms became fire racing through the air. His heaven and hell were her pleasure.

He rode the wave with her this time, allowing her to feel urgency building in his body. Giving her what she needed while he took another piece of her soul.

Doing his best to mimic human male responses, he allowed his hips to speed up so he carefully controlled the power of each thrust. Feeling her contract around him, he knew exactly when she was ready to fly. In that moment, he gave her a little more of his greed. His hand reached between them to firmly caress her clit. Tight circles forced her body to respond. Hard and fast, he pushed her over the edge and fell with her. Coming in her body was a pleasure he wasn't expecting.

Pushing deep in her, the sensations of her internal grasp shot flaming spears up his spine. It was blazing, feral delight in his possession of her. The beast gloried in his woman and would not be restrained.

At the first burst of come, the world exploded. Apparently controlling the power of his body's use of her had nothing to do with the power she could pull from him. His hips jerked, slamming into her in short thrusts as he emptied. Grinding his seed into her and sealing it there with his body. This wasn't the first time he'd come in a female, but it was the first time he'd lost control in that moment. She ripped away his ability to hide from her for those few minutes. His head jerked up to look at her face and see if she realized what had just happened.

Her eyes were closed, her mouth slightly open as she gasped through her own release. She didn't know.

Metaphorically grabbing his beast by the neck, Cord forcefully shoved it back into the cage of control before she could open her eyes and see what she did to him.

As the contractions in her body wound down, her eyes opened slowly. Gentle fingers trailed down her cheek as he gazed into her lazy smile. This woman glowed, she radiated the light of contentment and it blinded him.

"Kiss me," she asked softly.

His lips covered hers, but the touch was featherlight as he rubbed them back and forth, savoring the feel of her beneath him. It wasn't until she opened her mouth and ran her tongue over his lips that he took her kiss. Gentle, painfully gently, he kissed the wind.

He lifted his head but still couldn't smile. This had been much more than he'd intended. He had wanted to give her the reverent touch of an adoring lover. It never occurred to him that she could return that same touch with such painful honesty.

Cord didn't want to discuss it. Being a gentle lover meant time spent cuddling. He knew the rules, exactly what to do next. He just couldn't face it. Moving over her and off the couch, he slid arms under, lifting her to his chest. He strode out of the living room to the stairs.

"What are we doing?" Kelly wanted to know.

"Taking you to bed." He kissed her forehead as he lightly mounted the steps.

"Oh."

They were in her room already. He reached down and pulled back her bedspread. Placing her in the bed, he drew the blanket over her. Dropping to one knee, with an arm around her head on the pillow and one across her body, he kissed her cheek, her forehead, her eyelids, forcing her eyes shut. "Go to sleep," he whispered into her neck has he continued the soft kisses.

"Stay with me?" she whispered.

"I can't. When your baby runs in here this morning, she will find Mommy in Mommy's bed. That's how it should be. Now is not the time to change what you've taught her."

"What I've taught her?"

This time he could smile. "You've taught her the difference between what married people do and single people do. I don't want to get in trouble by not following the rules."

Kelly returned his smile sleepily. "Thank you."

Cord briefly dropped his head to the bed as he battled the urge to break every rule. Without lifting it, he made sure she knew what he wanted. "You know I want to stay, right?"

"I know, but thank you for supporting me as a parent. It means a lot to me."

Cord lifted his head to look at her. This was very important. "I know the difference between right and wrong, Kelly. I know what a difference it makes when raising a child. I will always support you, support instilling values, checks and balances. These are the things, the only things that Minuet will have to keep her a child of the light. Her power will tempt her to break all the rules, to take whatever she wants, to be anything she can imagine. Without a core set of values, she will be lost."

He could have gone on, but this wasn't how he wanted to leave her. Not with a mind full of worry and a heart heavy for the future. "Relax, baby. You know your daughter is everything right. She has an inborn concern, an uncommon awareness of those around her for a three-year-old. You're doing it right. I did not mean to imply differently. I'm trying to say that I support you and will continue to do exactly that."

Kelly nodded, but the clouds did not disappear from her eyes, and Cord wanted to kick his own ass. What they had just experienced was beautiful. He'd wanted her to drift off to sleep feeling safe and treasured, not worried and anxious. How was he supposed to walk out of this room if she was upset? It wasn't possible.

"Look, hand me that other pillow, will you?" he said. Unsure how to fix what he'd done, he figured it was time to just stop talking already. Every time he attempted to reassure her, he exchanged the shovel he was digging a hole with for a bigger tool, he had to shut up. Apparently this dragon was not eloquent.

Taking the pillow, he dropped it to the floor beside her bed.

Kelly shifted up on an elbow to look down at him as he stretched his long form on the floor. "You're sleeping on my floor?"

"Yeah, you're worried and upset, I can't leave you. If I keep talking, you'll never get to sleep, and I'm only making your concerns worse. If I get in that bed, you are not getting any sleep either. So this is it, you fall asleep and I relax. You stay up worrying and I'll be awake right here with you, except with a hard-on."

Kelly bit her lip to keep from smiling as the big beast below her firmly closed his eyes and folded his hands behind his head. "I see. So you on the floor is different from Minuet finding you in my bed?"

"Way different." He didn't open his eyes to respond.

Kelly relaxed back on her pillow but lay there looking up at the ceiling. "You'll know if I worry the rest of the night?"

"Absolutely. You'll know if I worry the rest of the night. Breathe in the air, draw it over your tongue. You can taste the worry as well as smell it."

She did as he instructed, marveling at how clearly she could identify the different emotions swirling around them. "Good to know."

Cord grunted from below her.

Outside the open window, the breeze picked up, bringing the night into the room with them. Kelly tested her new knowledge, inhaling deeply. Abruptly she sat straight up in bed. "Do you smell that?"

Cord opened his eyes but didn't bother taking the deep breath she had needed. "Yeah. Power is on the air tonight, and it's not us or Legion and Molly. We have company a lot sooner than I'd hoped."

"Who is it?"

"Lie down. I'm not sure who it is but they are far away. The power you taste is weak."

"You expect me to sleep?"

"You have to, Kelly. Humans can't afford to skip that much sleep."

Kelly looked down at him, his eyes were closed and his body seemingly relaxed. "Who do you suspect it is?" she asked.

The corner of Cord's mouth ticked up in a brief show of teeth as he acknowledged her intuition. "I think one of my cousins was sleeping within range when Minuet called me."

Slowly Kelly lay down as she thought through his response. "You are trying not to tell me it's a dragon."

"Go to sleep, Kelly. I'm tracking his every move and you've given me the power to take care of any problem that might arise. Your dragon is bigger, badder and a helluva lot more motivated than this guy could ever hope to be."

Kelly closed her eyes, seeking sleep, but she was pretty sure it wouldn't come. Cord was probably right. Sleep might be in short supply in the near future. She had to be rested. Had to maintain a normal life for Minuet, or as close as they could come to it.

It was an hour before Cord could be sure she had drifted into restless sleep. Dawn painted the horizon with a shy blush. He slowly stood and went to the window, hands on hips, gazing west.

He'd been afraid of this. On the other side of the mountains was the desert. People had been finding bones in the desert for a very long time. Human archeologists put them together in interesting combinations but sometimes they got it right. Sometimes getting it right meant they didn't believe what they'd found. This time a collection of bones had reassembled with no human help.

The dragon had to be extremely weak and hopefully he was deep in the uninhabited expanse of sun and sand. Left alone, eventually he would find a human and feed then they would probably lose track of him. At this point there was no way the starving dragon could understand how he had been reanimated. He wouldn't be looking for a power source as unimaginable as the one who had called him back to life.

It didn't matter, the creature had to be destroyed before he learned too much about the present. Cord and Legion would be hunting tomorrow. It was uncomfortable to leave the women so soon, but the risk of allowing an uncontrolled dragon to appear was much greater.

This brought him to the real problem. An issue he'd known was coming, but before discovering elemental witches walked the world again he'd had no way of addressing.

Dragons had not gone down easily in that last great conflict. Most of them had been gathered in two spots, fighting a pitched battle they'd been deceived into thinking was their biggest problem. In reality, irreplaceable blood had been sacrificed to draw them as a group to the two poles of the Earth.

The capture had been accomplished, freezing them instantly then burying them deep beneath what should have been endless icecaps. In that time, no one could have imagined humans would stumble onto a new method to ensure their own destruction by the evil that almost enslaved them once.

If the world lost the icecaps, it didn't matter how many bullets, bombs or flame throwers they had. None of those would kill a dragon. Most wouldn't even slow one down.

Ice-cold eyes gazed out over the peach-tinted world. Aristocratic nostrils flared as he drew in the information he needed. A slight movement drew his eye to Molly's backyard. There stood Legion, hands on hips, gazing to the west. Slowly the big earth dragon's head turned to look up at the second-floor window Cord stood in.

The two elemental dragons nodded with the slightest dip of chins. The job was clear. They would wait 'til the women were awake, but that's all the time their friend in the desert would have.

Cord clothed himself with a thought and slipped silently down the stairs to the kitchen. Fine coffee was a pleasure he had no intention of abandoning. Without little Miss Miracle around to monitor his actions, he appropriated some from an importer he knew in Miami, keeping the magic low and lean. He only required a small bag.

He had an hour, or he hoped two, before Kelly and Minuet came down the stairs. Enough time to study the pressing problem and see how bad it was. A few more small acquisitions and he had copies of the latest research available on melting ice shelves in the South Pole. The information was disturbing. There was little time, much less than he'd hoped.

Legion opened the back door and stepped into the kitchen. Cord glanced up but didn't acknowledge him any more than that. Legion pulled a chair around and sat down. He spent a few minutes reading the information spread out on the table, and hissed in silent frustration.

"We need Harrison and his witch." The earth dragon's voice was barely more than a whisper, but the low rumble held distinct menace.

"I know. It's fucking worse than I expected," Cord agreed.

"They really are amazing," Legion continued. "How do the shit-for-brains keep coming up with excellent ways to destroy their entire race? Even if there weren't danger in the ice, melting icecaps will change the world as they know it."

"They have no fucking idea they've been here before. The brink of extinction seems to be their favorite place."

Legion shrugged, his usually impassive face twisted into a scowl as he glanced toward the west. "Not our job to tell them. Our pal has found a human already, can you feel the change?"

"Wonder why he hasn't gone silent." Cord sat back and sipped his coffee.

"Probably thinks he's the only one." Legion held out his hand and a cup of coffee appeared in it. The coffee was pale with added cream and its sweet aroma told Cord there was perhaps a cup of sugar in it.

"There's someone besides the idiot. Did you feel the birds last week?"

Legion nodded and glanced at Cord. "Wizard power was all over them."

"How the hell long have you been here?" Cord wanted to know as he looked at the earth dragon with a raise brow.

Legion shifted and took a deep swallow of his sweet coffee. "Long enough to get tired of waiting for your ass to show up."

"What the fuck were you waiting for? You should've called me."

Legion smiled. "Was about to, but things sort of took care of themselves." Legion stood and strolled to the back door. "Meet you in a couple hours. Dust off the blade." Then he was gone.

Cord frowned at the closed door. He didn't want to tell Kelly where he had to go this morning, but she would know without asking anyway. He needed to stop concentrating on that concern before his two ladies came downstairs. He didn't want their home filled with the bitter aroma of death first thing in the morning.

He disposed of the materials he'd been reading and took his coffee into the living room. A wave of his hand removed all signs of the candlelit evening he'd shared with his Wind Witch. He sat on the couch and commanded the TV to show him Barney.

Half an hour later he was frowning fiercely. Now he understood Kelly's laughter last night. But a promise had been made, and as soon as little feet hit the floor upstairs, Barney would appear on the couch. It was going to be a long morning, well, hour at least.

Not long after, he heard the race of little feet rushing to her mother's room. Cord carefully put down his coffee cup. There was no way the big purple paws could hold it. Being an expert at assuming a new identity didn't mean it was exactly easy. In this case, it was the voice he was most worried about.

Shortly his two ladies came down the stairs so he stood. He hadn't added the tail until it was necessary to stand.

Minuet came around the corner and froze. Big eyes examined him from head to tail then she squealed, leaping from a standstill in a very good imitation of a little kangaroo. Barney caught her with the appropriate laugh. Kelly stood in the doorway and tried very hard to pretend she was only laughing because Minuet was so delighted.

Minuet adored her breakfast with Barney. The only really difficult thing was that Barney sucked at stealthily patting Kelly's ass. Kissing her good morning was out of the question, but there was an expected bonus to the situation. Kelly seemed to think his being willing to be Barney for Minuet was amazing.

Every time she touched him, he got a shot of near sexual power. The strength of her approval wasn't sexual at all, but that was the only equivalent he had to compare it with. Minuet insisted on eating breakfast in his lap. Her laughing joy was just as potent as her mother's approval. Being Barney got him huge points. A handy thing to remember.

Breakfast was cleaned up and Minuet sent upstairs to change out of her pajamas when Legion and Molly came in the back door. Barney had disappeared as soon as Minuet's feet met the stairs.

Kelly greeted them with a smile as she looked her friend over critically. "I don't see any broken bones."

"Why would you be expecting any? I was very gentle with him." Molly intentionally misdirected the concern.

Legion grunted, but there was a smile on his face as he glanced down at his Earth Witch. "Don't be fooled, she's very good at healing a body when she's done with it."

"As long as you're still useful," Cord grinned.

"Yeah, the important parts work." Legion boldly slid his hand down to pat Molly's bottom.

Molly grabbed his hand and pulled it up to her waist as she elbowed his ribs. "Get over yourself, Rot Wood," she snapped. "How long will you to be gone?"

"Not that long," Cord said casually as he turned to Kelly. Pulling her into his embrace, he looked into her eyes seriously for a moment. "It'll be all right. Call me if you need me."

Her arms circled his neck as she strained up on tiptoes. "Kiss me then come back to me."

Her request was more than it should have been to him. Her natural ease in displaying their intimate relationship in front of her friend and Legion made him proud. There was no hesitation, no shy attempt to deny his connection to her this morning.

His kiss was quick but fierce, claiming her, eating her and pulling away before it became too hard to do that. "Trust me on both those," he told her softly.

Legion was having a little more trouble letting go of his woman, but the two of them had to be out the door before Minuet came downstairs asking questions. In case anyone was watching, they climbed into Cord's truck.

Driving 'til they reached a deserted section of road on the way up the mountain, Cord pulled over and parked it out of sight.

"He is about two hundred miles away," Legion said casually as he glanced at the sky. "Better do angel of mercy. How's your shiny sword looking these days?"

Cord nodded. "Saintly. I'll come from the south. Go be the wrath of God."

Legion nodded. "Meet you at the body."

Both of them faded from the light range visible to the human eye and took off in opposite directions.

Chapter Nine

Minuet was mildly disappointed when she came down the stairs and Barney was gone. Molly thoroughly enjoyed the three-year-old's description of breakfast with Barney. Kelly acted as if she were laughing too.

Minuet dashed out to the backyard to play with Coco. Molly and Kelly followed her more slowly.

"So what do you think?" Kelly asked Molly. She didn't have to explain what she was asking. They were both living in a different world than they had been yesterday.

"We're in big trouble," Molly repeated herself from the day before. "But I guess it could be worse. They could like looking like lizards."

Both women chuckled as they settled into the patio chairs and watched the dog and child. The silence that was comfortable filled with tension. So many things they needed to discuss, new discoveries, new fears. Whatever it meant to be elemental witches bound them together. It was clear that their friendship had been influenced by a deep recognition. But that wasn't the tension the two women shared.

Sitting, watching the child while knowing the males who shared their beds had gone to face death put them in the company of every warrior's woman since the beginning of time.

Molly reached over and took Kelly's hand for a brief squeeze. "We shouldn't worry. They'll smell it on us when they get back and be all conceited about it."

"I know, but how do you quit?" Kelly wanted to know.

Molly shrugged. "I was hoping you knew."

"You know this threat in the west isn't their main concern, right?" Kelly asked.

"Yeah, have you asked what the real problem is?"

Kelly shook her head. "I figured he would tell me when he was ready. At this point, I'm taking things one at a time."

"Me too," Molly admitted. "You practice the craft yesterday?"

"Yes, it's amazing. Did he teach you anything new?" Kelly wanted to know.

"Several things, but they had nothing to do with the craft." Molly glanced at Kelly and laughed softly.

Kelly looked down and smiled, folding her hands in her lap. "I know what you mean. They can be so inventive."

Molly's eyes were twinkling as she looked at her conservative friend. "I never appreciated education this way in the past."

"Has he demanded you quit your job yet?" Kelly asked.

"Like the third thing out of his mouth," Molly declared with no small amount of disgust. "They seem to like ordering people around."

This time Kelly laughed. "I almost feel sorry for Legion."

"Don't waste pity on him. He can take care of himself," Molly declared.

* * * * *

Roughly two hundred miles to the west, Cord stood surveying the dilapidated shack. He was behind an outcropping of boulders that littered the bleak terrain around him. Terror flowed out of the one-room structure. Inside, the dragon had a victim. He was feeding on the endless supply of fear. It had probably transformed into a demonic shape, threatening the human and demonstrating his power by inflicting pain.

It was time. Cord allowed the change to flow over him, moving his form to the edge of the human light spectrum. In this guise, he appeared to glow. He added white wings and flowing white clothing to ensure the human's interpretation. Then he dropped shields. A thundering roar erupted from his adversary in the cabin as he felt the arrival of another dragon.

Cord flashed to the front of the cabin. The door burst open and a large, demotic form charged out. The beast had been feeding most of the night and now had a respectable power reserve. At eight feet tall, the dragon had put on a massive human-shaped body with blood-red skin. Black horns curled up from his forehead to create a ram's head configuration. There were more horns spiking down his back and across his shoulders. Black leather pants ended at his knees to reveal lower extremities with cloven hooves.

Yep, exactly as expected, this one was using proven methods to feed. It wasn't even that creative, and Cord was not impressed.

In the open doorway, a cowering old man crouched on the floor. Cord adopted a benevolent smile and raised the flaming sword in his hand, as if to engage horned dude. Stupid dragon was focused solely on his shiny white form and didn't sense the threat behind him. He was in mid-bellow when his head simply separated from his body and rolled a few feet away, freezing a shocked expression on grotesque features. A moment later the red form disintegrated.

Legion remained out of the human's sight spectrum as Cord calmly walked up to the sobbing man. Offering his hand in the standard human expectation of how a being who looked like him should act, he helped the man and to his feet. Placing his palm on the old guy's forehead, Cord manipulated a few facts and slowed his heart rate. The guy was in pretty good shape and didn't need too much help to avoid a heart attack.

Then Cord slowly faded out of the human's visual range, not wanting to add to the old guy's terror. In an afterthought, he wrote the words *Go To Church* in the dust at the man's front door. That should complete the impression he wanted to leave.

Appearing in a form the human could understand and draw comfort from made explaining the event unnecessary. What had happened was certainly a supernatural episode, so directing the man's attention to thinking a supernatural protector had saved him gave him the security he would need to live the rest of his life as a sane individual.

And who was to say things hadn't transpired exactly as a higher power directed? Cord's philosophy was, if someone needed to think he was the hand of God to feel safe, he'd be happy to leave them with that impression.

Cord and Legion quickly left the area. This time flying in tight formation just in case there was anyone who could observe them. Caution and deception were as much a part of their natures as the need to feed. Anyone watching the power leave would see one mark streaking in a different direction from where they would eventually end up. They didn't give away the women's location by using the opposite route. That would be too obvious.

The entire event had been accomplished in silence. Creatures who wasted time talking were seldom the last ones standing. A simple lesson that was almost impossible for an ego-driven aggressor to learn. Cold killers were not handicapped with the need to discuss the job at hand. Also, completing the operation in the shortest amount of time possible elevated the odds of success.

Minutes later, normal-looking human forms of Cord and Legion swung into the truck and calmly pulled on to the road.

"Feel anyone watching?" Cord asked Legion. The earth dragon had a slightly higher sensitivity to the vibrations being observed created, even if it were from a distance. The unavoidable boom of a dragon death could easily have drawn attention. No one in this age would know what they had heard though.

"Area felt clean," Legion confirmed.

"Good." Cord nodded.

"Only reason that one was here is because he's an idiot. Nothing will be that easy if the popsicles wake up," Legion stated mildly.

"I'm more concerned with the humans finding one. I don't think they can animate it, but now that we've met Minuet, we have to consider the possibility. Creative bastards that they are, humans always find a way to bring about the worst possible outcome," Cord continued. "Manipulating their perception of events will be impossible on a mass scale. You know the first person to stumble across a winged demon trapped in ice will have it on the internet ten seconds later."

"We'll be sure no one finds them," Legion answered in his usual abbreviated way.

Cord glanced at his big companion and raised a brow. "Good plan. Now tell me how to guarantee that."

They were almost back at Kelly's house. Legion shrugged. "You already have a plan or you wouldn't be talking about it. Let's hear it."

The earth dragon was a beast of few words, but there was no lack of thought in the ones he did use. They couldn't exactly be called brothers, but they understood each other well. The silent battle had been accomplished because there was no need to discuss it. The plan of attack was simple. Doing the job right meant no grandstanding. If a confrontation developed into a flashy show of strength, the hunter was doing it wrong.

"We need to find Harrison and his witch. We also need someone to go south and watch the humans just in case an idiot with a camera phone gets lucky. It wouldn't be wise to take Minuet anywhere near the popsicle fields, so you might want to practice your polar bear impression," Cord suggested.

Legion didn't answer as they pulled into Kelly's driveway. He slid out of the truck and walked around it to join Cord at the front door.

As Cord pulled the door open, Legion shot him a sly smile. "Cold means I warm her up."

Cord had to chuckle at the earth dragon's logic. He was right. Cold was an excellent reason to remain in physical contact with his witch. Lucky bastard.

Kelly and Molly were still on the back patio. The two large dragons strolled out the kitchen door, looking as if they'd simply been to the corner store for a few supplies, but the air around them told a different story.

It was natural for Kelly to stand and reach for him. Her mouth opened slightly as she pulled the taste of battle across her tongue. It was black licorice, dark with a hint of sweetness at the end. This must be what victory tasted like. Then she was in his arms and there was no time to analyze the air around him.

His mouth was on hers, and though the arm around her waist appeared casual, there was nothing relaxed about his tongue thrusting into her mouth in a quick stab of possession. Over as fast as it started, his head lifted and he smiled down at her.

"You missed me?" he asked. "I told you not to worry."

"Just because you said it doesn't make it so," Kelly told him forcefully. "But even if you are that bossy, I'm glad you're back."

Cord had to touch the roses on her cheeks as she looked up at him with that expression on her face. The back of his knuckles glided down her cheek to her chin. Words didn't really matter. She was taking something from him as much as he was drinking her touch. That didn't make sense. Her hand at his back was fisted in his shirt, and the other on his biceps clutched him too tightly.

The tension wasn't leaving her, and Cord frowned slightly. "Seriously, that was nothing. There was no danger. I should have made sure you knew that before we left."

Legion and Molly interrupted with their abbreviated goodbyes as Legion pretty much dragged Molly to the gate connecting the two backyards.

For an instant Cord was jealous then a short body barreled into his legs, wrapping herself around his thigh like a little monkey to laugh up at him. Looking down into Minuet's shining face as he stood with his arms around her mother, Cord couldn't think of one other place he'd rather be. The heat flooding his system was more than the power they couldn't help giving him. He was developing some aberrant need for this new mix of acceptance, concern and joy.

"I glad you back," Minuet declared happily.

"I'll always come back, precious," he told her with a smile. "That's a promise."

"I knows it. But Mommy like pomises," she told him seriously. "She petend not worry."

"Don't tell him all my secrets," Kelly laughed. "We girls have to stick together."

"We sticking to Cord," Minuet stated as her arms and legs tightened around Cord to show her mother she was sticking.

Kelly draped her arms around Cord's neck, giving him a quick hug as she agreed with Minuet. "You're right. That's a good idea."

Cord didn't know what to say. Minuet had a way of cutting through adult clutter to the heart of whatever she thought was important. In doing so, she wrapped her little fingers around whatever this dragon could call a heart and locked herself to it. Her intentions were transparent, pure as sunlight.

Cord cleared his throat and smiled at both of them as an arm circled each. "Tell you what, angel face, I'll promise Mommy whatever she wants. Is that all right with you?"

"No. That not right. We only gets what we needs. That rule. You can pomise be safe. That not selfish," Minuet reasoned.

"Got it." He nodded into her serious little face. "Thank you for keeping track of the rules. I don't want to get mixed up."

"I member good," Minuet continued. "I help you."

Cord fervently hoped she wasn't being prophetic. It was his plan to make sure they never came to a place where he needed her help. If they didn't succeed in securing the dragons trapped beneath the ice, she might be their only hope. However, the possibility existed that the opposite was true. There was no way of knowing.

There was another reason it was vitally important to make sure they never had to use her power. It was an unknown, its effect or consequences unpredictable. Simply being around her had a positive influence on both him and Legion. What if simply being near her had a positive response on a regular dragon? Could she wake them without trying? Could she unknowingly feed them by accessing her power for normal, everyday things, just because she was close to them?

Right now she was infusing him with massive amounts of power through her emotions. The pure faith of a child was magic on steroids. There was no way to test her abilities at this age. Teaching her to kill the frozen dragons would be an unimaginable horror. He wasn't sure he was strong enough to do it. Soon he would show her how to make sure she didn't harm anything, safety required it, but teaching her how to be a weapon was a revolting thought. No, he would be the only beast. If there was a battle to be fought, it was his battle, never hers.

An overwhelming wave of possession, protection, defense, washed through him as he looked at these two. They both felt the change in him and nearly identical frowns appeared on female foreheads.

"What?" they said in unison.

How was he supposed to explain this to them? A dragon was a greedy creature. He held what was his at all costs, defending with no conscience, no mercy and no remorse. Taking what he needed by any means. This was the beast who would never leave them.

"It's nothing. I'm glad to be back," he did his best to reassure them. Minuet accepted that that explanation with no question, unwrapping herself from his leg to run after Coco, who was barking fiercely at a rabbit that had been foolish enough to venture near the fence. The rabbit was long gone but Minuet had to investigate.

Kelly wasn't so easy. She remained standing in his embrace as Minuet ran off.

"Now the truth," she said quietly.

"The truth is, your beast is a nasty bastard who will do anything to keep you," Cord answered honestly.

"And the problem is?" She raised a brow.

"You're comfortable with that?"

Her smile was intimate. "It's one of the things I like most about him."

A purr rumbled in his chest as the air around them changed. She was flirting with him and completely unconcerned. "I'm not sure you understand, but I'm losing interest in explaining. Kiss me, witch."

She slid up on tiptoes, making sure her body rubbed up against his. His mouth met hers in a deep, demanding kiss. In it he told her how much he wanted to possess her right now. They broke apart as Minuet and Coco trotted back across the lawn to them.

"We'll finish this discussion later," he promised.

The rest of the day they spent making a game out of practicing magic. Going for a walk in the woods after lunch, Minuet quickly perfected her touch with small animals. Cord was amazed at how swiftly she learned control. Her touch was light. She fine-tuned it with innate ability and deep empathy. The child had no mean in her. If she even suspected she was hurting the creature, she'd pull away.

Returning from the walk, Minuet plopped down on the living room floor to watch *Sesame Street*. Cord and Kelly sat behind her on the couch. Soon she was absorbed in the show, though her attention was not solely directed at the TV. Minuet had an ever-growing capacity for knowledge. On the walk, they had discovered she naturally kept track of every creature within her range. It was a little bit scary for Kelly. Her baby was not only talented but she was brilliant as well, absorbing how to do things with all her senses.

What scared Kelly was the weight of the future. Minuet was different from everyone, even her gifted mother. There would come a day when she would be lonely. When that day arrived, it would last forever.

Gathering Kelly under his arm, Cord had kissed her forehead as they walked behind the little wonder, quietly reminding her that the future was not set. If there were miracles, and her daughter was one of them, there was always the possibility of others. Probably not exactly like Minuet, but the world continued to surprise him, and he'd been around a damn long time.

Kelly curled her legs under her on the sofa and leaned into Cord's side as he draped an arm around her. Resting in his arms was an exceedingly addictive habit. His large body surrounded her, creating the sensation of protection. He was the embodiment of every little-girl fantasy about knights in shining armor who rescued, protected and spoiled the princess of his choice. She left off the slaying dragons part. As the princess in her story, she could alter the fantasy.

Battling the lethargy of just surrendering to all that wonderful spoiling he was doling out, Kelly decided it was a good time to discuss a few things anyway.

"What now?" she asked, keeping the question generic in the hopes that Minuet would not follow the conversation.

"Molly and Legion go south for a while. Just to keep an eye on a situation we need to maintain under control," he stated. Being sure he used sentences that would not alarm Minuet he explained, "The three of us will find a friend of mine. Have you ever been to Scotland?"

Kelly's head was on his shoulder as she watched Minuet. "No, never went up that way. Are you asking or telling? Will Legion and Molly be okay?"

"Legion is looking forward to the trip," Cord said. "He likes the idea of keeping Molly warm while they take care of business. I'd like to be asking, but that's a luxury we don't have. It's something we have to do. We need the water dragon to find his lady." He could feel Kelly smile as he stumbled over softening the direction into a discussion.

"I hear Scotland can be quite chilly on occasion," she said with studied innocence.

"So they say," Cord agreed. "I'll be sure to check every inch of your body to make sure you're not cold. Regularly. Perhaps I should say relentlessly."

Kelly's head tilted to smile at him. "See why I'd like the beast?"

"Not so much, but don't pay any attention to my doubts. I won't."

Kelly's hand rested on his abdomen. She moved it up over his chest to tap his chin with her finger. The caress was oh so innocent and full of a woman's promise. "Good," she stated softly. "That's another thing I'm going to enjoy about the beast. He's dependable."

His eyes reminded her of steam pouring over her. The heat enveloped her, sinking into her skin, warming her bones. He didn't have to say a word as the heat moved over her lips, burned down her neck. She could feel him drag them back to her face. Building hunger was forced to a new level as she watched him try to pull back the distinctly sexual perusal of her body. It was one of the sexiest things she'd ever seen.

"Stop," he breathed.

"I didn't do anything. You're the one with dangerous eyes," she whispered back.

"You liked it. Don't invite the beast, baby. He doesn't play nice," Cord warned.

"Nice is overrated," Kelly stated.

Cord remained carefully still as he regarded the enticing Wind Witch. "You're pushing. Last night was only a taste. Understand what I'm saying?"

Kelly's bottom lip disappeared between her teeth. Her eyes remained gazing into the heat pouring from the male holding her. She nodded and little lines appeared under her eyes, her lip reappeared and she pressed into him with her body. A small movement only he could be aware of.

"Is that a promise?" she wanted to know. Her laughing eyes twinkled as she added, "You know how I like promises. They make me feel good."

Cord's entire body flashed to rock hard as she pressed into him and demanded he promise her the dominant lover she'd met last night.

"Count on it," he answered, his arm tightening behind her for a moment. "Feeling very brave, aren't you, baby girl?"

"Should I be afraid?" she asked boldly.

"Depends," he conceded. "Nothing compares to that path, it changes you. Teaches you needs that can't be unlearned, obsessions that will not let you rest. But if you go there, darlin', it'll be with me. I'll never let you crave what you can't have," he promised her.

Kelly studied his face, the humor leaving hers. "Why does it scare you? Your warning is dark, what we shared last night was not. You showed me a level of sensation that was new but I was never afraid."

"Scared? That's not the right word. I'm concerned. Being afraid is not the issue, exploring a new level of sensation is. You've heard of domination and submission, right? This is what you're asking for." He regarded her seriously a moment then glanced at Minuet who was still engrossed in her TV show.

Kelly settled her head on his shoulder, gazing blindly and the TV. "The two words you just used to describe what we did don't seem right. They bring to mind people with whips and chains, dressed in black leather all involved in making rules just to give them a reason to punish someone. Where you took me was nothing like that, so if that's what you're trying to warn me about, thanks. Forget I said anything."

"Good," Cord said mildly. "All the dressing up and carrying-on looks like a lot of playacting to me. I'm not interested in pretending anything. But that's not what I was referring to and it certainly doesn't have anything to do with our relationship. What we did was all about trust. It's not something you can pull out of the closet and dress up in."

Supper was light and early, a salad and some fruit. Minuet was a source of endless energy, but she was also a little girl who had spent the day learning. There wasn't much play after and it was soon time to get ready for bed. Minuet slowly got up and agreed with her mother that she had better kiss Cord good night now.

After they disappeared up the stairs, Cord found himself drawn to the back door. Stepping into the early evening gloom, he automatically rechecked his surroundings. The conversation with Kelly made him uncomfortable. He hadn't clearly explained his caution nor how incorrect her assumptions about getting involved in a submissive relationship with him.

Fire rippled down his spine as he inhaled. His body was instantly ready to shift and it had nothing to do with the conversation. He opened his mouth to breathe deeply, tasting the air as it invaded his being. Abruptly his mouth snapped shut in frustration. The information on the wind told him of clumsy eyes trying to see things they barely understood.

Whoever had sent the birds that had bothered Minuet was probably the same curious amateur. Perhaps calling the person an amateur wasn't quite correct. They had managed to narrow the search to this area. The explosion of power required to kill a dragon had not helped conceal them, but he had thought that kill had been made far enough away to appear a singular event. Apparently someone was much better at connecting the dots than he'd like.

What he smelled was bitter, the distinctive signature of a young wizard. Actually, there were three flavors. A little gang of them. They were perhaps one-hundred miles away. The three of them were currently engaged in a power search. Obviously no mature wizard had taught them the art of shielding.

It would be foolish to think that since the witches were just discovering their powers that the human wizards were in the same underdeveloped condition. Assuming the best possible scenario was inviting the worst possible outcome. No, he had to assume these three were trying to impress their superiors by striking out on their own to gather information.

Simply killing them would send a message, but it wasn't time to communicate with that adversary yet. The three delinquents had simply given away any element of surprise their superiors might hope to employ.

Legion stepped out into Molly's backyard and nodded at Cord. "We're leaving in the morning. How about you?"

"Same," Cord answered. "It would be fun to spank the pups and send them home."

"Yeah, I miss the old days too." Legion sighed. "Stay dark tonight. We don't have time to take care of both threats."

"Worry about your own situation." Cord grinned as he looked at the earth dragon. "I haven't noticed that Molly takes direction kindly."

Legion grinned and scratched his chin. "No she doesn't," he agreed.

Cord shook his head and turned back to the kitchen door, silently entering and locking up behind him.

Legion had no complaints about his sharp-tongued little witch, and it made Cord smile. It also reminded him how well each dragon had been crafted to fit the witch he belonged to.

Kelly came downstairs and was a little surprised to find him in the kitchen. "Are you hungry? Can I get you anything?"

Cord ignored her questions and walked directly to her, gathering her in his arms for a deep kiss. His palm cradled the back of her head as he took her mouth. She melted for him. Her arms gliding around his neck as she pressed into him.

Lifting his head reluctantly, Cord told her about the new threat. "We have company tonight, and I don't mean Minuet. I'm pretty sure the wizards who were using the birds Minuet didn't like are three apprentices. They've managed to narrow their search to this area. Legion and I could easily take care of them, but that would be sending a message to their superiors, who I suspect have no idea what these boys are doing. For right now we want to simply avoid them. A confrontation with an unknown number of wizards is unwise at this point. Our focus has to be on ensuring the frozen dragons remain undiscovered."

"What do you mean we have company? Are they coming for us?"

"No, they're about one hundred miles away, seeking any power signature. Remember what I said about making love? It's very difficult to completely shield that level of involvement. A sensitive within range will know something even if they can't pinpoint who or where the sexual activity is taking place," Cord explained.

"Seriously?" Kelly frowned.

Cord smiled down at her. "We'll be leaving on our journey tomorrow, using human means of transportation just to be sure to lose the little bastards. Tonight is the problem. No whisper of power can leak out of this house."

Kelly nodded. "So this means you have time to explain to me exactly what you and Legion are so worried about. What's to the south that Legion has to keep an eye on?" she stepped out of his embrace and went to the coffee machine. "Sit," she instructed. "I'll make coffee and you tell me everything."

Cord sat down obediently, grinning at her take-charge commands. "Everything? You know we only have a few hours and I've been alive longer than humans mark time. At least how they do it now."

"See, its comments like that that make me crazy. What do you mean?" Kelly wanted to know. "You act like history has been cut in half somehow. As if there was a before and there is a now. Time can be measured, but it can't be stopped and started again. There's no cutting it off and patching the new part on." Done with the coffee, she switched on the machine, turning to frown at him as she crossed her arms and waited for an answer.

Cord was mildly surprised at how clearly she articulated exactly what had happened. She was using the phraseology as an example of what could never happen when it was exactly what had happened. "Kelly witch, the ladies of your kind did exactly that. They stopped time. You know what happens in a video game when you hit the reset button?"

"Sure. Everything disappears and you start over from the beginning. Well, from where you last saved the game." She stated confidently "There is no way you can tell me witches are capable of doing that with a planet."

"Exactly why it worked, being the inconceivable option was its brilliance. So yes, I am telling you they can do it. You could do it if you had to. It wasn't simple and it wasn't easy. Taking that path involved the death of all life at that time. They saved an incredibly small number of humans in the hopes that they would build a new world, one without dragons. It was the biggest gamble imaginable. The choice was made because the vast majority of humans would rather die than live in the world as it was. There was no hope, no other method to gain freedom. So when every possible option is exhausted, all that is left is the impossible. Global reset."

Kelly stepped away from the counter, slowly coming to the table and pulling out a chair. She dropped into it heavily, staring at his face. They sat in silence as the coffeepot gurgled on the counter. Her eyes never left his as she tried to comprehend the huge concepts he was so confidently telling her. "The flood? As in the Bible?" she asked dazedly.

"Yep, that's the one."

"Are you saying there is no God?" she asked softly.

"No. There's no question in my mind that God exists. I fully believe God created the world and life in it. God had nothing to do with dragons. Brilliant humans meddling with the keys to life came up with the abominations that are dragons. Humans have tried it in this age too. They call it creating the perfect soldier," he explained.

"God's plan for life and how it should develop is perfect. Even though humans try it all the time, they have never managed to enslave the world under one rule. Humans are ruled by the original laws of nature that inserts checks and balances. Abilities that enable the oppressed to overthrow their oppressors. There is reason, compassion, that spark of Godlike inventiveness that envisions progress. Dragons were not so perfectly made. Once they gained global control, there would be no human power that could defeat them.

"The great mystery of you ladies called witches is the brilliance of God. You have the capacity to do good that is bigger than yourselves. God gave humans everything they needed to develop into masters of the universe. The only problem is, some humans keep getting impatient with evolution. They sense the power within themselves and seek to use it for all the wrong reasons.

"The dragon disaster was a human problem to solve. God's only involvement was that He'd even given humans the ability to fix something that horrific. Humans possessed the vision and power through the three elemental witches. Since humans had played at being God and created life, they also had to accept the responsibility of destroying it. Unfortunately it was not possible for that generation to destroy the abominations. They could only capture them and hope future generations would find a way to complete the job."

Unusually still, Kelly stared at him. The coffee had long since finished but neither of them stood to get a cup. "But you are here. How? I mean why would they..." She couldn't finish the thought as she looked at him.

"The three elemental dragons are the latest thing in dragon engineering," he said softly. "We were made differently, created for a different purpose with different abilities. Our makers learned from the mistakes of others and engineered creatures specifically designed to assist the humans. They knew that nature, as God created it, was infinitely resilient. It would take time but they had no doubt their kind, gifted individuals, would reappear in the world. We were made for the witches of the new world. Our mission concealed even from us it seems.

"The great deception in short was this. The dragon leaders were tricked into believing a final battle for control would be mounted by the humans at the South Pole. At the moment dragon forces attacked, the three witches gathered all the power at their disposal and shifted every tectonic plate. Think of how small a shift is that creates the earthquakes your world knows. Consider what happens when the shift is significant and universal. This triggered destruction on such a scale as to knock the planet off its axis.

"The result was an instant deep freeze at the poles. The rest of the world experienced volcanic activity, earthquakes, floods, basically the landmasses sank and new ones rose. Everyone and everything was destroyed except for one small group in a boat and the three dragons, whose job it was to ensure only that boat survived. You know the rest."

Kelly got up and went to the coffee machine. "Would you like a cup of coffee?" she asked calmly, as if they were discussing the weather.

"Please. Black."

She brought back two cups of coffee and sat down, taking a long sip before she said anything. "So if the icecaps melt, we will find dragons."

"Uh-huh," he agreed, letting her work it out in her mind.

"But finding them does not bring them back to life, right?" she pointed out.

Cord shifted in his chair, taking a minute for a drink. "We don't know. Those dragons were frozen instantly. The few stragglers who went to ground in other parts of the planet were forced into elemental sleep because there was no more fuel. We are fed by human emotion. When the witches destroyed the Earth, they cut off the dragons' source of power. Waking one of the dragons in elemental sleep is almost impossible. I say almost because Minuet is a new development, but the popsicle dragons could be different. They were not depleted, not starved into an elemental state. We don't know what will happen if one of those bad boys thaws."

Kelly took up the thought. "A dragon freed from the ice could be exactly as he was the moment he was frozen. And now there are lots of humans again… I see the problem."

Cord nodded. "Exactly."

"So what's your plan?" she wanted to know.

"Well, we thought getting you three ladies together would be helpful. Since the humans have somehow found a way to destroy their atmosphere, unintentionally this time, we are looking for a way to fix it. Keeping the ice intact will give us time to figure out a more permanent fix."

"If the people who created dragons couldn't figure out how to kill them, what makes you think we can?" she asked.

"We know exactly how to kill dragons," Cord said confidently "but it only works in small numbers. Separate a dragon from his head and the entire beast disappears. Since every dragon knows this, they're very good at protecting their necks. A couple thousand dragons in one place presents a problem. There aren't enough warriors to engage in one-on-one combat that beheading requires. Even if you dress the humans in asbestos, not enough of them will live long enough to do any real damage."

"And," Kelly said thoughtfully, "as soon as anyone gets a glimpse of a frozen dragon, they will be digging up that specimen for study as fast as they can."

"It will wake up and kill them," Cord observed.

"It does that and the world will be even more interested in it," Kelly said softly.

"So we're back to where we started," Cord agreed with her. "Curious humans who think they can control what they don't understand."

"You know I have no idea how to fix the atmosphere," Kelly said. "I'm the Wind Witch and I know less than you do about being that. Can you do it?"

"Not on my own. You are the source of my life, my power. The answer has to come from you."

Kelly frowned and stared down at her coffee for a few minutes. "Didn't they leave an instruction book or something? A book of spells and stuff."

"They've left you a dragon, Kelly. There was no way to ensure the information stayed out of the wrong hands. Imagine what would have happened if a wizard got a hold of such a book." Cord leaned across the table intently. "Their plan worked. We are sitting here doing exactly what they envisioned we would. That gives me hope that they thought of this aspect too. You do have the power to do what's necessary."

"My head hurts," Kelly avoided his insistent conclusions.

Instantly Cord was out of his chair and around the table, picking her up in his arms. "Enough history, baby."

Kelly relaxed into his hold as he strode into the living room. "I thought we couldn't, um, you know."

"We can do a lot of 'you know'," he contradicted with a grin. "I just have to be in complete control at all times. Something I don't have a problem with."

In the living room, Cord sat and adjusted Kelly so she was straddling his lap, but this time facing him. "Relax. Put your head on my shoulder and let me give you a massage," he instructed. His body was stretched out with lean hips resting on the edge of the cushions, making him a long, hard mattress.

"This isn't how it's usually done," Kelly mumbled. His hands were already moving over her spine firmly. Somewhere in the process, both of them had lost their clothes and the lights had dimmed.

"I don't do the usual," he assured her softly.

His chest vibrated with a low purr that she almost couldn't hear but resonated through her body.

"Oh my God," Kelly moaned as he worked muscles in her back, down her neck, across her shoulders. His hands knew exactly where to touch, and she was once again completely available to him. Except for the fact that they were both naked and he was freaking perfect, there was nothing sexual about his attention. And of course, she thought foggily, she was also the Queen of England if that were true.

He worked on her until it felt as if her body were made of butter. Then he slid from under her, laying her facedown on the couch and started on her legs. Strong, firm pulls on long muscles, deep circling caresses into joints. If she hadn't already been completely vulnerable to him, this would have sealed the deal.

How was a woman supposed to resist this? What wouldn't she do to get more of it? These questions had no answers because Kelly was too busy sinking into the world he created or her, the world where her body relaxed into oblivion as he worked each muscle and tendon with the same relentless attention to detail as he did everything else.

Cord had appeared in their world and become its center. He was a force of nature. He'd not needed to convince her of his place once she realized his role as her daughter's guardian. He'd insisted he was here for her, but that had never been her main focus.

Kelly was aware she needed help. Minuet's talents were so far beyond her own. She wasn't sure what she would have done if Cord hadn't shown up. Things had been getting critical. Then there he was. He'd brought a wealth of other issues, things she was struggling to comprehend, but the truth was he'd solved her problems in a big way.

Was she simply weak? Was accepting his presence in their lives so easily a sign of her faults? No, he'd been right when he'd stated that if even half of what he said was true, she'd have become his whore to protect her daughter. That wasn't weak.

He'd taken her surrender and made her his…what? What did one call a lover who would kill for his woman and her family? He and Legion had dealt death this morning. She didn't want to know the details, but she had tasted battle on him.

What did one call someone who worked at finding ways to wait on her? He watched her closely, supplying anything he thought she needed before she could so much as get herself a glass of water. What did one call a man who willingly impersonated the children's character Barney for her daughter just because it made Minuet happy?

Calling him the monster images that the name dragon brought to mind didn't fit. Whatever he was, he was truly content when he had her in his arms, pleasing her somehow.

She felt it in him. He literally lived to touch her. It was such an incomprehensible situation. There was nothing weak about him. There was no bend in his will, no hitch in his strength, and yet it was all directed at her and Minuet. What was the word for this male?

She had no idea when he'd added his lips to her massage. By the time she realized she was not only relaxed to the point of being molten chocolate, but smoldering on passion's embers as his mouth moved up the back of her calf, she had no hope of resistance. Of course, nor was she so stupid as to want to resist.

"What?" she mumbled on a moan as he licked the back of her knee. "We can't."

Cord blew a warm breath across the damp skin before answering. "We can't give away a hint of magic. That doesn't mean we can't do what regular people do."

"But I ah…" She couldn't finish the phrase for a second as his lips drifted to the inside of her knee. Who know that was such an erotic zone? "I can't control anything when you, when we…"

"I know," he whispered. "Relax, Kelly girl. Trust me to take care of you."

His mouth went back to its drugging task. Her legs were gently pushed apart as he turned to the other knee to give it the same attention.

Abruptly his head came up and his body tensed. She could feel it. A sheet swiftly covered her as he stood.

"Stay there. Minuet needs a drink of water. I'll be right back, and if you've move I'll spank that pretty ass." Cord strode from the room, fully clothed again.

Kelly's head turned to watch him go. She could feel Minuet's restlessness, but he'd been aware of it first. What did she call him? The person who rushed to answer her child's half-awake needs while ordering her sharply to remain decadently relaxed. Okay, so who cared what she called him, she really wanted to know what would happen if she moved?

Chapter Ten

Kelly closed her eyes and listened with her heart. Minuet could get her own glass of water. What a little girl needed was the security of knowing someone was watching over her. Cord provided exactly what she needed with natural warmth, cuddling Minuet a few moments after she drank her water until she settled back into sleep.

He quietly left Minuet's room and was coming back. Kelly took inventory of her limbs to make sure nothing had moved. She didn't really believe he'd hurt her, the command had been a sensual directive. Possibly he'd meant it as a test to see what she would do, to see if she was willing to move their relationship down that path. Being honest with herself, Kelly admitted she wasn't quite that brave.

Closing her eyes as he stepped into the room, Kelly did her own testing. What would his response be? She was in exactly the position he'd left her. Would he insist on taking them in the direction he wanted to go?

She should've known better. The sheet disappeared and he took up exactly where he left off, settling his perfectly naked body between her legs, and the thorough licking kisses continued.

As his tongue ran the crease where her bottom met her thigh, Kelly had to speak up. His attention had started as a slow burn, but now it was all burn and no slow. "Did I do something wrong?" she asked as his mouth moved over her.

"What makes you think that?" he wanted to know.

"You're punishing me by turning me on and then I get nothing?"

"Who said you get nothing?" His voice rumbled from the vicinity of her hip. His mouth never lifted from her skin as he answered.

"I'm dying here in case you hadn't noticed."

His body pulled up a little more as he nibbled the small of her back. His close-cut beard tickled the rise of her bottom as he moved over her. "I noticed, try to relax. You're not ready yet."

"I am so ready," she insisted softly. She couldn't help it, her hips moved under him, legs spreading in invitation. His body willingly sank between them. He continued the nibbling up her backbone, his hands caressing her sides.

"Remember the part about me being in control?" he asked. "I am, and you will enjoy this."

"Commanding me to enjoy it doesn't work," she groaned as his hands slid under her, grasping the sides of her breasts in a tantalizing caress.

This time his chuckle came from the back of her neck. "Denying you're enjoying this isn't what's not working, Kelly girl. I can feel the fire in you, I can smell desire in the air and there is no hiding just how much you love this from me. Now turn over. We have the whole other side to do."

He stood in a smooth motion and waited for her to roll over. Of course she did. This would make getting what she wanted much easier. Opening her eyes, she enjoyed the view of him standing over her. Long and lean, his body was hard-packed muscle. From this angle, his wide shoulders filled the room. The ladder of tight muscles down his torso led to a defined abdomen. Who in the hell had a defined belly? It wasn't fair to the rest of the world.

What was below that belly was what wasn't fair to the rest of the male population. He wasn't a man, she reminded herself, but damn, such hard, thick perfection was too much. Perhaps not exactly too much, she mused.

"Enjoying the view?" he asked softly.

Kelly realized his hands rested on hips as he let her look all she wanted. "Yeah, enjoying the view," Kelly whispered and licked her lips in natural reaction.

His abdomen jerked and a pearl of excitement appeared on the wide head of his cock. "Careful, baby girl," he warned softly. "I see that tongue again and I'll be tempted to give it something to do."

Kelly's eyes finally dragged up his body to his eyes. They were molten as he gazed down at her. The heat in them drove her, drew her into the sexual whirlwind swirling around them. There was no sound. No movement of air, the sweeping gale of emotion was contained between them. Kelly's body arched and her hands settled lightly on her breasts. She was rewarded with a ripple of tension down his body. His eyes followed her hands as she caressed herself, lightly plucking her nipples.

A muscle jerked in his cheek. Kelly smiled and felt fire low in her belly burn a little hotter. Her hands abandoned her breasts to trail down her torso, pressing into soft flesh, heading straight for the juncture of her legs. As her fingers passed her bellybutton, her legs slowly spread. Taking the suggestion from how he'd arranged her last night, she draped one leg over the back of the couch, the other with her foot flat on the floor.

Fingers combed down tight blonde curls and Kelly's eyes closed as she rubbed the center of the inferno consuming her. She couldn't stop watching him for long though. Her eyes barely open, she watched him watch her and both of them burned.

"Kelly," he said softly. But there was nothing else he could add to that. Nothing he could contribute as she opened her body and gave him this erotic gift. It was a pure gift. She was experiencing pleasure, but she knew she would have it anyway without lifting a finger to entice him. Hell, all she had to do was look at him and he wanted to fuck her.

Here she was giving him an amazing visual, and the woman was doing it for him. Momentarily he was afraid he was drooling. At least his mouth wasn't hanging open panting. Between his legs his cock was slick with his response to her. He could feel the hot lubricant dripping down his balls then her fingers disappeared into her body.

Cord dropped to his knees beside her, clutching the couch. He was behind her foot that rested on the floor, his view completely unobstructed as she slowly fucked herself. He could see the liquid pleasure. Hear it as she pulled in and out. Watch her body drip as pretty fingers invaded.

Her fingers pulled out of her body and her hand extended to him. "Give me your hand," she requested softly.

Cord had little control of his response as he placed his hand in hers.

"Give me two fingers. I want to feel you, but let me be in control. Please," Kelly asked.

His eyes shot up to hers as he realized what she was asking. His smile was dark. "Anything you need, Wind Witch, as long as it's me and you."

She grasped his fist, two fingers extended. Slowly she guided him to her entrance. He let her control the movements as she rubbed his digits through the soft petals of her center, coating him with her pleasure. Then she drew him down to her opening and slowly pressed his fingers into her body.

Kelly arched in pleasure as he entered her. He let her push him into her. He was in her body and it felt so good. Her hips jerked but she was enjoying herself too much to go fast. Pulling him out slowly, Kelly moaned in harsh delight as she pushed him deep into her body. Slight pressure told him she wanted him to twist there. He did.

Her other hand went to her clit, circling as she directed his fingers into her. Cord leaned down and nudged her fingers off that bundle of nerves to replace it with his tongue. That wicked muscle strummed her as she slowly released his fist. Cord continued the motions, his fingers screwing into her with a twist as he pushed deep.

Kelly was stretched out beneath him, moaning as his fingers delved into her sweet body. His mouth on her as she trembled with each thrust and it wasn't enough. She was feeding him power with every movement but he was about to lose control and mount her. Fucking her brains out was something he couldn't do this night.

His head lifted from her as he watched her carefully. Both his fingers pulled out of her as she thrashed beneath him. Turning his hand slightly, Cord slowly pushed his thumb into her body, his forefinger gently stroked the sensitive skin between ass and cunt. Her body jerked and pressed down on his fingers. She didn't pull away.

Focusing his attention on introducing her to new sensations controlled the magic flowing between them. The power increased with her excitement, but he could control it, drink all of it with the ravenous appetite of his kind. He could not afford to let her drive him to lose control, and she almost had.

His thumb pulled out of her cunt as his forefinger circled the pink of her lower opening. There was no question of lubricant. She was wet with her excitement, dripping down to the shy entrance he caressed now.

Looking up in to her wide eyes, he took control. "Breathe," he directed in a deep growl as his thumb entered her. His forefinger easily breached that lower clench. She jerked but then her response shot up to white hot as he held her with his eyes.

"That's a good girl." He fed her approval as she panted through the new sensations.

Her bottom clenched around the invader, her hips lifted off the couch as she froze. Looking into her eyes, Cord let her see the savage in him. Holding her gaze with unblinking demand, he pushed both fingers into her in a slow invasion.

"Breathe. Yes, little Wind Witch," he answered the question in her eyes. "Mine," he confirmed for her. His hands slowly pulled out and pushed back in. "Every pretty inch of you is mine."

Kelly's mouth dropped open as she panted through the barrage of emotions and sensations. Fear had flashed through her at his first touch, but it had only added another addictive shade to the fire of need he'd built in her. Her reaction to his demanding statements struggled to gain her attention. It was difficult for them to scream louder than the roaring heat consuming her from her invaded body.

His eyes devoured her surrender as she relaxed into new the sensation. "That's right," Cord approved softly. "Enjoy every bit of this. Fear has no place between us."

Fucking both ass and cunt with demanding fingers, he watched her closely. As her body accepted his invasion, she couldn't hide her excitement from him. He wouldn't allow it. Her body burned for him, for this, and only then did he release her gaze.

His head dropped to her clit and there was nothing but the sensations he was giving her. Sucking her sensitive nerves into his mouth, his thick thumb pushed into her cunt and two fingers stretched her ass. Fire shot through the shattering pleasure, racking her with its power.

The fingers pushing into her body became firm instruments of pleasure and torment. His mouth on her clit grew ravenous, and pleasure drew power from the torment. Sensations battled for supremacy and Kelly lost her soul to them.

That was the push she needed, Kelly's body clamped down on him and she flew apart, coming hard on his inserted fingers as he continued sucking her clit.

She'd never felt such a mix of intense sensations. The emotional surrender as he took her body added so much to it, sweeping her to a new high. Her body continued shaking as the contractions tapered off. His hands no longer in her, his mouth gently licking over shuddering folds as she slowly drifted back into reality.

Kelly squeezed her eyes shut and tried to figure out what just happened. It was difficult to sort out as his tongue swirled over her in lazy strokes. Everything had changed. She had changed, and he'd known she would. That's what he'd been warning her about earlier. The sensations were so intensely different from anything else. There was no comparison.

He had been in complete control. She hadn't been afraid because of that control. This wasn't what she'd expected at all. There were no trappings to it, no make-believe or pretend. It was raw power exchange between them. And it was as addictive as he had warned her it would be. She wanted more.

Kelly slid her elbows beneath her to prop herself up and looked down at the male between her legs. His head lifted, large hands were splayed on her inner thighs though he didn't have to hold her open. As his head came up to meet her gaze, he reminded her of a lion—large, beautiful and so dangerous that it almost hurt to look at him.

Their eyes held in silence for a few seconds then he prowled up her body on all fours, and again she could see the beast. No, he wasn't human. He'd told her that over and over, now she was beginning to understand. He knew exactly what they had done, where he had taken her and there was no regret in smoldering gray eyes.

"I'm proud of you," he said into her ear as his body lowered onto hers.

"Proud? Somehow I wasn't expecting that word," she said as he nuzzled down her neck. His arms pressed into the cushions to wrap around her body as if he had to hold her closer than he could get by lying on her with his massive weight. Kelly's arms circled his shoulders as her fingers absently stroked through his hair.

"You used the spice of fear to add to the return of pleasure," he said into her flesh. "I can feel you working through the experience and still there is no regret in the air around you."

"It was nothing like I expected," she admitted.

"There was no way to tell you that. You had to experience it to know," he said.

"Is it always that intense?"

His head lifted from her neck as he smiled into her eyes. "Again, baby, that was just the taste of how good it can be. Someday, when no one's listening, you'll understand what I'm talking about. But until then, trust me."

"Is there any question that I trust you?" she wanted to know, returning his smile.

Cord raised his brows with a slight smile. "I'm proud of you, baby. But we have a long way to go. I need your trust to be unconditional. There might come a time when it looks like I am the monster the world has named dragon. That will be correct, but I need you to know it doesn't apply to you. You and Minuet will always be the focus of my protection at all costs."

Cord watched her face soften and he knew she was about to deny that he could ever be a monster. It was pointless to argue with her, he was being a monster at this moment. Explaining to her what she needed to know without including any information that gave her power over him. She could control him even to the point of making him do something he knew was wrong for the greater good. For her, he would do anything. She didn't know it.

Telling her how to kill a dragon had been a deliberate risk. Trusting her with that information would make her believe he told her everything. He hadn't realized what he was doing until it was already done. The internal beast would always be a calculating bastard, subconsciously looking for an advantage in every situation. He was a predator. He had told the truth about her trust but omitted the part about his trust.

Could a soulless being trust another? He had trusted his maker and look how much she had concealed from him. That was the root of his struggle. Kelly had never given him a reason to doubt her, but then nor had the other Wind Witch.

Aware of his weight, Cord pulled her up with him as he sat so he could lie down with her on top.

Kelly let him move them, following his lead. As he lay beneath her, she relaxed across his body, her head sinking to his shoulder.

"Will you ever trust me?"

Her question shocked him. He hadn't expected her to read him so well. "Your skill at reading the air has improved, little one."

"You're avoiding the question."

"It's not your fault," he told her quietly.

"I know that. I suspect it's my predecessor, were you lovers?"

"Never. She was like a mother. She withheld so much from me. She couldn't bring herself to tell me the real plan. There has to be a reason she didn't trust me."

"Perhaps it wasn't a matter of not trusting you."

"How can you say that? Her secret plan stripped you of choices. I was created this way. You were a free individual before I arrived."

Kelly lifted her head to look him in the eye. "If she had told you the complete plan, she would have removed your choices. How can you not see that? By not telling you what she hoped you would do, she gave you free will. I think she invested all her trust in you, not just enough to believe you would follow the plan."

Cord gazed up at the ceiling and felt a winter wind blow across his body then incredible warmth as her words rattled around in his head. The female logic was making a strange kind of sense. If Kelly was right, the deception he felt was all in his head. There was a big *if* in front of that statement, it bothered him.

"That's an interesting train of thought," he murmured cautiously. "Instead of hiding things from me she was trying to give me a future?"

"Silly dragon, what else would it be? By not telling you about me she took an incredible risk, leaving the future totally up to you. And I'm guessing here, but I'd bet the part about killing the witches when they reappear was cooked up by you three dragons. It's predator thinking. I almost said male thinking but it goes beyond that. Am I right?"

"Sorta." Cord reached up and rubbed his jaw as he thought back on the events that happened so long ago.

The six of them had been together when the witches revealed their plan for destroying the dragons, and that he, Harrison and Legion had been created for this event. They were the hope of the future, and the witches had actually asked if they'd choose to take the mission. At the time, he hadn't paid attention to specific wording. The situation around them had become critical to bring them to that point. There was no safe place, nowhere to hide. In that atmosphere, destroying the world had made perfect sense.

"It was a chaotic time at the end," he said quietly. "Knowing they were planning to destroy the world was an incredible burden. If even a whisper of it had gotten out, it would not have worked. Obviously we were desperate."

"Think about it," she said.

"Go to sleep, baby girl."

"Aren't you taking me up to bed?" Kelly wanted to know, her voice showing how tired she was.

"In a minute. Relax."

"I have to ask. Don't you feel sexual excitement like the rest of us do? I mean, after all of that and you want to go to sleep? Doesn't this," she rubbed her belly across his hard shaft, "bother you at all?"

"I've never been something else, so no idea if what I feel is the same," he lied. "This isn't a problem to concern yourself with. It is my concern."

"Are you telling me it doesn't matter to you?" Kelly wanted to know carefully.

"Matters a great deal to me, however, I take my responsibilities much more seriously than my wants. And I do want you, baby, but for me to come, you have to be capable of shielding or consuming a great deal of power. Someday you'll be able to, but not tonight."

"So the answer is sort of?" Kelly asked, puzzled at the contradiction he seemed to be. Fierce and so sexy it rolled off him in a fog when he walked by, how could he be casual about sexuality?

"No. How to explain this? I want you and that means keeping you alive and safe first. Having the pleasure of fucking your brains out is a result of keeping you safe. See?"

"That was exactly how to explain it," she said softly.

He chuckled. "As soon as we're safe and Minuet is somehow occupied, expect the dragon, honey."

"If you're trying the scare me, it's not working," she informed him.

"Good. Now go to sleep before I'd lose my mind," Cord growled.

He was keeping it light for her, but the drive to claim his woman had reached a new level. The intoxicating taste she'd given him was as addictive as he had told her it would be. For humans, the practice of domination and submission was all about power exchange. The public view of a relationship at this level was a caricature, a cartoon of what the reality could be. Knowing that Kelly was not afraid to go there with him had the same result as waving raw meat in front of a hungry tiger. Unpredictable and powerful were the responses she drew from him.

His need of her was unpredictable because she overwhelmed him, the craving could become ruthless. He would certainly become more dangerous as their relationship deepened. He had nothing to gage what they were doing by. As far as he knew, no dragon had ever truly claimed a mate. The three elemental dragons being created to need exactly that had been another gamble, the next generation in power.

What he was feeling, what humans called emotions, translated to primal survival instincts in a beast. Dragons did not possess emotions. Protecting his new family at whatever cost was an imperative. Developing a growing need of them was a new outcome.

This was the elemental change Marelda and her cohorts had worked in them. Need was a foreign concept to dragons. Dragons took what they wanted. Taking is a basic activity, concern is not required. The welfare of any other not considered unless there was another agenda.

Cord found his agenda had changed dramatically. Luckily the welfare of this society would have a positive impact on Kelly and Minuet. Keeping dragons well hidden from humans was necessary to best protect them. If that were not the case, he doubted he would have much interest. But Kelly would. Through her the old witch had indeed ensured her agenda. It was a very effective circle, brilliant even.

Kelly woke in her bed. The sun was already up and she could smell coffee tempting her from the kitchen. Not only that, Minuet was downstairs laughing at something Cord said.

She got up slowly, sitting on the edge of the bed for a few moments. She knew they were leaving today. Should she pack? Probably not. They were leaving to elude the ones looking for them, so it would be important to look normal. Not as if they were running away.

After a quick shower, Kelly arrived in the kitchen just as Minuet finished her bowl of cereal. Minuet hopped up and ran to fling herself against Kelly's legs in a hug.

"We fly airplane," Minuet declared in excitement. "Cord said."

"That's right. We're going on an airplane today. Do you know what that is?" Kelly asked her daughter as she lifted her for a big morning hug.

"I knows it," Minuet declared indignantly. "It shiny wings in sky."

"So when do we leave?" Kelly asked her daughter.

"Anytime you're ready," Cord answered as he slid an arm around her waist and dropped a kiss on her forehead.

"Don't these planes have schedules?" Kelly asked a bit amused as his hand glided down her back and over her butt.

"I'm sure they do," he said casually. "But since we have to drive off and not head for an airport, I've arranged for us to drive to the mall and be picked up in the parking lot by a limo. We have to get to the East Coast to catch the commercial fight, so we'll take my jet to New York."

"No bags?" Kelly asked as Minuet returned to her seat and Kelly took the cup of coffee Cord had fixed for her.

"No, we'll get what we need when we arrive," Cord assured her.

"I guess I'd better call my prospective employer and tell him that I'll not be showing up Monday." Kelly took a long sip of coffee. It was made perfectly.

"I'll be happy to take care of that," he said a bit too quickly.

Kelly was slightly surprised at Cord's offer. "He's never met you. How could you do it?"

"Pick up the phone and tell the person on the other end that you will not be available for that job," Cord supplied.

"Ah, that's okay. I'll take care of it," Kelly assured him, unsure what this really was about. It seemed strange for Cord to make that offer.

"Here's your cell phone," Cord pulled it out of his pocket. "I cancelled the land line a little earlier. Hope you don't mind."

"No." Kelly took her cell from him, her puzzlement growing. "We'll not need it now. Did you call and cancel the appointment?"

"I paid the workman and sent him on his way half an hour ago." Cord turned to the stove. "Would you like scrambled eggs on toast? Minuet and I have perfected it. She puts the toast in and I supply the eggs when it's done."

"Sounds lovely." she smiled at Minute who'd run to the toaster. There was a stout wooden stool for her to stand on and she was carefully dropping two slices in the slot. "You are very good at that."

Kelly stepped out the back door to make her call, unsure why she was uncomfortable to do it in front of Cord and Minuet. Her prospective boss answered his line and was not surprised to hear from her. Molly had spoken with him yesterday and mentioned that Kelly's plans had changed as well. The man was abrupt. Kelly could understand that. He'd just lost one highly skilled employee and the other person he'd hired. Now he had two vacancies instead of one.

Cord's eyes were on her as she returned to the kitchen. He took the frying pan off the heat and strode over to her, taking her coffee cup and putting it on the counter before gathering her in his arms. "What did the bastard say? I can maim him for you."

Kelly gently grasped bulging biceps as she looked up at her bristling dragon and she had to laugh. "What? Of course he was upset. He needs someone doing the job. Two of us just bailed on him."

An eyebrow on Cord's forehead rose slowly. "I couldn't care less. If he was rude to you, I'd like to know," he said, the rumble in his voice sinking right down to her bones.

"He was civil," Kelly said around a smile tilting up her lips. Her body rubbed up against his as her arms went around his neck to pull his head down. Her voice was barely a whisper in the hopes that Minuet would not hear it as she directed. "Now kiss me, sexy beast. Jealousy seems to have turned me on."

Cord growled as his lips dipped willingly to her mouth. The kiss sizzled with frustration as he plunged into her. His back to Minuet, Cord took full advantage as his hands grasped her ass and pulled her into his body.

Needing to express desire was foreign to him and yet inescapable. Never before had he sought what he wanted from Kelly now. He was seeking her response, hungering for her in ways that had nothing to do with feeding from her. It wasn't comfortable.

His tongue swept in her, and fire shot down her body. Kelly rippled in pleasure as he took her in that kiss. Oh yes, the dragon was possessive. It was immensely flattering though unwarranted in this case.

She was a little uneasy about what would happen if someone did make a pass at her. It wasn't as if it happened all the time. She saw herself as very average looking, except for the tall part. Men liked to look at tall women, they lost nerve past that. But who could think about stupid men when a dragon was doing this?

A little body barreled into the back of Cord's legs. "We hugging?" Minuet asked. "Me too."

She wiggled around and Cord reached down with one arm, lifting her easily to be included in the hugs, which was all they were doing now.

Breakfast went quickly. Minuet was too excited to let Kelly linger over it.

"Can I bing bears?" Minuet needed to know.

"Of course, but only one," Kelly admonished.

The list of questions was endless. It was impossible to stem them. Her quick mind kept jumping to pertinent questions. "Does shiny wings has potty?"

Cord left most of the answers to Kelly as he checked the house and locked up. It was ten a.m. when they climbed into Cord's truck and headed toward the city. They left the truck in the mall parking lot, getting directly into a waiting limo.

The big car, while exciting at first for Minuet, soon lost its glow as they still had to drive an hour to the large city. As they entered the suburbs, Minuet became quiet. Shortly she was cuddled up beside Kelly, her eyes closed.

"Tired, sweetie?" Kelly asked.

"I sleep," Minuet agreed.

Cord observed the active child's subdued behavior with growing concern. In the short time he'd known her, Minuet hadn't take a nap and only wound down late in the day. Considering her excitement about the trip, this change in behavior was even more unexpected.

"Is she okay?" he asked Kelly softly has as Minuet dropped into sleep.

"I don't know. I didn't expect her to be this calm about traveling," Kelly said as her hand moved over Minuet's hair in a comforting mother's pet. "She doesn't have a fever and I don't see any other signs of illness."

"Her body is working properly," Cord assured Kelly. "I can monitor her heart and several other involuntary functions. I'll let you know if anything changes. For right now, if she wants sleep, it's probably what she needs."

At the airport, the driver was able to take them on the tarmac to park next to Cord's plane. Minuet woke up but was strangely groggy. Cord carried her on to the plane.

Having no bags made boarding and takeoff occur with amazing speed. It seemed to Kelly that everyone they met in the process managed to bow slightly to Cord. Perhaps that was the influence of money.

Cord certainly knew how to make things happen, always ready with a plan and the means to execute it. It was more privilege than she was used to.

Cord settled them in plush chairs and Minuet dropped back into a deep sleep. A few minutes later the pilot taxied onto the runway and they had a short wait for their turn to take off. Once in the air, Minuet sat up slowly.

"How are you feeling, honey? We have chocolate I think. Would you like a candy bar? If it's okay with your mom," he corrected himself quickly.

"A chocolate bar sounds good," Kelly agreed. The boost of sugar in Minuet's system might help, she figured.

Minuet went with Cord to find the chocolate, behaving more like herself. Cord's jet was exciting, but this time she settled in the window seat with her candy. They had food and a potty on the jet as well. Minuet approved of the arrangements.

As they approached the East Coast, Cord made a point of watching Minuet's reactions. Sure enough, the closer they came to the mega-populated area, the more subdued Minuet became. By the time they landed, Minuet's head was in her mother's lap and she was sleeping once more.

The jet pulled to a stop. "Stay right there," he told Kelly. "Let Minuet sleep. I have a feeling I know what the problem is, I have to make some arrangements."

"Well? Tell me what you think it is," Kelly said sharply. "And is there a problem? Is there something you don't want to tell me?"

"I think the problem is the density of population. She's too young to understand what's pressing on her through her gifts. Self-preservation is natural instinct and the very young don't question it. Sleep is a way of cutting herself off, calming all the different things she feels that she has no way of communicating to us.

"I was going to take you ladies shopping this afternoon, but right now I just want to get us out of here. She'll be fine when we reach Scotland. The population where we're going is even less than the town we just left."

"I hope you're right," Kelly said worriedly.

"Me too," he agreed quietly. "We can't be sure until she's ready to talk about it."

Cord went up to talk to the pilot. Unfortunately he needed an international pilot and that would take a little time. As long as Minuet slept peacefully, it would be okay.

He needed a way to shield her from whatever was crowding into her soul. Until Minuet found a way to talk about the problem, there was no way he could enter her mind and figured it out. Without her consent, an attempt would make him part of the problem. Knowing all this didn't make it easier to watch her fight her own battle. That was his job and she didn't know how to let him help.

All he could do was make his ladies comfortable and get them out of here as quickly as possible. The plane was fueled and ready for the international pilot when Minuet opened her eyes and grasped her head.

"Bad, berry bad. Make it stop," she cried softly.

Kelly had her in her lap. "Honey, what's bad? What can we make stop?"

Cord dropped to his knees in front of them, his arms going around both as he questioned. "Show me, Minuet. Show me in my mind so I can help."

In the next slot, another private jet had just pulled up. Minuet showed both Cord and Kelly the evil she couldn't escape in sleep. Aboard the jet were several passengers whose sole purpose in life was death. They carried death with them, on them, in them. Immediately Cord recognized assassins.

Minuet's impressions were not specific, she simply felt the complete absence of mercy in them and it physically hurt her.

"Minuet, will you let me help you sleep like I did for Mommy when she was hurt?" he asked softly. "I have to go take care of a problem and I don't want you to be in pain."

Big eyes gazed at him for a moment. "Cord gonna fix?" she asked.

Little Miss Miracle went to the heart of the issue again. "Yes. I can't let them hurt people, you know that."

Minuet regarded him a few more seconds. "I sleep."

"Good girl. I'll be back in a few minutes and everything will be all right," he assured her as he placed his hand on her forehead. Minuet closed her eyes and a moment later she was deep in sleep again. It was Kelly who looked at him with the worried face.

"What are you going to do?" she asked.

"Take care of the problem." Cord stood. "This is what I do." He faded from the light spectrum humans could see and made his way to the other jet.

Cord stopped beneath the plane to reach for cold control. Enjoying the kill was a dark danger of the animal DNA. Lack of emotional involvement had always been an edge for the three dragons of the elements. They made deadly opponents because there was nothing that mattered to them besides reaching the goal. He was different now. He hoped that difference would not be a handicap in combat.

The short episode in the desert had gone well, but he realized he hadn't been detached that time either. His goal had been protecting Kelly and Minuet. The single-minded drive to achieve that objective had given him the familiar coldness required for efficient combat.

Aware of his new limitations, Cord was cautious as he approached the parked airplane.

No stairs had appeared for this plane. That wasn't a problem for a dragon. Climbing into the bowels of the plane through the wheel well, he easily gained access to the cabin. Inside were four males. The papers in front of them and their conversation betrayed their intentions to the invisible guest standing beside them. The targets were elementary schools. They planned to blow up three schools on the last day of classes to maximize the chaos.

Their plan was detailed, the objective date over a year away. This was going to be the last time three of them saw each other.

Cord refrained from helping them to that goal instantly though he had to consciously stem the rush of saliva to his mouth. The beast wanted a kill, up close and personal. Something with fangs and talons would have been gratifying. Considering all the possible outcomes, four dead bodies would cause too many problems. He needed an outcome that exposed their plan to the humans and allowed him to get Minuet and Kelly out of here as fast as possible. A murder investigation would accomplish none of those goals.

That was a compelling reason, but not the one that saved these men's lives. He would not bring death on his plane with Minuet. She would feel it and this trip was already difficult enough.

Cord needed security forces to raid the plane but a few political issues stood in the way. The men arrived as employees of an embassy though they planned to disappear shortly. The plane was property of an American ally from the Middle East. Since they hadn't entered the terminal, they were still in international space. The only thing that would get U.S. personnel on the plane was an emergency that required an investigation. Cord would make sure there was something to find during that investigation.

Cord exited the plane, sealing the closed cabin door from the outside by directing heat to fuse the metals. Under the plane, he needed something slow burning with a high smoke yield. The tires would work. In case the boys inside knew they could escape out the wheel wells, Cord sealed those hatches as well.

With a thought, he heated the rubber of a wheel and billowing smoke erupted. Emergency proceedings started as a worker noticed and fire trucks were scrambled. Flames lick up the wheel wells to heat the cabin as Cord watched. The men inside realized their plane was on fire and tried to get out. Now they were banging on the windows. Cord pulled back the fire with a thought. Dead was not how he wanted them, at least not yet.

A little smoke in the cabin and its occupants passed out. Cord made sure it was done just as emergency crews were pulling open the door that hadn't opened for the men inside. He directed the events while standing under his own plane, still cloaked. With this many people around, he had to continue moving very slowly. Just because the humans could not focus on him didn't mean he wasn't there. His movement caused a ripple in their visual field that could be followed.

Soon coughing men were led out of the plane and being taken to the airport medical facilities, just where Cord wanted them. As soon as an investigator got in that cabin, he would find a reason to hold the men. After that their plan would be exposed as well as where they had just come from. Cord and made sure the investigators would have enough information to be looking for this sort of plot in the future. They were in New York, a place where investigators were particularly sensitive to foreign nationals with bomb-making instructions and carefully marked locations on a map.

The last conspirator to exit the plane stiffened as his feet hit the ground, his head turning swiftly to gaze directly at the private jet Cord was standing under. His expression did not change but his eyes did. For less than a second they glowed as if under ultraviolet light and then it was gone. That look shot through Cord with the power of a lightning strike.

The man could not see him, but eyes, even strange eyes, were not the only thing evil used looked with. Now Cord was doubly sorry he couldn't simply dispatch them. There was more to these people than he was comfortable with. He was distinctly disturbed by the fact that he'd never seen anything like this before.

Shielding his activity while using this much paranormal energy could be tiring. Had he let a little hint of what he was slip out? No, he'd been standing beside this man in the plane and the individual hadn't known he was there. That left a much more disturbing possibility.

Had the guy felt Minuet? That was the more likely answer and one that caused Cord's lips to draw back over gleaming fangs. The reaction was instinctive, his transformation to savage instantaneous at the hint of a threat to his family. At least he remained cloaked from human eyes. It was definitely time to go.

Chapter Eleven

The international pilot arrived in the confusion. Cord entered the plane and went to the back to materialize as if he had been in the sleeping quarters. Moving through the cabin, he dropped a kiss on Kelly's forehead as she looked up at him with knowing eyes. In the cockpit, he conferred briefly with the pilot on their flight plan. The tower let them know takeoff would be delayed because of the chaos beside them but only for another ten minutes.

In the cabin, Cord sat across from Kelly and Minuet. Closing his eyes, he reached out with senses to continue influencing the men investigating the contents of the neighboring airplane. He also ensured the four occupants being treated for smoke inhalation were detained. By the time the pilot called back to tell them they were clear for takeoff, the four men were under arrest and the investigating officer had an amazing amount of clear evidence of the plot.

They pulled away and Minuet's eyes opened to look directly at Cord. "Bad man mad," she stated flatly.

"Did he talk to you in your mind?" Cord wanted to know.

"Yellings," she said. "Him think I big."

"Have you answered him, Minuet?" Cord asked calmly.

"No."

Cord smiled at her. "Then he wasn't yelling at you, baby. Don't worry about it." He tried to sound casual for her.

"I not worried. You berry big an he feels it."

Minuet closed her eyes and sank into sleep. That surprising episode told Cord several things. First, he could help Minuet sleep but only if she consented. Her power could override his commands anytime. The second was that though he'd been aware of the conspirator's paranormal sensitivity, he hadn't heard the man's voice. Minuet heard it.

This future with its human villains was not like his world. He operated on the parameters from a bygone age. Would it be possible for him to learn the range Minuet heard from? Was he even capable of it? He damn well better be. This was the job he'd been created for. He'd be really pissed if the woman who made him had handicapped him with her inability to envision change and therefore made him incapable of adapting to it.

Cord had directed the pilot to head straight out to sea instead of up the coast and across the Atlantic on the northern route. He wanted them out of range of this population as fast as possible for Minuet. Taking them across the widest part of the ocean wasn't a problem though the human pilot would worry. Flying to the range limit of their fuel tanks was not the risk he thought it was.

There was no possibility they could crash. Even if both engines went out, having the Wind Witch and Air Dragon aboard meant the craft would continue to fly. With Minuet aboard, the engines couldn't fail, nor could the craft run out of power.

As they moved away from the coast, Kelly asked, "Are you going to wake her up?"

"I don't have to. She can wake up any time she wants. Instead of putting her into a deep sleep, I think I simply taught her how to do it herself."

Kelly's brows went up. "She's that strong?"

"You are too. You don't trust your power like she does. She's too young to doubt what is natural to her."

Minuet stirred in Kelly's lap, gradually coming awake. Looking around her, her eyes quickly lit with the sparkle of childish delight. She hadn't been awake long enough to finish investigating the plane. Sitting, she asked Cord if she could explore in very polite three-year-old speak.

"I look Cord's toys?" Minuet asked.

"Sure. I think you'll find something interesting in the bedroom," he suggested.

Minuet squealed, reading his intentions easily.

During their stop in New York, he'd acquired several things from gift shops, doing it in dragon fashion by leaving money in the register and blank spaces on the shelves.

Cord settled in the chair Minuet had vacated. The armrest between the wide leather chairs had been lifted so Minuet could sleep on Kelly's lap. Cord scooped Kelly up and set her across his lap.

Minuet would be fully occupied for a few minutes and he intended to take advantage of the opportunity. His mouth came down on hers in a hard kiss, thrusting into her, sweeping up her taste as if he were starving for it. Kelly's response was a gratifying low moan as her arms move naturally around his neck and her body relaxed.

All too soon Minuet dashed out of the back compartment to show Mommy her treasures. Cord's arms tightened to let Kelly know he wasn't letting her in her chair yet. He needed the contact, even if it was casual.

Minuet bounded up to them with absolutely no surprise at how they were sitting.

"Mommy, Mommy, look what I has." She held up a Barney and a purple, stuffed dragon. "Cord an Barney. It Cord an Barney."

Kelly's laughter wrapped around Cord, stroking his body with each note. His need of her was physical in every way but there was no question that Minuet's presence made everything better, and it had nothing to do with the power issues. She completed the circle of life and it felt right to have that beautiful little soul interrupt deep kisses. It was another thing in the natural order of life Cord had never experienced before—children.

He also realized he had needed to put smiles on Minuet's face. Her comfort was critical, and helping her deal with the difficulties of traveling, a drive he would kill over. No, that was wrong. She kept him from being a killer, forcing him to find another way. The thought made him smile as he watched Kelly admire the two purple toys.

"They're beautiful," Kelly said. "What do you say to Cord?"

Minuet climbed up them so she was sitting in Kelly's lap, still holding both Barney and the dragon, she wrapped her little arms around Cord's neck and kissed his cheek soundly. "Thank you."

"You're welcome. I'm very glad you like them. I wanted Barney and the dragon to be friends and I thought you could help me with that."

"I berry good make friends," Minuet informed him. "But you berry good make Minuet happy. An Mommy happy. Cord have pretty heart."

"That's an interesting thing to say. Why do you say Cord's heart is pretty?" Kelly asked.

"Because, him make happy. Him heart makes pretty," Minuet explained.

Cord was a little concerned with what Minuet was seeing. Her abilities could become uncomfortable for adults. He wasn't sure what she meant by seeing his heart. In this form, he had the physical vessel beating in his chest, but that didn't mean he had a heart as humans knew it. Like everything else about him, it could move and change shape, becoming something entirely different in some forms.

Minuet scrambled down and went to sit in the chair across from them to play with her new toys. She was completely natural and accepting of the adults holding each other. Talking with them almost continually as she made up games and personalities for her purple possessions.

Sitting on his lap, Kelly couldn't help but notice the hard bulge beneath her hip.

He wanted her to feel it, feel his response to her. She needed to know the contact with her was not just drinking the power she gave him so freely. He wasn't simply using her but also holding her for selfish reasons.

The flight was long and eventually Minuet nodded off into normal sleep.

The events of this trip had highlighted the limitations and advantages of the gifts in each of them. In the ladies, checks and balances were a natural order for power to develop. Cord appreciated the fact that innate power came with a certain cost for humans. The fact that he also was saddled with limitations was comforting for the first time. The feeling of belonging, shared experiences bound them together. He found it an unexpected gift from his maker.

Kelly draped a blanket over Minuet and came back to him. She stretched out with her legs in her seat and her torso settled naturally into his embrace. Cord pulled a blanket over her as well.

"How confident are you that this Harrison is in Scotland?" Kelly wanted to know.

"It doesn't matter if he's there, he'll show up. He has a castle overlooking Loch Ness. People think it's a dilapidated shell, but actually it's a den. As soon as we enter the property, he'll know. He's got it protected so it alerts him to trespassers. Here's what has never made sense to me. He's a water creature and the only one of us with a permanent home on land that he actually lives in occasionally. You'll see what I mean when you meet him, he's different."

"I wouldn't be throwing around phrases calling someone else different if I were you," Kelly laughed softly.

Cord grinned and found her teasing made him feel good in a weird way. It was unlike the rude insults the three dragons often addressed each other with. Not that they spent much time together, but when they did, communication was correspondingly arrogant. Having spent no time in conversation with the other type of dragon because he'd always been busy killing them, who knew what their interaction was like.

Conversation with Marelda had been personal, but it still wasn't even close to the relationship developing with Kelly. It wasn't as if he hadn't spoken to millions of women, he just never done it for long periods of time. That had to be his problem. He wasn't used to it.

"You'll see," he assured her with a raise eyebrow. "Dragons are never wrong, you know."

"I see," she said. "Apparently humble is one of the things they never are either."

"If we're never wrong, how can we be humble? It would only confuse the humans, and we like to be clear when giving direction or stating facts." He baited her with the attitude and enjoyed the hell out of it as his little Wind Witch looked at him with female amusement written all over her face.

"I'm guessing there are no female dragons, right?" she asked.

Cord frowned. "Why would anyone make a female dragon?"

"Seriously?" Kelly asked her face registering disbelief. "I didn't realize I wasn't joking."

As the conversation turned to a subject she was curious about, Kelly asked, "All dragons were created? There are no dragon eggs?"

"No such thing," Cord confirmed. "Procreation is strictly a God-given ability. Even though we have the equipment, there has never been a dragon baby."

"Wow," Kelly marveled. "You were created an adult?"

"Yes. We had an adult body though some development is required to gain experience. Our instincts are fully functional, which was the original problem. We are predators from the moment of consciousness. The longer we live, the better we get at it. That's the only growth correlation we have with humans. Experience breeds skill. However, innate predatory skills from the start far exceed an adult human male's abilities. You can see how this would not work out well for creators."

"Sounds like male thinking to me. From what you say, they were building an army, not interested in raising children. Still it's stunningly stupid," Kelly observed. "How did they expect loyalty?"

"The wizards realized that, but it was a little late. They attempted to make adolescent dragons, but that created a whole new set of problems. Childlike killers are vicious and totally out of control. They have to grow up to access some of the skills required to control their abilities. They would prey on people but could only control the very weak ones. That was children, the sick or old. The one we found in the desert was a juvenile. I've always assumed that dragons not captured at the poles were these adolescent creatures."

"How sad," Kelly murmured.

Cord regarded his softhearted Wind Witch and marveled at her capacity to feel sad for child killers. "You think a house for wayward dragon children would've helped?"

"I can feel bad about something without having any idea how to fix it," Kelly informed him from his chest.

Kelly was completely relaxed, her body turned into his arms and her head on his shoulder as they talked. Her eyes closed, though he could feel her interest in the subject. A little tired, Kelly was unable to sleep, so he continued as his hands moved up and down her back. The gentle massage started because she needed to relax but continued because he needed to soothe her. Her feelings of safety and contentment were a sweet reward.

This desire to be the source of her every comfort was growing. It pleased him to supply whatever she or Minuet needed. Examining the source of pleasure might not be a wise use of his time at the moment. As they drew closer to the British Isles, the next problem was looming.

Cord had been mildly worried about Legion before he knew the big earth dragon was already there. Mildly worried because he had Molly handy to introduce to Legion. That situation, while possibly dangerous, had been one he was sure would work out with Legion realizing he could not kill Molly.

They were going to find Harrison, the water dragon, but had no idea where the Water Witch was. Explaining the new plan to Harrison would be tricky if Harrison was in the middle of trying to execute the old plan by killing Kelly and Minuet. Cord didn't want to kill Harrison. For the new plan to work, they needed the water dragon and his lady.

His eyes on Minuet, Cord considered the options. She could be the key. Apparently Minuet had been the power that attracted Legion to the area she lived in. Legion had worked out the imperative that he must protect Minuet, even if he had to do it from a distance. Cord was still pissed that the bastard hadn't contacted him as soon as he encountered Kelly and Minuet.

Kelly distracted Cord from his thoughts as her head turned into his body and her lips glided over his neck. Exploring him with lips and tongue she ate her way up under his chin, nibbling along his jawbone. He gave her about two minutes to explore then he'd had enough.

Intoxicating witch had no idea what she did to him. He'd been as gentle as he knew how to be so far. Trying to ease her into accepting what he was. Last night's restraint had cost him more than he cared to think about. Her tongue licked through his control with the same destructive power of a wildfire wind walking a California forest.

Hard lips captured her mouth, punishing the little explorer for lighting the fuse on his libido. He loomed over her as his mouth demanded she open for him. Her melting acceptance only slightly mollified the beast. One of his hands moved from her back to cup her head, holding her under his mouth as he plundered the sweet interior.

The kiss was hot, urgent and a drawn-out journey into sexuality. He thrust into her with leashed power, letting her know exactly how he'd like to be thrusting into another part of her body. His firm hand palming the back of her head demonstrated the control he would take of her pleasure. Ruthlessly extending the kiss into an endless demand showed her that next time would last a long time.

Kelly moaned, her body shifting under the blanket as heat bloomed between them. Her breasts suddenly felt heavy, the nipples aching. His mouth would not release her so she pressed into the hard ridges of muscle and tried to relieve the ache by rubbing over him. And still he plundered her. Her hips rolled as she rubbed her legs together. A firm hand grasped her hip bone, holding her still.

As he lifted from her mouth at last, holding her immobile at head and hip, Kelly sucked in a sharp breath. His eyes were shielded by lowered lids but they were molten smoke. Yesterday she had thought steam was the color of his eyes. Today he looked at her through the gray warning of fire within.

He let her see the sparks rising in him as the hand on her hip moved around to cup her core.

"Remain perfectly still," he directed in low tones that were not quite a whisper but definitely a command. His eyes flicked up over her to Minuet's sleeping form and back to her gaze. The reason for his direction was perfectly clear. Under the blanket with her body turned facing his, any movement of his arm was hidden from Minuet if she should wake up.

The hand cupping her crotch lifted to unsnap her jeans. His eyes holding her gaze captive, his large hand pulled down the zipper and palmed her trembling belly. Sliding down under her panties, his fingers curved around her body to invade damp folds.

His fingers were hard and firm but moved slowly. They explored, caressed down to her entrance. Still his gaze burned into hers as two fingers pushed into her body. The invasion was thick and slow, deliberately taking her. He pulled out as slowly as he had entered. His hand left her to firmly drag her jeans and panties down her legs by using the strength of that arm straightening.

"Lift up," he commanded softly so the material would slide down her thighs. He left them at her knees and returned to the juncture of her legs. Pushing between her constricted limbs, he again boldly caressed the petals of flesh guarding her entrance.

Kelly's mouth opened in a soft pant.

"Hush," he demanded in that soft rumbling tone.

Kelly swallowed and nodded, unable to come up with any other response as again thick fingers pushed into her body. He had effectively bound her legs together with her jeans and panties at her knees and yet still pushed into her, all the while holding her gaze. If she had had any doubt that he could take her any time it was thoroughly erased.

His fingers moved over her boldly. The strength in that single arm could have lifted her above his head, she was sure of it. Knowing all that and feeling him enter her as he wished was fiercely erotic. The blaze behind his eyes burned her alive.

His thumb stroked over pussy lips with relentless rhythm, each pass grazing the top of her clit but not lingering. The finger-fucking continued, heating her from the inside out. His fingers pulled out of her and burrowed up between her outer pussy lips to capture her clit in a sawing grip. Pushing and pulling in long strokes.

In her mind, his deep voice rumbled. *"Tempting the beast?"* he asked. *"Do you not know I hunger for you? Not to feed, little witch, something much more dangerous than that."*

Two fingers pressed into her body as he continued. *"What I want is to ride this portal to heaven's gate then show you how delicious the fires on Hell's shores taste. Deep and fast, the animal will take this cunt. Hard and long, the demon will ride his witch. I have yet to show you what truly enters your body, tastes this nectar."* His fingers pulled out of her and he brought them to his mouth, licking her taste off them with slow enjoyment as she panted in his lap, staring up at him.

"Nothing to say?" he questioned in softly savage tones. "No begging for mercy? No pleas for gentle love and lighted candles? Say something, Kelly."

"What should I beg for? I want more. You're licking the proof of what I want," Kelly replied.

"Damn it, I have to stop," he hissed in her mind. *"Don't push me to be the dragon."*

"I didn't push. I kissed the one who watches over us. That's not pushing," Kelly insisted as his hand grasped her pants and panties, firmly pulling them up her body. Swiftly the zipper rose and the button were fastened.

Cord's eye sparkled and the irises elongated to slits as he glared down at her. Kelly didn't recoil as she stared into the eyes of a beast.

"Now you're showing off and it doesn't scare me," she stated firmly. "No matter what skin you're in, you are Cord."

"I'm trying to warn you. Restraint is not my best thing where you're concerned," he confessed, closing his eyes as his head dropped back on the high seatback. "I'm sorry. These feelings are unfamiliar. Please do not kiss me, nibble on me or lick me until I get a better handle on controlling them."

"What?" she asked softly.

"Which part didn't you understand?" he wanted to know. His eyes opened and they were normal human orbs again.

"The 'don't touch' directive," she replied dumbly.

"I'm trying to protect you. What happens when you reach for me is different. I need to analyze it to understand why I react this way."

The fire licking around his eyes contradicted the normal tone of his words. There certainly was an inferno roaring in Kelly's womb and her entire body was trembling as he looked into her eyes. His calm was a mask, the rock-hard body beneath hers gave him away. Every muscle tensed, rippling with the blaze he was containing.

"You don't understand your response to me?" she asked cautiously.

Cord raised a brow as he regarded her. "It has unusual elements that quickly get out of control. I do not wish to harm you or embarrass you."

"You've never felt this way before?" she pressed.

"I am a creature of control. That is the only responsible way to handle power. If control is eliminated, I become the abominations we must kill," he corrected. "My response to you initiating intimate contact is dangerous. You must refrain."

Kelly smiled and glanced down to hide her eyes. He didn't have a clue what to do with being emotionally involved. He was used to being desired, but feeling the rush of validation when someone he desired wanted him back seemed to have completely unbalanced the big beast.

He was in love and had no idea what that meant. The heat of that knowledge would not let her off the physical high they'd just reached. She saw no reason to give him a pass on it if she was going to suffer until they could be together in private.

"I want you, Cord," she said softly in his mind to ensure privacy. Her eyes looked directly into his as she said it.

"I will have you Wind Witch, and when I do, you will understand. I will enter that pretty body as you face me. I will have it with you turned away so you're only stimulation is the sensation entering between your legs. I will have you," he promised in a dark growl, his chest rising on harsh breaths as he answered.

Kelly swallowed. She had to look away from those eyes. Find a way to live with the fire eating her from the inside out. Lust was crawling under her skin, wrapping around the sensitive centers of her body and hanging on. His words only drove lust's talons deeper into swollen flush. But she had the deep satisfaction of knowing he was just as turned inside out.

The pilot's voice startled her even though the volume of the speaker system was low. "We'll be landing in ten minutes, folks. Welcome to Scotland. It has been a pleasure flying your jet, Mr. Windweaver. I hope we can do business in the future. Just contact my agency when you're ready to return."

Before Kelly could open her mouth, Cord continued to her softly, "Don't think for a minute that you're the only one who wants and is denied." He sucked in a breath through his teeth. "Next time we are alone, I won't be seducing you. Not the first time and probably not the second."

Across from them, Minuet stirred in her sleep. They felt her waking slowly as the plane descended. Minuet sat up and beamed at them, naturally happy upon waking.

Cord had directed the pilot to make the flight plan straight into Scotland, avoiding London. In fact, he'd chosen the smallest airport he could that would accept private, international flights. Watching Minuet as they drew closer and closer to the medium-size city, Cord was slightly relieved. Perhaps it was the lethargy of waking up from a nap, but he suspected it was the population they were entering that had her subdued. However, she didn't appear to need to separate herself from reality this time.

As soon as Minuet had stirred, Kelly sat up in her own seat. She folded the two blankets, settling beside her daughter to watch as they neared the airport. It was day, Scotland time, however for them it should've been night according to Kelly's body. Minuet's nap and the bouts of sleeping throughout the day would make her ready to face the Scottish day normally.

Kelly supposed that Cord didn't need sleep the same way she did, so it was only going to be her who was exhausted. Not just exhausted but strung out wanting a dragon who was very good at keeping her that way though he had no idea what he was really feeling. He also had no idea what was coming. A tired, sexually frustrated woman usually did not make a pleasant companion. Emotionally she was extremely satisfied though, it made up for several other things in a big way.

As she sat beside Minuet, watching the ground get closer and closer, every breath she took rubbed sensitive nipples against the lace of her bra. If she shifted, the stiff material of her jeans dug into the throbbing folds between her legs. She felt a little lightheaded and decided it was because all the blood in her body was busy making her miserable.

They landed and passed through the obligation of customs. They couldn't actually forget anything for this trip, Cord simply summoned Kelly's passport when he needed it. Minuet was still on her mother's documents from an earlier vacation to Canada.

Kelly was occupied taking care of Minuet as they've moved in the airport. Cord was always either right beside them or directly behind them, a protective presence that she avoided touching. A few times his hand had rested on the small of her back to direct their movements, forcing the burn in her body to flame. A car waited for them at the terminal door.

As they pulled away from the airport, Cord explained they were going to a bed and breakfast well outside of town.

Deep in her chest, a tight fist of power twisted. Kelly became aware of the new sensations as her body burned around the feelings. They were not so much feelings as knowledge. Whatever it was, it was buried too deep for her to pull it up to examine it, but she felt it coming on its own. As if the heat of her frustration had cracked some internal shell. The possibility of that being true made illogical sense.

If she had some internal birthright that had been hidden from her all her life, emotionally committing to Cord and receiving the same commitment from him, even if he didn't realize what had happened, would trigger her gifts. He'd been puzzled by her lack of faith in her own powers, telling her over and over again that it was her belief that would free it.

If this was the birth of her gifts into full strength, Cord had been wrong. It was her lack of him that had been holding her back.

The slow unfolding of knowledge washed over her, and Kelly was amazed at the new awareness it gave her. She was still frustrated as hell, and she was also quite sure that her dragon didn't have a clue what he'd triggered in both of them. He was completely focused on her sexual overdrive problem.

They left the city and entered picturesque countryside. Minuet became more active, peppering Cord with questions. He answered her questions with an endless supply of good humor. A little over an hour later they pulled up to a charming country inn that sprawled in the middle of a wildly flowering garden. Natural stone paths meandered about the property, disappearing and reappearing around the exuberant shrubbery. The place could have been clipped from a magazine.

They didn't even have to check in. Pulling up to the far end of the building, away from the central structure, Cord produced a key and opened the door on a charming suite. It managed to appear as if they were walking into the past. Antiques for furniture were scattered about the comfortable sitting room that welcomed them. The space included three bedrooms. Minuet was delighted and seemed to sparkle as she explored the rooms.

A small kitchen was attached to their common sitting room. The back door of that kitchen opened onto one of the garden paths. Suddenly a beautiful terrier appeared outside the screen door, sitting with its tail wagging furiously. Minuet was instantly captivated, running to meet her new friend.

Cord smiled at Kelly as he suggested, "Why don't you take a nap while Minuet and I have a walk with our friend?"

"Are you sure that dog is safe?" Kelly wanted to know as she eyed the friendly creature that was trying to lick Minuet through the screen door.

"I'm sure I can control any beast that size. It's the woman-size one I'm having trouble with," Cord said. His tone was full of amusement.

Turning to Minuet, Kelly smiled brightly. "Would you like to go for a walk with Cord and the puppy?"

"Me run," Minuet corrected her as she dashed to Cord and grabbed his hand, dragging him toward the back door. "Me and Shawn wants run."

Cord let her tow him through the kitchen. The low rumble of his laugh moved like the brush of male fingers down Kelly's back.

"The dog's name is Shawn?" he asked Minuet as they went out the door.

Kelly didn't hear any more as she closed the door to her elegant bedroom. Stripping off her clothes as fast as possible, she headed for the shower. Damn it, a girl needed relief and she needed it now. A cold shower had never looked so inviting in her life.

Ten minutes later, Kelly gave up on the cold water and lay on top of the covers of her bed. Completely nude, she hoped her body would calm down as the air dried her. The door opened and the dragon entered.

Chapter Twelve

Her door closed behind Cord with a soft click. Kelly sat up jerkily, reaching for something to pull over her. The urge to hide was immediate. On the heels of the thought flashed the question about Minuet. Naked didn't matter anymore, but before she could get the question out he answered it.

"Minuet is playing with the owner's daughter. Lori's mother is watching them. Lori is about her age. Harrison owns this place and I have every confidence in his choice of employees. Minuet is fine." His big frame had not moved from the door.

Kelly's eyes widened then her body relaxed.

Cord rigidly attached his back to the door, giving her a few seconds. It was all he had. The scent of her arousal was thick in the air. It went straight to the animal responses. She was in heat and he would kill to get to her, to fuck her. The animal kingdom was not polite about reproduction and he was holding on to the few human responses he could muster as his eyes tracked over her naked body.

Her relief at knowing Minuet was okay was relaxing for a second. Then she was aware of the male before her. Dragon in human skin was standing rigidly at her door with fire behind his eyes. Those molten metal eyes traveled over her and Kelly felt the heat of the earth's core. An elemental reaction shot through her, causing her body to gather, preparing to leap somewhere. Escape.

"Don't do it," he cautioned. "Don't bring the hunter. Let me be gentle."

His sentences were sharp, powerfully minimal. He was asking for surrender, cautioning her not to run. Kelly felt his threat burn down her body, a flash fire to already smoldering responses.

"You told me there would be no gentle," she reminded him in cautious tones as she relaxed, slowly lowering her body to the bed. She couldn't remove the watchful looked from her eyes. Fear, excitement, whatever, he brought them all to the room. This was what she'd wanted but the tension was difficult to work through.

"Gentle is relative. I want you to be sure. For about two more seconds I can turn around and leave this room. After that, asking is over. Say yes."

"Yes to what?" Kelly wanted to know. She was lying naked on a bed and the man wanted her to say yes. What did he need, sign language? How much more yes could be required?

"Say it, Kelly," he rumbled.

His insistence on hearing the simple word raised big, loud, screaming warnings. His reluctance to explain what the yes was about dotted those warnings with flashing red lights. This naked woman was going to ignore all the flashing, screaming, blinking warnings because the dragon at the door had just removed clothing with a thought and she was all out of time to think.

"Yes."

Cord crossed the room in a fluid motion. Coming up her body from the foot of the bed his arms scooped up her legs and as his face rose above hers. He held her stretched and open. The thick head of his cock pressed at her opening. Her eyes wide, she gazed up at him.

His attention was fiercely focused as he looked down at her and his hips thrust forward. He didn't push in. The beast rubbed himself over her, his cock furrowing up damp fold for a few brief moments.

"Not wet enough," his deep voice rumbled. His hand reached between them, hard fingers ruthlessly finding her clit. Teasing her with maddening circles as his eyes held her gaze.

It was so nakedly intimate. He was expertly manipulating her body, driving her to respond with a touch that would not let her do anything else. A new type of control she couldn't deny as long fingers stroked down to check her entrance. Sliding into her easily and still he wasn't satisfied, returning to her clit.

"More," he snarled. His hand left her to grasp the back of her knee. Pulling her wide, his head dropped to her cunt. Hot lips nibbled at the swollen head of her clit as two fingers of the other hand held pussy lips open. He sucked her into his mouth, rolling her clit with tongue and lips as the two fingers now messaged her opening. Dipping in and pulling her lubricant out to paint it firmly around the tight entrance.

He kept working her, sucking but not giving her enough sensation to take her close to the edge. His fingers rimmed and stretched her until three fingers slipped into her easily. With a low grunt his mouth left her body.

His entrance was fast and forceful, even after his attention, he stretched her, thick cock filling her body with a hard push. He didn't stop, pulling out as swiftly as he had entered to shove himself back home, deep within her. Her legs over his shoulders held her immobile beneath his pounding hips.

If she hadn't been so hungry for him, so totally primed into wet anticipation, this might have been painful. As it was, the slap of his hips against her created a sting that added sharp sensation to the already thundering crescendo crashing through her system. With each movement, his body stabbed through her most sensitive nerve endings, sending shock waves of pleasure ripping up her belly. Sparks cascaded around her body as he repeated the demanding sensations.

There were no words passing between them as his body took her. Helplessly, she responded, her channel clenching around the merciless invader. That's when his eyes changed again and Kelly suspected he didn't so much control that change as allow it to happen.

The cock slicing into her body continued relentlessly as the face above her showed her that hint of the predator. Looking into feral passion, Kelly found she loved being fucked to within an inch of her life by the beast. His control was complete and almost lost. He was both. She was the one who took him there. He had taken the time to ensure her readiness, but it had been different this time, a basic, animalistic demand.

His hand reached between them and grasped her clit.

It was too much and so powerfully right. He was losing control. His need had nothing to do with feeding and everything to do with getting in her. Sensation, emotion and screaming lust combined as release took her on a fast dizzying ride. He didn't slow down.

Kelly's hands gripped his shoulders and Cord's lips drew back in a snarl. He swiftly grabbed her wrists, pulling her arms overhead and holding them there with one hand. The other hand went to her breast and griped soft flesh. He kept slicing into her. Holding her beneath him as his eyes burned down at her.

Kelly's breath came in harsh gasps as somehow the power in his hips turned up a notch, slamming at blinding speed. The smack of every contact sounded louder as he continued to fuck her with harsh, driving thrusts.

"I need," he growled through his teeth.

Her body was tightening again, answering his demands. His hand kneaded her breast as he snarled his vulnerability. Primitive gratification joined the vortex of sensation and emotion swallowing her alive.

This male held her under his pounding cock, her legs ruthlessly immobilized over his shoulders and her hands stretched above her body. He was taking her as basically as he could and her body was going crazy. His control of her movements was complete but the fire leaping in his eyes told her she drove him. The knowledge was erotic and edgy.

Again an orgasm rocked her, drawing a scream from her lips. At her cry, his head whipped back and her unfocused eyes followed his every move as his mouth opened. She thought he would howl, but what came out of his mouth was much more demanding than that. It was a quiet roar that ended in a long, drawn-out purr as his body continued fucking her.

That's when Kelly realized he was still controlling himself to a great degree. The beast entering her body was being as gentle as he could be. The instincts driving him could be recognized as an animal to some degree but there was something else too. Something much bigger and darker.

The purr stopped, his head came down to look at her. "Need more."

Kelly simply looked at him. "More what?"

"More submission."

"I don't understand," she panted the words.

"Predators need more. Must control them," he said again insistently. The words were almost unrecognizable as he growled them. His lips drew back, displaying gleaming fangs where teeth had been before. "Trust me."

He abruptly released her and pulled out of her body. His hands grasped her hips, flipping her on the bed easily so she was facedown. "Knees up," he snarled. "Do it for me."

It sounded as if he were strangling on the words as he demanded her acceptance. Kelly came up on all fours and there was another muted growl behind her.

"Head down, hands over head. Offer mate."

He was directing her to expose and offer her body to him. Her arms trembled and she dropped to elbows, her head sank down as she laced her fingers behind it. Doing as he demanded shot a potent mix of erotic awareness through her.

"Spread legs. Arch back. Must have more."

Her body shifted as directed and she heard another long hiss from him as his hands grasped her hips. His thighs moved to the inside of hers, ensuring she remained spread as he directed, his cock brushing her entrance. He held it there, moving on her folds in a circular tease. The rumbling purr continued. Kelly realized he was watching. Looking down on the spread of her ass and cunt and purring.

One of his hands reached around her hip so he could pull her folds open from the front with two fingers, exposing her more fully for his view. He pushed into her body as he held her open, sliding into the wet channel easily, slowly this time, sinking into her in a deliberate rhythm. The fingers holding her folds went to work caressing, moving up and down as he stretched her round his cock.

His fingers left her but not for long. Wet with her excitement, he painted the puckered opening of her ass as he continued to slowly push into her weeping cunt. Kelly jerked in natural reaction as she realized his intent. His hand on her hip tightened but there was no other response as he continued stimulating the other entrance to her body.

Kelly's head came up and her arms straightened as she looked behind her. That did get his attention.

"Mine," he stated softly in that gravelly growl. His body stopped moving as his eyes burned in to her face. "Mine now," he repeated slowly. "Submit."

"What if I can't?" Kelly croaked.

"Can. Breathe," he said, and was still looking into her eyes as two fingers entered her body. Cord didn't move fingers or cock as he watched her take dual sensations. "More," he demanded, and began moving slick fingers in and out, slowly twisting them to loosen tight muscles. Her channel tightened around his cock, telling him the new sensations came with pleasure.

His hand left her hip and in it appeared a sensual toy. The plug was small but Kelly gasped as she looked at it.

"Only this now," he said. "Trust me."

Her eyes clung to his for a moment then she slowly turned to face forward and lowered elbows to the bed, her hands lacing behind her head as she gave him the submission he needed.

The plug was already lubricated. He pulled fingers out of her bottom and placed the tip at her opening. "Breathe," he demanded. Slowly he inserted the training plug as she drew in deep breaths. Both of his hands grasped her hips and his body began working her channel.

Looking down at his cock stretching pink folds around its thick girth while her other opening clenched on the plug pulled a rumbling purr from his body.

Then there was no more control he could give her. The thrusts into her body became harsh. He felt the fire eating up his legs as his balls tightened. Fucking her hard he let sensation claw through him. This was his mate and she was taking him, submitting to him. He was safe in her as she was safe in him.

His animal nature was almost fully in charge, and Cord reached for the release it gave him. The magnificent woman under his body again tightened around his cock as she responded to the hard thrusts. At this moment it didn't matter that he could not give her a piece of himself in a baby. All that mattered was that she had bent her body to his will. This was his temple of life, and he would both have and protect her at all costs.

The release boiled up from the dark dregs of his body. Flames consumed all knowledge of yesterday in this basic act to ensure tomorrow. His thrusts became short, hard digs to seat himself exactly where he needed to be. Then his cock swelled and all he could do was grind into her as hard bursts of seed splashed into her. Over and over he emptied into her and still his body held him there, driving his engorged member with powerful thrusts.

A storm of sensation ripped through him. The prolonged orgasm shredded any remnant of control he might have clung to. She took him out of his body and there was nothing but Kelly.

When he could finally opened his eyes, he was crouched over her, grasping her hips, still jerking her on his shaft. He couldn't leave her body. The size of his cock had not diminished in any way. He realized what part of his DNA was at work. His cock remained closing the entrance to her, sealing his seed within her. Wrapping an arm around her hips, he took them to the side so she was lying in front of him, his body curled around hers. They were locked together physically as surely as they were in reality.

Kelly struggled for breath, her body clamping on the thick invader. The sensations sent bolts of erotic charge through him.

"Relax," he commanded. "You must relax. The stimulation is too much, I can't leave you."

"I'm not doing that on purpose," she said through her harsh breathing "Are you?"

"No."

"How long?" she wanted to know.

"Don't know. Never happened before," he admitted. "Try to breathe."

She didn't respond as they lay silently. Both their bodies were damp with sweat. His hands petting up and down her torso. Fingers lightly brushing over clit, up her belly, her ribs, her breast to her neck and back down.

"That's not helping me relax," she said as he continued the soft strumming over sensitive body parts.

"It's helping me relax," he told her softly in a more normal tone. "I need this freedom to touch. Touch all of you." As he spoke, his hips again thrust at her in small movements.

He wasn't pulling out as much as he was pressing in over and over again. The sensations were intense but not only sexual. For him it was a possessive confirmation. He was petting her internally.

Shudders rippled down Kelly's body. Was it possible to be sexually shell-shocked? If it hadn't been before, it was now. Still deep inside her, thick and hard, his hips moving in short, lazy thrusts not only nudged the cock in her body but pushed the plug in her ass. His big body curled around her radiated heat like a furnace. His hands moving over her wouldn't let her think.

Something new had just happened. She'd wanted him, needed him with a burn that would not go away. Nothing had tamed the want, not cold water, not logical thought, nothing. Then he appeared and her body came unglued. His demand that she say yes to begin with had flipped the switch in both of them.

Securing her submission that easily, he'd then taken her to a place of intensely sexual eroticism and her mind seemed to have embraced it. What they had done had demanded total awareness of every sense. He had pulled away the normal world as if it were a disposable wrapping, exposing the woman within.

She was naked in a way that involved much more than exposed skin. The woman lying in his arms with a toy in her ass and a huge cock in her cunt was someone Kelly had never met before. This woman's body was wriggling with sexual excitement. She gloried in the feel of him unable to pull from her body.

This was different. They were different. Perhaps he would understand what triggered his need for the assurance of sexual submission. He was hers in every way. The power of that knowledge was blinding. Such a contradiction from the modern world Kelly used to inhabit.

The world she lived in now involved life and death on a basic level. It was half his world and half hers. He must remain a killer. She needed him exactly like that. Protection and defense had become personal battles, not something one could call the cops for. For him to be proficient at the job, the original elemental witches would have made very sure Cord's abilities far outpaced those of normal dragons. To do that he had to be more of what they were. Beast with a capital B.

Embracing what he was, what he could be, was the only way for her to be what he needed. He needed her submission, and when she surrendered it to him, he became what he was. In his transformation, hers occurred. She was exactly the woman who would ride a dragon.

She knew what to do, how to help them move to the next level. There was no fear because he was hers. Understanding that freed her from inhibitions that could hurt them both, but she wasn't sure the dragon was able to put a name to it yet.

Kelly's body stretched slightly to press her bottom firmly against his groin and a moan slipped out her mouth as the plug moved in her. She had relaxed around it as her mind relaxed around the idea of what it meant. Her trust was the key. All she had to do was hand it to him and there would be no limits between them.

A rumble moved up Cord's chest as he felt her press into him. Her body moved in his arms. Her leg lifted and she opened for him. He grasped her bent leg, holding it up, and she mewed softly in consent.

"I need more," she told him.

"There's only one more submission," he said just to be sure she knew what she was asking for. "Are you ready for that?"

"Are you?" Kelly wanted to know. "I said yes."

The sound from Cord's throat was not a chuckle but not a growl either. "Wind Witch is a demanding mistress." Rolling them over, he rested on top of her body. Her head turned to the side, his mouth was at her ear, kissing down her neck.

"I will have what's mine," she told him.

"Yes, Kelly girl. This is yours, only yours."

His body slid from her channel as they spoke. He leaned to the side and grasped the plug in her bottom. His thighs pressed hers wide as he pulled the toy from her. His arm snaked under her hips to lift her and slip the pillow beneath her. She had not fully settled her weight on the pillow when he grasped the globes of her bottom, opening them as the damp head of his cock pressed into her tight clasp.

He paused, his breath suddenly coming in harsh draws as he looked down. Her back arched and a little more of his wide cock disappeared into her body. She did that herself. There was no doubt that this woman wanted exactly what he was giving her.

Her acceptance raced over him with a forceful punch. He took her and she gave the power exchange of trust. Her trust was pure nectar delivered in a fireball. Whatever he thought he had gained from women in the past, even from her, did not compare to the pure mainlining of the drug she gave him now.

His hips pressed into her slowly, opening that small entrance. The greedy moans escaping her mouth fed him. Her body straining back to take more made him drunk with the sweet taste that was Kelly.

Had he been leashed to her before? No. What she gave him now bound him in ways he hadn't imagined were possible. She made him what he was, and in that moment, it was something that had never been before. This is what the lady witches of his past had hoped would happen. He understood it now. None of them were able to comprehend it before because it had not existed. He had not existed, not like he was at in the hands of the witch Kelly.

Fully seated in her, Cord leaned over her body, his hands tunneled under her to grasp her breasts. His mouth opened over her shoulder and gently clamped down to secure her beneath him. Then there was nothing but the incredible, irresistible sensation of drinking her submission. Feeling her move beneath him in pleasure that was nothing like pleasure had ever tasted before.

This time his movements were steady and slow. Around them, erotic excitement thickened into a dense fog of emotions. It didn't take long for her to overwhelm him, driving him to the edge of physical release. He refused to go there alone. Whatever was left when they were finished, it would be new and he had to have her in that world with him.

Reaching around between her legs, he knowingly strummed her center of sensation. Giving her every pleasure he could, but it was still nothing like she gave him. He was sure of it. His fingers plucked and stroked her clit with increasing pressure as her body drove him into the gates of complete oblivion.

Cord closed his eyes and hung on to the sleek Wind Witch in his arms. She took him with her into a reality created for them, by them. Her orgasm wrenched through her body, his eyes rolled back and the stars exploded. Empting his seed into her, shattered the world.

As soon as he could scrape together the composure to return to the present, Cord carefully pulled out of her body. It felt like hours passed, anything was possible, but he hoped it hadn't been quite that long. He was shaking. Lying facedown, she didn't notice and he was grateful for that. Whatever he had called an ego was now prostrate at her feet, he had no question of that.

Getting up, he stumbled into the bathroom and did the necessary cleanup. Jamming a fresh washcloth under the warm water, he refused a glance up at the mirror. Call him a coward but he wasn't sure he could face the creature looking back at him.

Taking two washcloths, just to be sure, he returned to her and carefully cleaned sensitive folds. Doing her this service did nothing to dispel the need to express how he was feeling. Kelly moved for him, letting him handle her with her head still in the pillow. He suspected she was a little bit embarrassed and that almost amused him.

Her vulnerability drove the emotional confusion to a new level. Adorable was what she had been before. There were no words for how she looked to him now. His hands moved over her with reverent care.

Dropping the washcloths by the bed, Cord lay down and gathered Kelly into his body. Holding her against his chest, he wrapped as much of himself around her as he could. She hadn't said a word yet. He was aware that their time alone was running out. It seemed as if someone should be doing some talking.

"I can't apologize," Cord said into the back of her neck. "I'm not sorry. I'm a little overwhelmed, but nothing could make me want to take one minute of that back."

"Good."

Kelly's response was brief and gave him no clue what she was thinking.

"Are you all right," he asked in an attempt to get a little more out of her.

"Dunno."

"Come on, give me something to work with." Cord tightened his arms in a gentle hug. "I'm trying to figure out if you're upset."

"Not upset," Kelly stated. She was waiting for him to say the words. Own what had passed between them.

"That's a start. What would you say you are?"

"A little tired. A lot blown away."

"Still doesn't give me any clue to your emotions," he pointed out.

"I have never experienced anything like that." Kelly had to let him work this out on his own. He knew something was completely different but he had to identify the emotions.

Telling him he was in love would be cheating him, stealing the opportunity for him to find that depth of emotion in himself.

Cord frowned at her answer. It didn't help him. Not being able to see her face was a distinct disadvantage. Her tone was soft but not hesitant.

"You surprised me," he tried a different approach to get more than short statements out of her.

Kelly took a deep breath. It wasn't exactly a sigh, just an excuse to not say anything for a few more seconds. "Everything surprised me," Kelly confessed. "That doesn't mean I regret any of it either. I guess I have some questions about what happens now."

"What do you want to happen?"

"That's a good question. There's so little I control about what is happening that it's hard to figure out what I want to happen. I think I'd like to understand what did happen first." Kelly slowly turned to face him.

Cord gave her a rare smile as he met her eyes. "I'm not sure there are words for what I feel. Emotions are not supposed to be important to my kind. Some doubt we have them, I've doubted it in the past. I no longer doubt."

Kelly searched his eyes, a small frown on her forehead. "You didn't think you had emotions?"

"Not so much," he confirmed. "We have instincts, a lot of drive and very little concern for others' needs. I'm not sure if that means we have no emotions, but I've never noticed them before now."

Kelly bit her lip as she regarded him seriously. "The guy who made himself Barney did it because he wanted to. Not because it would make the three-year-old happy? I can see what you mean. Dragons have absolutely no ability to be concerned about anyone but themselves. And all that standing guard and being fierce is just because, what, it's fun?"

Cord scowled at her mocking face. "That's different."

"How?"

"Well, I was mostly making you happy. If I make you happy, I get more of your attention. See how self-serving that is?"

Kelly's face was very serious but her eyes were laughing at him. "Of course it is," she agreed with him.

Still scowling, he studied her as her point sank into his brain. "Are you saying you think dragons are emotional?"

"Nope. Never said that. I suspect if someone called you emotional, you'd be handing them their ass."

A wolf's smile spread across his face. "Well, if you put it that way, call me emotional all you want. Handing your ass is the most amazing thing I've ever done."

A pink flush lit Kelly's cheeks and her eyes dropped to examine his breastbone. "It was amazing, wasn't it?"

The smile left Cord's face as he gazed down at her. "More than amazing, much more," he agreed.

"I liked it," Kelly whispered.

"I know," he growled softly.

She was still blushing furiously, both hands resting on his chest because she needed to touch him. Feel the heart beating beneath hard muscles. He was getting close to understanding himself. It was sort of cute to watch him work it out.

"We have to get dressed," Kelly changed the subject. "Minuet will be looking for us soon."

"I know where she is and what she's doing," Cord said causally as he sat up. "Take your time, I'll get dressed and go find her," he assured her as he stood and moved into the bathroom.

Kelly stretched out on the bed, pulling the sheet over her because she really wasn't that casual about being naked. It was silly. Her eye strayed to the bedside table where the toy rested. He came out of the bathroom and she had to pretend she was looking at the clock.

A wave of his hand and the plug disappeared.

"Where do things go when you do that?" Kelly had to ask as he pulled on his clothes. He could undress with a thought, and yet there he was, dressing normally. So many things about him didn't make sense.

"Usually they go to my place. All dragons have lairs. For me it's just a place to store things. I don't live there."

Cord only had jeans and boots on as he sat on the bed and gather her and the sheet into his arms. The need to hold her had rushed through him unexpectedly but he continued with the conversation. "I use it as a sort of holding place. If I own a thing I need, I retrieve it. Or return it there. Creating a tool can take a great deal of energy and knowledge of its construction, time consuming when the thing is complicated, so storing things is a time-saving tool. I'll take you and Minuet there when we have time."

Cord's cheek rested on the top of Kelly's head as he spoke, his arms wrapped around her. "I think I'd better get Minuet. She's getting hungry," he stated, and gave Kelly a gentle squeeze before releasing her.

After he left the room, Kelly tried to hurry through another shower and dressing but she simply couldn't. Languid satisfaction would not let her rush. Everything felt more vibrant, touch, scent, even her hearing. She supposed being exposed to dragon senses might rub off just a little. Finally getting herself out to the kitchen, she found Minuet and Barney making a very late lunch.

Minuet was instructing Barney and the big purple dinosaur got everything wrong. Laughter lived in the room with them, and Kelly found she could see the color of joy as well as taste it in the air.

The three of them spent a pleasant evening exploring the gardens after the meal. Minuet splashed in a fountain for a while, played on all the equipment in a lovely playground area they found and ran when she wasn't doing something else.

Bedtime came early for all of them as the crash after traveling caught up with Kelly and Minuet.

That night, Cord stayed in her bed all night. They didn't make love but he couldn't stop holding her. Kelly had to smile as her big dragon struggled to understand his needs.

The idyllic calm didn't give them much time. The next morning as they drove to Loch Ness it was shattered with the coming conflict they could not escape.

Chapter Thirteen

"Him coming," Minuet said. "Him berry mad."

Cord pulled the car to the side of the road. "Which way do you feel him, honey?"

Minuet pointed ahead.

Cord got out of the car quickly. "Stay here," he directed, and walked to the front of the vehicle. He stood still, reaching out with senses. Harrison came at them fast. Without Minuet's warning he might not have noticed the change in atmosphere soon enough. Harrison was using a lot of energy to conceal his approach.

To the two watching from the car, Cord appeared to shimmer and disappear in a short burst of bright light.

Kelly gasped and searched with her senses. Then she felt him. He was the air and light, moving at rapid speed to the north. Minuet had been sitting between her and Cord, now she was clutching the dashboard as she leaned forward to gaze out the windshield. There was silence, suddenly a great gust of wind swept along the road causing dirt devils to spin out and die on the edges of the gale.

"Can you hear anything?" Kelly asked Minuet.

"They yelling," Minuet said. "Dat other one argues Cord."

"Just argue? Not fighting?" Kelly asked worriedly.

"Playing. Liked me and Coco with ball," she explained.

Kelly hated to rely on Minuet for the details of this fight. She wanted to distract her from something that could get very ugly, but since she had no way of following the action and

Minuet seemed quite comfortable with it, she had no other option. The wind around them died down to a normal breeze.

Abruptly Minuet jumped with a yelp of pain. In the next instant a structure appeared several yards away in the rocky field beside them. An instant later Cord materialized beside the unusual building.

"Me talk mean dagon," Minuet stated as she scrambled behind the wheel and out Cord's side of the car.

Kelly was up and running after Minuet but wasn't fast enough to catch her as she came to a halt beside Cord.

From inside the structure a loud roar was followed by a racket as someone pounded the walls. The building was an ornate castle, but only about nine feet tall and fifteen feet around. It had Barbie-pink rock walls, bright-purple tiled roof and golden bars on every window and door. It glittered in the morning sun. Every surface sparkling.

Cord, Kelly and Minuet stood about ten yards away from it as the roaring, pounding and now cursing continued from within.

Cord put an arm around Minuet's shoulders. "It's a very pretty castle. Why did you do that?"

"Him hurt Cord," Minuet stated. "Him want hurt Mommy."

"I know, sweetheart, but everything was all right. I didn't need help."

"Mommy say fighting bad. It a rule."

The noise from the structure suddenly ceased. There was silence as the three of them waited for what would come next.

"Cord! What the hell is this?" boomed out the little castle.

"I believe you're in Barbie's dream castle," Cord informed his questioner.

"What the fuck is that? Get it the hell off me!"

"Clean up your language, and I didn't do it. Look out the front door window and you'll see who wants to talk to you," Cord instructed sharply.

"Who the..."

"Curse one more time and I'll show you something you haven't seen before," Cord threatened softly, cutting off the voice from the castle. "If you can keep a civil tongue, perhaps the little lady holding you captive will reconsider. The problem is, if you take too long getting a grip she will forget how. Three-year-olds can't write down the original spell."

A face appeared in the round window of the ornate front door. The man had rippling blond hair and startlingly blue eyes the color of a stormy ocean. Below the eyes dark smudges of exhaustion made him appear old. A straight nose and chiseled features would've been extremely handsome when he was young, and if the individual wasn't scowling. Just looking at his face showed he was severely underfed.

The face regarding them did not stop scowling as his eyes moved over the three people standing there.

"The lass did this?" a slightly calmer tone questioned.

"I do it," Minuet stated firmly. "You not hurt Mommy or Cord. I makes sure."

"Cord, you better be explaining," the male in the castle said softly, his eyes never leaving Minuet's little form.

"Harrison, meet Minuet," Cord introduced them. "I suggest you start believing what you're sensing. If you had listened to a word I said instead of sinking talons into me you'd have a clue what's going on. As you can see, she likes things pretty and sparkly. Tick her off some more and you might find yourself turned into something pretty and sparkly."

"What is your little friend? I've never encountered her kind," Harrison said cautiously, still addressing Cord as he kept eyes on Minuet.

Minuet stepped from under Cord's arm. Little hands landed on her hips as she faced the sparkling castle. "I Minuet," she told him firmly. "You be nice. No more mean. It hurt you berry lots. Now you sick."

The voice from the castle was suddenly tired. "If by sick you mean I'm about to fall on my, ah, rump, you're correct. Mind giving me a chair in here?"

The front door of the castle disappeared. In its place bars blocked the entrance. Behind them a slender man was now sitting in a chair that looked exactly like one in Kelly's living room back in America.

"A crafty little witch you are, lassie." He smiled. "It's clear I can't hurt anybody." He shrugged casually. "So somebody start explaining what's going on."

"Cord say you good." Minuet crossed her arms as she took over the conversation. "I feels only frowns in you. The laughing all gone." Minuet paused as she studied the man. "You needs the laughing," she finished softly on a puzzled note.

"You read well but that doesn't explain what you are, my little prison keeper," he responded to her.

"She is a dragon caller," Cord supplied. "Something new. Part of what has changed the mission. Feel her, feel the strength in me and where it comes from. You're a stubborn sea donkey, Harrison, but even you have to admit this is not how they said it would be. Are you ready to listen?"

"Dragon caller? Never heard of such a thing." His head tilted as he regarded Minuet. "I may be weak but I'm fully aware that you have a Wind Witch feeding you power. You're no longer balanced enough to follow the plan. I was simply trying to aid you."

Minuet took another step closer to the castle and the male inside stopped speaking. His eyes on her little form, he leaned forward. "What is this? She is... She is power. Come closer, lass," he invited softly.

"No," Cord said firmly as he pulled Minuet back to his side. "First you listen. Then we'll see if she wishes to help you."

Minuet looked up at Cord. "Him much sick."

"I know, honey. But he is also a sneaky dragon who loves to play tricks."

"Him much sad. Need laughing or he gone and Shelley die," Minuet stated.

Cord raised a brow as he looked down at the child who read them all so clearly. "Who is Shelley?"

A furrow appeared between Minuet's eyebrows as she looked up at Cord. "Shelley is him heart." Minuet pointed at Harrison. "She afraid. Him make her dying."

Cord dropped to haunches, his hands clutching Minuet's hands. "Is Shelly in danger? Can you show me in my mind?"

Minuet shook her head and tears formed in her eyes. "I can show him but no you. She afraid and I hurt her if you look her."

"Wait. What the hell are you talking about? Don't hurt her," Harrison snapped, coming out of his chair to grip the golden rails in front of him.

Cord didn't even glance at the man grasping his prison bars. "Minuet, this is very important. We have to save Shelley. Where is she?"

A tear slid down Minuet's cheek as she gripped Cord's hands as tightly as she could. "I don't know. I don't know all the places yet. She hurt."

"It's okay, baby," Cord tried to soothe her and his own emotions as well.

Kelly knelt beside Minuet and turned her, gathering the child into her arms. "It's okay, honey. You're doing your best." Looking over Minuet's head at Cord, Kelly continued. "Whatever you have to do to make him understand, do it. She's too young for this, for this responsibility. If he can't grasp what's going on, I'll take care of him myself for putting her through this."

Cord stood in a fluid motion and strode to the castle. Reaching through the bars he had a hand around Harrison's neck. Moving so quickly it was difficult to follow the action was completed in less than a second.

"Here it is, and I'm only going to tell you once. Our creators told us half the story. We were made to match the witch who shares our element. When Minuet called the woman named Shelly your heart, she meant Shelley is the Water Witch. She couldn't have been more accurate. We're connected to our witch both by instinct and DNA. Use what little strength you have left to feel what I am."

Cord glared into Harrison's eyes as the water dragon consciously touched him with senses. Harrison's whole body shook in reaction to what it touched in Cord. But that involuntary reaction was Harrison's only indication of his understanding.

Cord remained holding him by the neck a few moments longer. Harrison's eyes went to Minuet and he ignored the large male holding him in such a vulnerable position. "Miss Minuet, I apologize for not understanding. Please forgive me," he stated simply.

Cord slowly released Harrison and stepped back. "It's okay, honey. Harrison is sorry for being mean. He knows if he tries any tricks I will be very mad at him. Could you come talk to him over here?"

Kelly stood, holding Minuet's hand. Both of them approached the castle door.

Harrison dropped to one knee. He didn't say a word but held his hand out through the bars, palm up, silently inviting Minuet to touch him.

Cord could read the water dragon but he doubted his judgment was as good as Minuet's. Whatever Minuet was feeling from the person she called Shelly could be distracting her enough to give the dragon in front of her an opening. If the bastard even hinted at a wrong move, Cord would be ready to use deadly force. That was a last resort. They needed the water dragon and his lady. Needed them desperately if there was going to be any hope of a future.

Minuet placed her palm in Harrison's hand. Long fingers closed over her tiny hand. Harrison paled even further. His body was racked with involuntary shudders as Minuet touched him with power. Cord knew the excruciating pain of having Minuet's power flooded a starved body. It force-fed nutrients into withered muscle and bone. Encountering Minuet before one had touched his witch was painfully difficult.

Harrison's teeth clenched, his lips drawing back in a grimace as tears dripped down his cheeks, but he held on.

Minuet's other hand reached through the bars to flatten on Harrison's forehead. The dragon groaned but leaned into her touch. His eyes closed as he drew air swiftly through his teeth.

Kelly frowned and glanced at Cord. "What's happening?"

"Minuet is forcing power into his system. He's accepting it as fast as he can, but she wants to make it go faster. She is trying to show him what she knows of the Shelley woman. For him to be able to hear her at that level he needs to recover a bit more. I don't know if she will ever have the power to make this less painful, but she doesn't now. When it happened to me, I thought I was dying," Cord explained softly.

"Will he be able to hurt her?" Kelly wanted to know.

"Only if he wishes to die," Cord said in a low growl. "But when has anyone wanted to hurt Minuet after they've touched her?"

Kelly shook her head and ran a hand through Minuet's hair. "Does it hurt her?" she asked Cord. She wasn't sure Minuet could hear her. Her eyes were locked with Harrison's and she seemed somehow distant.

"I don't know. When it happened to me, she was so worried about you I guess neither of us focused on that. Now she is sharing the pain of the Water Witch and again I don't think she can separate what is her pain and someone else's.

Harrison's hand opened and Minuet pulled back.

The water dragon was no longer gaunt. The hollows in his cheeks were gone as were the dark bruises under his eyes. Ash-blond hair flowed back from his forehead in a smooth fall. His shoulders were wider than the door he knelt behind. Power rippled around him as if someone had thrown a stone in a lake.

He remained on his knee, looking at Minuet. "Thank you, Miss Minuet. You know what I must do."

The sparkling castle around Harrison disappeared but the large man remained where he was, looking into Minuet's eyes. Then he stood slowly to face Cord. Cord was still larger but not by a whole lot.

Harrison nodded then he was gone.

Kelly looked around. "Where did he go?"

"He go save his heart," Minuet stated confidently.

"That's it? We came all this way for that?" Kelly wanted to know.

"Yep, looks that way. Minuet, do you know where he's going?" Cord asked casually as he took the hand of each of his ladies and turned them back toward the car.

"I don't know. I show picture and he go," Minuet said proudly. "Him not sick anymore. But not laughing. Him need laughing."

"When he finds her, he will find his laughter," Cord told her. "Did it hurt you to help Harrison?" he asked as they got back in the car.

"No, me and sister like help. We still go big deep water?"

Cord started the car and pull on the road heading in the same direction they had been going. "Sister?" he asked. "Don't you mean Mommy?"

"Mommy like help but sister just learn it."

"Are you calling your new friend Shelly a sister?" Cord asked, trying to understand.

"No. Sisters and brothers come from mommies, right?" Minuet asked as she looked between them.

Kelly smiled down at her. "Yes they do, but a mommy has to carry them in her tummy for a while. You know what being pregnant is. Remember Aunt Penny was pregnant? Her tummy was big and you could feel the baby moving sometimes."

"I member," Minuet agreed confidently. "Look." She pointed out the window excitedly as they topped a hill and a huge expanse of water came into view. "Big water!"

Kelly looked over Minuet's head at Cord. His eyes met hers for a brief second. Both of them were silent as Minuet chattered about what she saw outside.

Cord calmly found a place to park overlooking the loch. It was a relatively warm summer day and there were several other groups of tourists scattered though the area though it was by no means crowded. Minuet ran ahead toward the water before Cord could make it around the car.

Taking Kelly's hand, they followed Minuet's path. Still neither of them said a word except for Kelly calling after Minuet not to go in the water. Minuet grabbed a stick and was playing in the sand at the water's edge. Cord and Kelly stopped walking a few feet away from her.

"Um," Kelly started to speak hesitantly.

"It's not possible," Cord said quietly.

"Why not?" Kelly wanted to know with studied calm. "We've never used protection."

"There is no need. My kind do not have that ability. We are not actually sentient beings. Mixing DNA in a dish does not result in something God would allow to breed."

"You are ascribing a whole lot of disapproving judgment to God. Didn't you say you are very different from the original dragon type? Made to save humans? A job you willingly expected to do with no thanks, no acknowledgement until you died? Sounds a lot like a plan God would approve of, though I don't think he'd make it as bleak as you do."

Cord stood rigidly beside her, his senses continually scanning the area and every person in it. Animal senses he could not turn off and didn't want to. He was not the creature she so desperately wanted to believe. He'd known she needed the illusion of his being human, having human emotions, human needs. Now she was trying to convince herself that God could extend some of the regard He held humans in to an abomination.

Kelly went on, her tone softly casual as they watched Minuet find smooth stones and start piling them up. "The people who made you firmly believed that eventually there would be unusual humans in the world again. Humans with abilities that make us almost alien to the original human model. They did not see these differences as the work of a devil, but as God-directed development in the species, natural evolution. Correct?"

Cord held her hand gently, but that was the only part of him not rock hard with tension. He nodded curtly to her conclusion. She was building a lovely case for an outcome that simply would never be, no matter how one wrapped up the process.

God made humans and the normal animals. They had a logical developmental path lovingly guarded by the laws of nature. There was order to that world. Perhaps an afterlife or some thought of a next life. He'd never paid much attention to human religion. He considered it none of his business and possibly blasphemy for him to poke around God's relationships with his children.

Creatures created outside the laws of nature were fucking on their own. Of that he had no question. He'd seen God in action. The flood was a plan God had approved. The word for his creators was witch now. It had been something else in the time before, closer to High Priestess, Daughter of God.

No, he was pretty sure God had been pissed at the humans inventing dragons. He'd judged the entire population of humans in the process, but it was the dragons who God had wanted destroyed completely, except for the three of them.

Cord frowned. *Except for the three of them.* The thought echoed in his brain. Math was one of God's most elegant natural laws and Cord often employed it when something didn't make sense. If something could be figured in an equation, it could be understood. Now the numbers were screaming at him.

The number of humans saved from the flood in relation to the total number of the global population. The number of animals saved in relation to the total population of said animals. There was a correlation to the number of dragons saved in relations to the number of the total population at the time.

But the equation fell apart because the population of dragons had not really decreased. They were still present, just in altered states.

Kelly continued voicing her thoughts. "Why would you think there could be no positive development for dragons as well?"

A muscled ticked in Cord's jaw. "Because we are the abominations that brought about the destruction of the world, Kelly. Not just some of it, the entire world. Could you forgive the creature who destroyed your child? Much less billions of your children? Forget it. Whatever you'd like to believe, this is reality."

"I'm not God. My capacity for forgiveness isn't in question. Besides, you didn't do it personally. Humans created the problem. As I understand it, dragons were created by greedy humans for the purpose of enslaving the world under a human's control. It seems to me you're holding a grudge for God, it's rather vain of you to assume you carry God's judgment for an entire species you didn't create.

"You are part of the solution in a plan you admit God approved. Get over yourself, Cord," Kelly finished and let go of his hand to go play in the sand with Minuet.

Cord remained where she left him, his arms crossed as he stood guard. His eyes quartered the area in relentless precision as his mind turned over her words.

About a mile away another couple was arguing, completely ignoring their two children who were playing close to a little cliff over the lake. Cord wanted to be totally absorbed in his own problems, but he couldn't stop watching the eight-year-old boy who was teasing his younger sister as mercilessly as his father was disrespecting the mother.

He was aware of that group as well as every other human in the area. It was not difficult, a natural function of his abilities. That situation was becoming critical though. One more step and the little girl was going over the edge backward, head first. Below her, the shore was rocky, no soft sandy beach.

He had several options. Forcing the parents to look up at their children would just transfer the stress they were indulging. The anger would be turned on the children. Nothing in the family situation would change. More likely the obvious negative spiral would continue, creating a sullen, destructive teenager of the boy and a defensive mouse of the girl.

His other option would shock the parents. It would still be their choice, but it opened a possibility for a positive difference in the family. There was no time left. Cord mentally sent Kelly a brief explanation and disappeared from the human light spectrum.

An instant latter he reappeared at the cliff. Remaining at the edge of human's ability to see him he again glowed in white light, large white-feathered wings rested on his back as he gently caught the girl. Her scream of terror at falling had gained her parents attention at last.

Cord carefully carried her away from the danger, giving her a gentle squeeze as he put her down. "Be careful," he murmured softly as he put her on her feet again. "God needs his angels on Earth too."

The little girl's wide eyes studied him, taking in the white robe, white wings and glowing body. There was no fear in her. Cord looked up at her parents, who were gaping at him. His face became serious as he stood holding the child's hand.

"You have only one chance to raise them. Don't waste it," he stated seriously. Deliberately using words that would let them draw their own conclusions about what he was. The core truth of his statement could not be misunderstood, regardless of their personal beliefs.

Cord faded quickly then flashed back to Kelly and Minuet. Both of whom were sitting in the grass, beaming at him as he reappeared. Minuet jumped up and ran to him, barreling into his legs as she laughed in delight.

"My Cord make pretty!" she declared. Holding up her arms, she demanded he lift her.

Laughing with her, but a little confused, Cord scooped her up and lifted her high over his head. Squeals of laughter echoed across water as he settled her on his arm and walked down to Kelly.

"What did I make pretty?" Cord asked Minuet.

"The peoples," Minuet informed him as she scrambled down. "Look, we made a fort." Her attention already skipping to a new subject, Minuet pointed at the construction she and Kelly were working on with the smooth stones.

"It's a lovely fort," Cord admired.

Kelly stood and grabbed his hand, going up on tiptoes to kiss his cheek as she smiled at him. "I'm proud of you," she said quietly.

Cord turned his head to capture her lips briefly. "You are? That was just a little preventive maintenance."

"No, that was you doing what you do. What comes naturally to you," she corrected patiently.

"Anybody else ready for lunch?" Cord asked to change the subject. The warmth of her approval and Minuet's delight was gratifying, and for some reason a little embarrassing. Cord couldn't remember the last time he'd been embarrassed and the feeling was distinctly uncomfortable.

As they turned and walked to the car, he thought about it a little more. Embarrassment was not an emotion dragons possessed. Their limited repertoire consisted of anger and satisfaction as far as he knew. There was amusement too, he acknowledged.

Driving back to the inn, they stopped in a small village and enjoyed making a picnic out of a few things bought at the market. After eating, the general store saw a substantial uptick in income.

Minuet appeared completely comfortable in this environment. Whatever had made her uncomfortable on the flight was absent now. Cord took the opportunity to encourage his two ladies to shop. Minuet quickly had herself outfitted. She then had very definite ideas about what Cord should buy as well.

When Cord refused to purchase a tartan, he failed miserably in his attempt to explain the importance of colors and pattern in this culture. The general store's proprietor had no problem taking up the explanation of family and clans. Minuet was enthralled with both his accent and his tales of Scottish warriors and bonnie lasses.

As Cord was finally following the women out of the store, the owner nodded and said to him quietly, "I fair think the plaid of the loch would do well on ye, sir."

Cord paused to look into the man's eyes. "The Laird of the Loch may be handing those out, but he has not done so yet."

The elderly man beamed. "Give him my best." He slapped Cord on the back and waved to them from the door as they pulled away from his store.

Minuet had been comfortable in the village, yet there was knowledge there, things not said were understood. The people of the Scottish countryside were an interesting lot.

Returning to the B&B, Minuet wanted to go play with her friend, so Kelly took her to the owner's cottage to meet them herself.

When Kelly returned, she found Cord standing in front of the main room window, his back to her in that powerful male stance. His arms were crossed, accenting wide shoulders above a dramatic vee down to slim hips, drool-worthy ass and powerful thighs. His widespread legs spoke of aggression though his head tilted down said he was lost in thought. Unsure what to do for a moment, she had to smile at her own hesitation.

The dragon knew she was there. Thinking that she was bothering him would be foolish. Going into another room to let him work through his thoughts equally dumb. He had once made a statement she didn't understand at that time. He had said that he wanted to experience the pleasure of her touching him simply because she wanted to, not because she had to. Now she smiled at that memory.

Walking up to his back, she leaned against him, wrapping her arms around his waist. Her head rested between his shoulder blades as his arms immediately covered hers, welcoming her touch. Kelly wanted to know what consumed him but not enough to break the silence and somehow change the atmosphere of the room.

He had a lot to consider and some new possibilities to think through. Minuet's comments about a sister were uppermost in her mind. She didn't know if Cord was sensitive enough to feel the beginnings of a new life in her this early.

Cord turned slowly in her arms. His head rested on the top of hers and she settled into his chest. They still didn't say anything but his arms tightened fiercely, holding her to him as if something were trying to take her away. His big body shuddered once as he took a deep breath.

Kelly smiled but didn't bother to open her eyes. The dragon had gone seeking in her body and found something he wasn't prepared for. His reaction told her everything she needed to know. So this is what a terrified dragon felt like.

He was rigid beneath her arms, every muscle pulled tight. Apparently he had been that sure of his own conclusions. Well, the women in his life were going to teach him things no dragon had ever known before. How to be a daddy.

Chapter Fourteen

Much later that night, Cord lay staring at the ceiling. Kelly was sleeping in his arms, her head on his chest, a leg slung over one of his thighs. He was fiercely erect, a condition he'd been in for hours. He hadn't made love to her this afternoon or evening. After Minuet went to bed, they had talked casually about Legion and Molly. Then speculated on where Harrison had gone to find his lady, Shelley.

Neither of them wanted to traumatize Minuet by questioning her about the danger she had sensed surrounding Shelley. Cord hoped Harrison knew enough to call for help if he needed it. He'd contacted Legion to let him know what had happened earlier today but had left out the news he was carefully avoiding.

Kelly hadn't questioned him. She was treating him with the kind of gentle care one showed a shock victim. He supposed he deserved it. He was in shock. Everything he'd known about his life, what he was and who he was seemed to be a lie. Not exactly a lie. Marelda had never said he couldn't have children. In fact, she never actually lied to him.

She'd simply not told him that his assumptions were untrue. He hadn't thought to discuss the impossible with her, perhaps his first mistake.

Large hands gently stroked up and down Kelly's back as a smile inched across his lips. He was the product of several sets of DNA, knowing about those predators had been an important part of his development. Marelda insisted he study each one to better understand himself, and hindsight showed him all he needed to know was in that study. She had also disclosed that the human DNA in his makeup was from her family. The significance of her directions were growing on him now.

Each of the predators in his makeup not only mated for life but was only able to procreate with a single partner.

Marelda's family was made up of people who held themselves to the highest standard. In human form, when he looked in the mirror, he was looking into Marelda's eyes in his own face. The shape of his jaw matched her husband's. He was their child. She may not have carried him in her body, but she had created him with the love of a mother and given him the strength of a father.

What was the difference? The mixing of human male and female DNA, did that make him something other than a dragon, other than an abomination? Were the three elemental dragons actually a different species?

"Are you done yet?" Kelly asked from his chest.

"With what?"

"With being shocked and whatever," Kelly said.

"Don't think so," Cord confessed.

"It's been hours. Do you need help?"

"What are you going to help me with?" Cord wanted to know.

"I thought I'd start with explaining where babies come from," Kelly said seriously. "Then we'd move on to what it means to be a daddy and a mommy."

"I know what it means to be a daddy and a mommy," he said firmly. "It means getting married. Would you like to do it here?"

Her head shot up to glare at him. "That was you asking me to marry you?" she demanded indignantly.

"Ah, of course not. That was clearly all wrong and something I would never do," he assured her. "I was wondering if you'd like to be asked here."

"I would love to be asked here," Kelly purred. "It's a very romantic setting and I'm sure a smart dragon can figure out how to make it memorable."

Her head settled back on his chest and now Cord was frowning at the ceiling. There was silence for a few moments as he tried to decipher the woman speak.

"Let's pretend you're talking to a dragon dumb as a box of rocks, one who has no idea how to get his witch to marry him," Cord started conversationally. "If he came to you for advice, what would you tell him?"

"I'd have to ask him something first," Kelly said thoughtfully.

"Really? What?"

"I'd ask him if he had told his witch he loved her?"

"That's big for humans," Cord agreed. "Then what?"

"If he had, I'd want to know if he thought he had convinced her. Because as you know, the only way she'd say yes it is if she believed he loves her," Kelly continued. "After that it's easy."

"Right, easy," Cord mumbled.

Kelly bit down on her bottom lip to keep from smiling. She didn't want him to think she was laughing at him. She understood exactly why he was having this conversation. Who else was he going to ask? There was no one but each other.

Again the room was silent for several minutes. Kelly shifted against the hard dragon holding her, but he only patted her hip absently as if to settle her.

"You know, I'd have more advice for him," Kelly prodded.

"More? Something specific?"

"Not exactly specific. Just some suggestions I suppose. This dragon was coming to me for advice on relationships after all. I could be very helpful to him," Kelly stated confidently.

"Oh yeah? What would you tell him?" Cord wanted to know as his hands began stroking up and down her back again.

"First, I'd be sure and let him know that even though witches are humans, they really enjoy the beast in their dragon. I'm guessing he's feeling hesitant about that. I've noticed dragons in love get self-conscious."

Cord rolled them over so he was resting on his elbows above the little smart-mouth witch. "Oh, you've noticed that, have you? I can't imagine where you get that idea. Dragons are not known to be shy," he growled softly into her openly laughing face.

Kelly's hands framed his handsome face. "I didn't say he was shy. I said he might be feeling hesitant and self-conscious. I want to assure him that his witch enjoys every minute of her dragon's attention. I mean she probably will understand that he's been knocked off his game with the love issue. Of course, if the witch is pregnant, the dragon is probably seriously traumatized. It's never a good idea to let the pregnant woman know the guy who got her that way is panicking and incapable of reassuring her he wants the baby by making love to her. Humans have a blue pill that fixes the problem. No idea if it works on dragons, but I guess I'd want him to try it if his shock was overwhelming."

Cord lowered his hips, using his knees to spread her thighs, settling the hard length of his erection on her soft belly. "I've never known a dragon to have blue pill problems. I suspect it would take a helluva lot more throwing him off his game to accomplish that, though his beautiful witch being pregnant is a damn good attempt."

Kelly's legs gracefully rose to circle his hips as she smiled up at the beast looming over her. Oh yes, regardless of his other reactions, his beautiful body was responding perfectly. Went to show that the animal within was completely comfortable. It was the human part of the dragon who was kicking around disbelief. Interesting turn of events.

Cord licked the smile off her lips with slow deliberation, finally leaning down to take her mouth in a deep, slow kiss that explored her. The rumble started low in his chest, vibrating into her breasts. It was amazingly erotic. He was holding most of his weight off her, his hips moving in deliberate strokes, dragging his cock over soft, damp folds. His mouth lifted but only to allow him to worship her lips before he sank back into her again.

The sweet kisses went on forever as his body lightly caressed the rest of her. He seemed in no hurry to move on. Kelly had been suffering on low burn for hours, waiting for him to get over whatever it was. At first she thought he was upset, but that thought was quickly erased as his attention this evening had been overwhelming. It just hadn't been sexual.

Now he was torturing her with attention. Gentle, careful attention. She was sure she had been clear explaining that a witch needs her dragon. Perhaps he hadn't gotten the message. It wasn't as if he wasn't interested. The thick rod between her legs, moving painfully slow, was certainly ready. What would it take to get his attention fully focused on what she needed?

Time to find out what it took.

"Please roll over?" she asked softly.

His body lifted off her quickly, his brow furrowed in a worried frown. "Are you okay? Did I hurt you?"

Kelly followed his body, straddling him, but his firm hands held her off his cock as he studied her face.

"I'm fine, really, but I need to try something. Would you mind letting go?" she asked.

"What, what do you need to try?"

"Trust me," Kelly whispered.

Cord still frowned but his hands opened. Kelly smiled and moved her legs so she was kneeling between his thighs. Ignoring the frown on his face, she concentrated on the beautiful body her hands were trailing down. Such a lovely beast he was. At her touch his, muscles jumped and tightened.

At last her hands framed the hard evidence of his animal nature.

Cord watched the Wind Witch kneeling between his legs. He wondered if it was possible for a dragon's brain to implode. He knew what she was about to do, but the expression on her lovely face was almost more than a beast should have to take. Especially after the difficult day he'd had.

Her mouth opened in a light pant as her body bent. Her warm hands circled the base of his cock, holding him up for her attention. She had to grip him with both hands, and Cord had his answer. Yes, it was possible to lose one's mind at the hands of the witch.

Her pink tongue circled the head of his cock with slow enjoyment. She licked up from the underside of the mushroom head to press her tongue into his slit. Her mouth lifted as she savored his taste on her tongue.

A mysterious smile crossed her lips and her mouth opened to sink over him. Licking around as he sank into her. Then her lips closed around the thick post she was sucking and her fists tightened at his base, stroking with each strong pull of her mouth.

Perhaps there was some heaven beyond this Earth, but at this moment, Cord strongly doubted it. If this wasn't as good as things got, he wasn't at all sure he was strong enough to survive something more. His eyes slowly closed as his mouth opened to pant through his Wind Witch's attempt to give him a heart attack.

Blood pounded through his body. His hips thrust toward her mouth, and he had very little control of the movement. He tried to keep from forcing himself farther into her. She was small even if she thought she was tall.

Then she changed things. Her head twisted as she pulled off him to swirl that wicked tongue of hers around the cap of his cock. Her fists began pumping in earnest, and Cord stopped thinking. There was no possibility of thought as she tried to suck all reason out of him through his cock.

Reaching down, he grasped her under her arms and lifted her body over his hips. Her legs straddled him and he didn't hesitate to set her down on the instrument she had been preparing for this. His cock plowed through her soft folds and he was briefly grateful the she was wet. He wasn't sure he would have been able to stop if she hadn't been. He needed to be in her. Deep in her body.

Rolling them over, his hands gathered her arms above her head, one hand shackling her wrists as his hips thrust steel into her body. Reaching down with the other hand, he yanked her leg high on his back. His hips never stopped moving as they pounded into the wet welcome her body gave him.

Above her face, his lips drew back from his teeth as he grimaced through the crashing sensations entering her gave him. Her licking had only served to make his nerve endings more sensitive to the sweet tightness of her channel.

Holding her arms above her head, her body impaled on his thrusting cock, Cord found he couldn't stop. He couldn't slow down. She robbed him of control and she'd known what she was doing.

Looking down at her, he felt his eyes change. The face over her was indeed the beast. He was taking her hard and deep, fucking her brains out and not able to slow down enough to give her an orgasm first. All that knifed through his brain as branding fire licked up his spine and backdrafted down to his balls. It was too late.

His mate, it burned through him, melting the past into a meaningless mass. This was true. There were no rules, no limitations. In her was the only place he was complete. He needed this, her, more than life, more than death.

His head hitched back and at least he held in the roar that wanted to rip into the night as his seed jetted into her. This time he knew the temple of life below him was fertile for him.

Even though she was already pregnant, the knowledge added a hard edge of possession to the pleasure, this overwhelming, shattering pleasure of pumping her full of his mark.

With each explosion of seed, his cock swelled further, locking him in her body with his animal responses. Still his hips slammed the vee of her thighs in grinding jabs. Fire licked through his veins instead of blood.

His body gradually relaxed, opening eyes slowly, he looked down at her cautiously. He was still locked within her tight channel, but at least the mist of a reality was wandering around the edges of his brain again.

She met his gaze. Cord clamped his mouth shut. He had been too rough. Taken no time to ensure her readiness and then used her hard. The loss of control was humbling.

Even more humbling because it was clear she had intended it to be so. This time he had no doubt the witch knew she had picked up the leash to the beast. She spoke of love but her actions showed him control. He should have been ready for this. No one had ever said these women were stupid. It was a nice, hard lesson in remembering his place, his duty and his obligation.

She had an even tighter rein on him than he could've ever dreamed up. Being shackled to her through his DNA wasn't enough. His mate was so much more than an instinctive response, and now the life in her womb ruled him as nothing else could have. He would be exactly what she wanted, when she wanted it.

That realization convinced his body to let her go and he could finally pull out and roll over. Cord swung an arm over his eyes, unwilling to even face the ceiling. He lay there, his body soaked in sweat and still throbbing. He heard her move. Her hand landed on his chest as she curled into his side.

His jaw clenched, his brain rebelled against his instant response to her touch.

"What is it? I can feel the anger. I don't understand," Kelly said as she looked down at his grim face. She couldn't see his eyes. His arm was still obscuring the upper part of his head.

"Give me a second and I'll take care of you," he said tightly.

"You make that sound like a chore," Kelly observed softly.

His arm came off his eyes as he looked at her. "A service," he corrected.

"A what?" Kelly sat up abruptly. "You're going to service me?"

"Yes ma'am," his low voice confirmed as he raised a brow though no other expression moved his features." I'm very clear on my place beneath the witch." He sat up. "Now if you would lie down and spread your legs I'll clean the animal off you with my tongue."

Kelly's body jerked as if he had slapped her. Her eyes grew wide then she swiftly turned her back on him as she scrambled off the bed. "Relax. Go to sleep," she stated sharply as she moved swiftly to the bathroom.

"Is that an order?" he snarled as she closed the door.

"Yes."

It was ten minutes before she returned to the room. A robe tightly belted around her waist, she ignored him and disappeared out the door. Cord watched her silently. The emotions swirling in the wake of her rigid back were toxic darts aimed directly at him.

She was mad. He opened his mouth to breathe the air over his tongue then snapped it shut. Not only was she mad, she was hurt. The taste of that hurt was tinged with bitter copper, almost the taste of blood. Cord jackknifed out of bed and took two steps toward the door and stopped. Turning on his heel, he retraced the two steps and stopped again to swing around and face the door.

He needed to think. She was feeling exactly the pain he had felt at her using him. Why was she upset? She was the one who had taught him a lesson. He was just being honest about it.

From the other bedroom he heard the unmistakable sound of muffled tears. Cord's hands clenched into fists as he listened to her cry. All right, he already knew something was seriously fucked up. Kelly's crying required a response from him. His nature could not tolerate it and he damn well had no clue what to do about it.

Cord started pacing and went over exactly what happened in the last hour. It began so well. They had indulged in soft teasing as he stumbled through asking her to marry him. Her answers made him think she wanted what he wanted. Then her actions had told him how thoroughly she could control him. That was the sucker-punch he'd reacted to.

In his experience, a creature's actions were the true indicator of intentions. His instincts demanded he put more importance on physical display. Listening to pretty words and ignoring all else often resulted in fatal surprises.

Maybe he'd read something wrong. He was swamped with emotions and very few useful tools to handle them. Women could be tricky, he'd always known that. She'd hurt him when he realized that she intended to control him. He'd lashed back when she decided to talk about it after. His only defense had been hollow words. He was under the impression they were clearing up the power issue. They both knew she could do whatever she damn well pleased and he'd take it. Was that what had brought the tears?

Could be he'd hurt her when he'd fucked like an animal. Maybe she was crying because of that.

Cord stopped in the middle of the room and swore viciously in every language he knew. Each soft sob sliced into him and cut a strip of flesh off his body, over and over again. It had to stop. He was her dragon and it was his responsibility to do whatever it took to make her happy. His designers had ensured he couldn't live any other way. Getting his head around that issue was his responsibility. His fucking pride was a stupid lie anyway. He'd never truly possessed the freedom to indulge in pride, not for a moment. Being ignorant of that fact didn't make it untrue.

Yet pride could not be his main problem. The pain of listening to her cry was more than the bloody death of his pride. It went way beyond that.

Swift strides took him out of the room and down the hall. Her door was unlocked and he didn't bother knocking as he stepped into the dark room. She was in the bed, facedown under the covers with the pillow over her head. It didn't matter. Every breath she took was a stiletto hitting the soft tissue target of his new emotions.

Cord sank to his knees beside the bed, his hands barely resting on the mattress. "Anything. I'll be anything you want. Do anything you need. Please stop crying."

"Go away," was the mumbled directive from under the pillow.

"Anything but that."

The crying diminished to hiccups. The lump under the blankets was trembling though. She said nothing.

"Please tell me what to do," he begged softly.

Her head came out from under the pillow. She looked at him in disbelief through red-rimmed eyes. "We tried that once. It didn't work so well."

Kelly closed her eyes a minute and took a deep breath. "Look, I'm sorry if I offended you by lusting after your body, your attention, and most of all, lusting after your heart. I've learned my lesson. It won't happen again. We're stuck together by more than just saving the world. I'll do my best to keep in line."

Cord hadn't thought he could sink any lower than he already had. Her words tore through his ego, showing him what he'd been hiding behind. He was terrified. Terrified of her and the power she could wield over him, so he had decided she was doing exactly that. He was the one who had forgotten the difference in their species. She was not a dragon. She did not react like a dragon would. Like he would, like he had.

He sat back on his heels putting distance between them. Her head sank to the pillow, eyes closed, shutting him out, and he knew he could not live with that, even for second.

"I love you," he stated nakedly. It was all he had to offer. She made him capable of this, able to be something he wasn't and he had tried to crawl back into the shell of the creature he understood. Being an animal was simple. Being her lover was more important and the most frightening thing he'd ever faced. The end of the world didn't come close to the devastation losing her would bring about.

Kelly moaned as if she was in pain, but her eyes did not open. "Don't. Don't hurt me anymore. I can't take it."

"I'm not hurting you. I'm trying not to hurt you. I love you, Kelly. How can I prove it to you? Love is not a thing. I'm trying to give it to you but I don't know how."

Her eyes did open this time and she studied his face. A frown rippled across her brow and then was gone. "Then explain it to me. If you love me, what was all that after we made love?"

"That was the jackass DNA at work. I thought you had deliberately stripped me of control to prove you could make me do anything you wanted. I was hurt. I hurt you back because I had no other defenses. No idea how to handle being in love with a woman who can destroy me like that. Tell me what to do and I'll do it."

Kelly rolled over and sat up, her eyes never leaving his face as she moved. "The only thing I need," she said in a trembling whisper, "is to believe you love me."

Cord was still kneeling beside the bed. Her words were the most effective weapons he'd ever encountered. She had done exactly what he asked, told him what she needed. The problem was, a dragon had no idea how to provide proof of love. At least he knew better than to ask her for a quest to prove it. That dumb-ass move had been used throughout the centuries by idiot men to no avail. He would have tried it if he hadn't seen it fail so many times.

Desperation and pain floated around the room as they faced each other in silence. Looking into her face, her sad, tear-streaked face, forced him to understand how truly limited a creature he was. There was a barrier between them that neither could remove. It was a glass wall. He could see her, see what he needed but he would never be capable providing what she needed.

Her eyes suddenly changed as she looked at him. Surprise and amazement skittered across her expressive features only to disappear into calm composure. Perhaps she was finally seeing him for what he was. A beast limited by his animal heart. He couldn't stand it anymore.

One arm was braced against the bed as he knelt a slight distance from it. He turned his head to drop it on his biceps for a moment and gather the strength to release her. It didn't matter if he looked weak to her. She already knew what he was. Giving her what she needed to be happy was his only option. Finding a way to live with what it required of him would be his battle every moment he remained sentient. So be it. He could do this. He had to do this. God, he didn't know if he could live through it.

How was he supposed to let go of the child?

Remembering what he was, a soulless abomination should do the trick. All that nonsense he'd thought when his dick was engaged was exactly that, nonsense. Fantasies of a bastard animal taking what he needed. His child would not be that.

Born of a woman, his baby would have everything he couldn't provide for it. He would only cripple an innocent with his small, narrow understanding of what it meant to live.

She deserved a man who could give her what she needed. The baby deserved love and support from parents who knew how to provide it. Not the harsh handling of a killer pretending to be something he wasn't.

He would always be there. He'd come at her call anytime she wanted, but he would stay out of her bed. He had no choice but to serve her as her dragon, but that service had to include letting her build a life after this crisis was resolved. He had no doubt that the three witches of today were just as powerful as the ladies from the past. They would find a way. When the child was grown, he'd fade away. The other two dragons were more than enough protection for a world without the threat they had brought with them from the past.

She had to be happy. That was the beginning and end of it. They all, the three of them, deserved someone who knew how to provide happiness. He must give them the freedom to find what they needed. Cord stood and turned to the door.

"Wait," Kelly asked hesitantly.

He stopped with his back to her. He couldn't look at the tears on her face. Not right now. Later he'd be stronger.

He heard Kelly slide out of the bed. Her light footfalls thundered in his mind as she neared him. *Please,* he begged silently. *Please don't touch me. I'm not that strong.*

Kelly came to stand in front of him. She was naked. Cord stared over her left shoulder at the door. "What?"

She reached up with a single finger and traced a damp path down his cheek. Taking her finger away, she stared at liquid evidence.

"Where are you going?" she asked.

"You asked me to leave. I can at least honor your requests." She didn't move. He couldn't look down at her.

"You said you love me," Kelly countered.

"I do not lie to you. I will never lie."

"Then hold me or something," she suggested with a hesitant smile.

His eyes cut to hers. "If I touch you, I will not let you go." Cord's hands clenched to keep from reaching for her. Changing her mind now was confusing and he was dangerously low on resistance. Working up the strength to leave her was a onetime deal. He had no illusions about being capable of doing it again. "Choose now. I'll never be a human, Kelly."

"Thank God, and I mean that sincerely." Her hands lifted to his shoulders as she stepped into his body. "I was afraid for a minute that you were going to be a jerk and run away. That's what a human would do."

Cord's arms wrapped around her as he buried his face in her hair, pulling her tight against his body. "Why would a human run away?"

Kelly groaned, her legs left the floor to wrap around his hips. "Because it's hard to be in love, the real thing. It means we can hurt each other and sometimes we don't even know we're doing it. Love is risky business, only for really brave guys like dragons and such."

He carried her to the bed as she explained. "What happened to proving I love you," he wanted to know in a guttural growl.

"You did."

"Yeah? Explain that to me, but later."

Cord carefully lowered her to the sheets. Again he had no control of what was going to happen next, but it didn't matter. Worshiping her with his mouth from head to toe was a compulsion he had no intention of resisting.

"I love you," Kelly breathed as he leaned over her, dropping kisses along her hairline.

"I know. God help us," Cord growled as the Wind Witch blew through him. She was pure magic. They were magic.

What they had become was new. Creating a life was certainly proof that nothing was as he'd known it before.

Drawing back, he looked into the eyes of a future that was free. Not free of responsibility, not free of danger, but it was theirs to make. It wasn't set in some master plan they had no control of. Succeed or fail, they would be the crafters of this future.

Chapter Fifteen

A month on a luxurious, private sailing yacht was not a difficult way to cross the Atlantic. Kelly stood at the rail and watched as Minuet and Cord swam with a pod of dolphins. Minuet's abilities had blossomed at sea, as had her own. They were getting close to the East Coast though and soon they'd have to start acting like normal people again. No more talking with animals.

Cord glanced up at her and grinned. Of course he knew exactly what she was thinking. He was more a part of her than the air she breathed.

"We will be back on the water with our friends soon," he promised, his words carried on the breeze instead of telepathy. "Our job in the glades will not take long."

No, not long, Kelly mused. A few hundred miles off the Florida coast she had no trouble detecting wizard signature emanating from the interior marsh. The air told her everything, and the poor, arrogant fool had no idea what he was broadcasting. The man considered himself a grand master wizard and he had many followers who agreed with him. Indeed, he probably was, but he was way out of his league with real witches and dragons.

It had been disciples of this fellow who had sent the birds. That seemed like a lifetime ago. It was certainly a different age, one where this fellow was probably the baddest thing in wizardness. She felt kind of sorry for the man.

Cord and Minuet came out of the water and they pointed the sleek, three double-mast yacht at a secluded cove on the Florida coast.

"He's an evil soul. How can you feel sorry for him?" Cord wanted to know. "You've seen what he does. What he wants to do. Believe me, this time the wizards will not be in control of anything."

"Of course not. I just felt sorry for his humiliation factor. He's about to experience a long fall down the ego ladder," Kelly responded with a smile.

"See, and I'm looking forward to making a fool out of him." Cord chuckled. "One of the perks of this stop. There's the reason we need you ladies so much. Compassion. I would have done things differently and probably made a martyr of him. Your plan gets his followers out of the way too."

"Mmmmm," Kelly confirmed, and unconsciously smoothed a hand down her belly. There was only a slight bump, hardly noticeable. "What can I say, he's the guy who scheduled his big show so helpfully. I will never understand that drive to show off. I'd get it if he were trying to conceal what he's capable off."

* * * * *

Much later that night the boat lay silent and dark as three people floated just above the water to shore. Minuet between Kelly and Cord was thrilled to be joining them. Actually they could not leave her. Even a weak wizard was dangerous. Not to Minuet, the danger was what she would do if threatened.

There was no way to measure her power, no norm to gage it by, so how could a person express the fact that it was increasing as her control and knowledge did. This part of the coast was thick with would-be witches and wizards, the risk of one them stumbling on an enchanted boat was slim but still too great to be ignored.

Using a combination of each of their powers, the three of them were outside the human sight spectrum and any supernatural creatures as well. The combination made them something new. It was probably way too cautious, but Cord insisted.

The plan was simple. Uber wizard had called a hundred of his best buddies to see how splendid he was by showing them he could kill a person with his mind. He was going to torture the person first, all telekinetically, then finally deliver the death blow without actually touching the person. Thwarting his little show would be simple and make him look like an idiot, thus dispersing his followers, at least that was how it was supposed to go.

The event was taking place at an abandoned sugar warehouse. They had just stepped in the door when Minuet gasped. She didn't do it audibly, they were just as invisible as they'd previously been, but both Cord and Kelly heard her shock.

"What," Cord asked telepathically.

"Him has dagon."

Kelly and Cord were scanning the crowd, the dark corners of the filthy building, the rafters, everywhere and couldn't find a dragon.

"Where is it?" Kelly asked calmly.

"Besides him." Minuet pointed at the makeshift stage. *"Dagon is hiddy, like us."*

"Does it see us?" Cord wanted to know.

"No. Feels us," Minuet said softly. *"Feels me. Dagon running away."*

"Don't let him out of your sight! We'll follow you. Minuet, we must capture him or he will use another human to create this same evil. He needs it like I need you and your mommy," Cord flashed to her.

He should have explained this. Should have told her how other dragons were different than he. It's just he thought there would be more time. If she were a little older, maybe the complete evil would not be so horrific. Right now he needed her to follow the dragon only she could see.

He'd been fucking wrong about something else. There were old dragons walking the world, not just him and the other two like him. It had been supremely stupid not to suspect that. An excuse for the stupid was why he'd never run into anther dragon.

Well shit, here was why. This one knew how to shield from him. Stood to reason there would be others who had figured out the plan and found a way not to starve into elemental sleep, keeping sentient by consuming only the minimum. Using humans to create the emotions they needed. Never stepping beyond that line so he or the other two guardians suspected a dragon.

Minuet hesitated and then she was after him, Cord and Kelly flashing with her.

"Wizard no hurt lady?" Minuet wanted to know as she took them after the dragon.

"It was always the dragon, honey. The guy is not a wizard without him. We'll make sure the lady is safe," Kelly explained to her daughter. *"But we have to catch the dragon before he gets too far away. Can you put in him a castle like you did Harrison?"*

One a.m. in the morning, deep in the everglades, Barbie's Dream Castle sprang up in the marsh, complete with a roaring dragon thrashing inside. They were much farther than human hearing could detect them from the warehouse. Scanning the area said there wasn't a human for over fifty miles in any direction. There was no one he could be calling, no human or immortal, so why the roaring?

Allowing the dragon to see them, Cord asked conversationally, "Why the racket?"

"Pain," screamed the dragon. "Why torture me? Kill me, I beg you!"

"Torturing you? You deserve it but no one is torturing you," Cord responded, puzzled at the dragon who continued to writhe and howl as if they were removing his organs while he still lived.

Minuet started to tremble, her emotions clear to them as she empathized with the dragon.

"No, baby, don't connect with him." Kelly dropped to her knees and turned her from the castle, trying desperately to distract Minuet's soft heart from the hideous scene.

Suddenly there was silence. Not even the night animals made a sound. They all looked at the glowing pink castle. Kelly and Cord could hear the dragon breathing in deep gasps. He was lying facedown on the castle floor, unmoving. In human form, he was filthy and disheveled. His clothes were old to the point of rags that appeared draped over a boney frame.

He was the first one to speak. "What the hell did you do?"

Cord looked down at Minuet and Kelly. "What did we do to him?" he asked Minuet.

"Him fixed." Minuet smiled at Kelly then Cord. "No more crying."

"Minuet, what did you do?" Cord asked. "You're not in trouble, but it is very important. Tell us exactly what you did to him."

The man figure in the castle slowly stood up. "What is she?" he demanded.

"We hurts him berry much. I change his," Minuet paused and looked her mother pronouncing the big word slowly, "orraahs."

"Oh." Kelly smiled reassuringly at Minuet. "You made him shine?"

"No, silly," Minuet laughed. "Shiny must come from him heart. Can't gives it. I jus helps him know he wish it. Our shiny hurtted him until he wished it."

"What is she talking about? What the hell are you all?" the dragon snarled, but his gaze was focused on Minuet.

"You distract her from explaining and she might think you look better as a pink pony," Cord stated in with a smile.

"It should be clear she's capable, or do you need another demonstration to keep quiet?"

"Sweetie, how did you help him wish it?" Kelly asked. "Helping anyone in pain is good. How we do it matters a lot. That's all we are trying to understand."

Minuet frowned slightly in her "thinking hard" face. "I look in him like I look in animal. I look for the happy. Him only has a little wishing for the happy. I make it bigger than the wishing for the mad. Now him like Cord."

"Like me? What does he have that's like me?" Cord asked.

"Him want his family. It was in him, I jus help him wish it most. Now he no mad all a time. Him sad but be happy when him finds family."

Cord laughed softly and bent to kiss the top of Minuet's head. "What a brilliant little miracle you are. That was a very good idea, sweetie."

"Now that you're all proud of the little creature, perhaps you could explain?" the dragon in the castle asked coldly.

Looking at him, it was evident Minuet's changes were having a profound effect. He stood in clean clothes, though still slender, he was no longer a starved skeleton.

Cord turned to the male and regarded him, scanning him ruthlessly as he did so. The male stood completely still, not resisting the scan in any way. What Cord found was something he recognized and yet was a bit speechless at the simplicity of the change that could be so complete.

Minuet had altered the dragon but not like one would expect. She'd gone seeking in his soul and found a spark of goodness. A tiny kernel of caring. Using what was already within, she'd changed the balance of a few chemicals. Her ability to know which ones to use was the magic. It was that part of her nature that set her so far apart from the rest of them.

She had taken nothing from the dragon, given him nothing new. Her touch on his soul was profound and so light it was barely there.

"There is good news and bad news." Cord stepped up to the imprisoned male. "Good news is I'm not going to kill you. Bad news is you are in love." Cord chuckled. "You have no idea what to do with it but there it is. Finding the woman who makes you whole will be a challenge. Convincing her to love you even more…ah, interesting."

The male scowled. "Dragon's don't love. Not part of our nature."

"Yeah, that was before, this is now," Cord stated. "The thing I want you to grasp clearly is I know who you are." Cord's form shimmered and changed. In his natural state he stood fifteen feet tall, the white glow off his form almost blinding as he continued to explain the dragon's new situation. "I can track you at will. Are we clear on that?"

The captured dragon looked up at Cord then at Kelly and smiled. It wasn't so much a friendly smile as a knowing one. "Seriously?" he said softly. "She gives you that much?"

"Try to focus, buddy," Cord snapped. "I don't have time to babysit you, but one day you're going to want some advice and I'm the only guy you know who can give it to you. Don't disappoint me."

Cord changed back to his human form. "Minuet, your new friend can be let out of his castle."

"Him doesn't has a name," she stated as the Barbie castle dissipated into the marsh mist.

"He'll get one on his own. We have to go do something about his former followers though."

"Hey, wait a second…" echoed after them as they moved away from the dragon standing in knee-deep swamp.

"He'll be fine," Cord assured Kelly as she worriedly glanced back at the tall man they'd just abandoned. "Minuet's answer to his pain didn't exactly strip him of his ability to defend himself."

"I know. It's just he's so clueless right now," Kelly said.

"Small price to pay for all this," Cord growled as they entered the old sugar warehouse again.

The crowd had disintegrated into a jeering, churning mass as the man onstage failed to deliver even one of his promised stunts. The woman tied to a pole was too terrified to even weep. The air stank of mounting violence as the crowd lost all respect and consequently all fear of the man who had made himself their grand wizard.

The one thing this human had taught the people he called disciples was violence. He had ruled by fear and pain, exactly what the dragon controlling him needed. Now the crowd was calling for his subjugation to them.

Cord turned Kelly and Minuet from the scene, taking his family outside. In the distance, sirens were screaming their way to the remote structure, but there was no possibility they'd arrive before there was blood on the floor.

"Cord," Kelly said softly.

That was all it took. He knew what she wanted. Her compassionate nature required they stop violence before it began. If it were up to him, they would leave this place and let the wizard experience his reward. But that was not the world Kelly and Minuet lived in. It was not the world he'd allow anywhere near them, so it was his responsibility to ensure…something.

Returning to the warehouse, he materialized onstage beside the wizard, all fifteen feet of him in blazing white. White wings for good measure. Abruptly there was utter silence. The crowd drew its own conclusions and eyes darted to the wizard and back to the glowing being.

Right, they would think that. Cord scowled at the crowd. Looking down at the wizard, he spat on the man's head. The wizard fell to his knees in terror.

Cord allowed a flame to light on the tip of his finger as he pointed at the kneeling, crying wizard. "You are a liar," he stated in a booming whisper. "And a thief. You have broken every Commandment and defiled every life you touch." Looking up at the crowd, Cord breathed in and allowed himself to expand. The humans stumbled back as far as they were able.

"Do you follow this idiot pissing himself before you?" he demanded.

No response, but all eyes looked at the puddle around the wizard's knees. He was probably not the only guy in here that terrified, yet that act of cowardice before them sealed their opinion of him.

"Then go." The sirens could be heard by the humans now. They left in silence, melting into the everglades amazingly fast. Cord shifted to his human form and strode to the woman onstage.

"The police will find you here in a second. You must press kidnapping charges. Do not admit to seeing anything supernatural, his story will convict him. All will be well with you now," he promised.

She nodded and he shimmered out of human view as the police burst in the door.

The fact that the local cops had raced here with sirens blazing told Cord that at least some of them knew exactly what was going on in the warehouse. They expected to find it empty. The tied woman onstage and wizard still kneeling in his own piss were a surprise. One they could not ignore as State troopers noiselessly arrived on scene.

Time to go.

Back on the yacht, they silently cruised out into the open ocean. The air dragon and Wind Witch had no need of the motor attached to the old-world sailing yacht. Nor did they need the crew that usually came with a vessel this size.

Cord was seated on a deck lounger with Kelly in his arms. Minuet slept soundly in her cabin below as they left the Florida coast.

Cord kissed Kelly's forehead and asked, "Where would you like to go?"

"Thought we were headed south to help Legion and Molly," she murmured, far too content to lift her head.

"No need. Minuet just showed us what to do with an awakening dragon," he stated. "It was a risk to expose them to Minuet in the first place. I showed Molly and Legion what she did. Molly can do it easily. Well, not exactly like Minuet did, but very close. Molly is also able to see if there is no spark of compassion in a dragon and take the correct action. Teaching Minuet to be an executioner is not something I could permit.

"We still have to come up with a fix for the hole in the ozone but the danger isn't as critical as it was. There is a new problem though. Might be quite a few males looking for their mates soon. I'm guessing they will each need a witch."

Kelly lifted her head to turn and look at Cord in alarm. "Dragons looking for witches? Don't you think we'll have some trouble with that? I mean, it just seems dangerous."

Cord grinned at his Wind Witch and kissed those worried lips. He'd meant to kiss her briefly but should have known better. Much later his answer to her question was whispered in her ear. "It will be incredibly dangerous, for the dragons."

Also by Gail Faulkner

eBooks:

Any Price

Ask For It

Darius

Ghost Unit 1: Full Ride

Ghost Unit 2: Slip Knot

Ghost Unit 3: Wanna Play

Into His Keeping

Jamie's Cherub

Romeo

Stealing Carmen

Wicked Beast

Print Books:

Ghost Unit 1 & 2: Knot Tonight

Ghost Unit 3: Slip Knot

Into His Keeping

Jamie's Cherb

About Gail Faulkner

Hello everyone. If you're reading this, I hope it means you've enjoyed reading one of my books. If you have some other opinion of them, feel free to lie to me anyway. I hereby absolve you from all possible guilt and consequences for flagrant, adjective-saturated lying to the author.

I'm a chronic fantasizer. Every good romance novel ended too soon. After a while, I started making up stories when I had a few minutes to while away. So now, instead of sitting around with a blank look on my face, I've taken to writing them down.

Because of my father's job, we moved every three years in my early life. My first memories are of Bermuda, and then we were in several African countries. It was a wonderful childhood. I gained a rich cultural background in the world community, but never learned to spell. As an adult, I avoided writing at all costs, embarrassed over my limitations.

But the writer will not stay silent forever. She broke out, and insisted on learning the mystical world of grammar and spelling. Haven't mastered all of it yet, but they let me write for you anyway. Bless every editor on the planet. They give dreamers a place to send fantasies and save us the embarrassment of owning our shortcomings.

The author welcomes comments from readers. You can find her website and email address on her author bio page at www.ellorascave.com.

Tell Us What You Think

We appreciate hearing reader opinions about our books. You can email us at Service@ellorascave.com (when contacting Customer Service, be sure to state the book title and author).

Why an electronic book?

We live in the Information Age—an exciting time in the history of human civilization, in which technology rules supreme and continues to progress in leaps and bounds every minute of every day. For a multitude of reasons, more and more avid literary fans are opting to purchase e-books instead of paper books. The question from those not yet initiated into the world of electronic reading is simply: *Why?*

1. ***Price.*** An electronic title at Ellora's Cave Publishing runs anywhere from 40% to 75% less than the cover price of the exact same title in paperback format. Why? Basic mathematics and cost. It is less expensive to publish an e-book (no paper and printing, no warehousing and shipping) than it is to publish a paperback, so the savings are passed along to the consumer.
2. ***Space.*** Running out of room in your house for your books? That is one worry you will never have with electronic books. For a low one-time cost, you can purchase a handheld device specifically designed for e-reading. Many e-readers have large, convenient screens for viewing. Better yet, hundreds of titles can be stored within your new library—on a single microchip. There are a variety of e-readers from different manufacturers. You can also read e-books on your PC or laptop computer. (Please note that Ellora's Cave does not endorse any specific brands.

You can check our website at www.ellorascave.com for information we make available to new consumers.)

3. ***Mobility***. Because your new e-library consists of only a microchip within a small, easily transportable e-reader, your entire cache of books can be taken with you wherever you go.
4. ***Personal Viewing Preferences.*** Are the words you are currently reading too small? Too large? Too... ANNOYING? Paperback books cannot be modified according to personal preferences, but e-books can.
5. ***Instant Gratification.*** Is it the middle of the night and all the bookstores near you are closed? Are you tired of waiting days, sometimes weeks, for bookstores to ship the novels you bought? Ellora's Cave Publishing sells instantaneous downloads twenty-four hours a day, seven days a week, every day of the year. Our webstore is never closed. Our e-book delivery system is 100% automated, meaning your order is filled as soon as you pay for it.

Those are a few of the top reasons why electronic books are replacing paperbacks for many avid readers.

As always, Ellora's Cave welcomes your questions and comments. We invite you to email us at Service@ellorascave.com or write to us directly at Ellora's Cave Publishing Inc., 1056 Home Avenue, Akron, OH 44310-3502.

Lightning Source UK Ltd.
Milton Keynes UK
UKOW02f0314180816

280960UK00001B/72/P

9 781419 968280